CONTENTS

The Coldest Dish

Prologue

October 2001

I wonder if they will come for me again tonight.
I hope not.
My weals are still raw, my bruises still tender.
My ears are pricked, my eyes alert.
I cannot sleep.
I scan the darkness, backward and forward.
A slight noise.
A shaft of light.
To my relief, it is the boy from next door.
My only friend.
He utters a language I cannot understand, but his kind eyes speak to me.
He strokes my head.
I curl my tail under my paws and fall asleep.

CHAPTER 1

December 2022

The middle aged man had left his *local* slightly earlier than usual as he wasn't feeling well. He had found it hard to concentrate on the last game of dominoes and, conscious of the fact he faced a twenty minute walk home, bid farewell to his drinking buddies, citing the need for an early night.
He hoped he wasn't in the early stages of an exacerbation of his emphysema when lethargy, nausea and sleepiness sometimes preceded the more classical respiratory symptoms.
The bracing Aberdeen December air hit him as he swung the pub door open. He pulled his jacket collar up to its full extent and, taking advantage of the shelter afforded by the canopy above the door, inhaled a few lungfuls of cold air in an attempt to clear his slightly muzzy head. Apart from triggering a spasm of coughing, the deep breaths of air failed to affect any beneficial change. He shrugged his shoulders and took his first, slightly tentative, step towards home.
"Sad bastards," he muttered, in the general direction of the two doorstep smokers he left behind. There was no trace of irony in his voice despite the fact it was only six months since he himself had ascended to the moral high ground from the smoking lowlands.
As he trudged somewhat wearily along the street, he was only vaguely aware, through the darkness of a winter evening and a clouding consciousness, of someone else leaving the pub.

Despite the familiarity of the route, progress was unusually laboured and he stumbled on a couple of occasions.
Those bastards in the pub must have served me a bad pint.
Having negotiated the first few streets the ground under his feet changed from concrete hard to a softer woodland path as he entered the riverside route, which connected the urban start and finish of his journey. Through the darkness, he could hear the hum of the adjacent river Don, almost but not quite silent, against the stillness

of the surrounding trees. The noise of an occasional twig breaking punctuated the darkness and he assumed a fox, or perhaps even a deer, was on a nocturnal mission.

By the time he was half way along the path, he was feeling even more lightheaded and dizzy and barely noticed the unusual presence of a dark coloured van parked close to the walkway. There were no official roads in the woodland, and the van must have taken one of the dirt tracks, occasionally used by ghillies or council workmen, to access the spot. With a clearer head this would have at least piqued his interest, or perhaps even put him on alert, but he was, by now, solely focused on the increasing challenge of getting home before his legs gave way.

He never saw the attack coming.

A sickening blow on the back of his head encouraged his already wobbly legs to give way altogether, and he fell heavily to the mud, gravel and crushed twigs that constituted the surface of the riverside path. He was vaguely aware of powerful arms twisting his wrists behind his back, and a cable tie was rapidly ratcheted to a tight closure. He then felt a cold, more substantial, chain placed around his neck before he was bundled unceremoniously into the back of the van, where a further cable tie secured his ankles.

His pulse accelerated rapidly, and the hairs on the back of his neck stood on end. Even through the fog of what he now assumed was a drug induced drowsiness, he attained a level of awareness denied to him since he left the pub. His senses were on as high alert as the head injury and sedation would permit, and he was terrified at what they were telling him.

A large man wearing a full length apron, who made no attempt to conceal his determined face, stood before him. Even in the semi-darkness it was possible to see that the walls and floor of the van, behind and below him, had been covered in thick polythene. In his left hand his abductor held the other end of the chain that was around his neck, and in his right hand a large knife.

He realised he was about to die.

CHAPTER 2

Tuesday 10th December

Andrew Mitchell was a 3rd generation butcher in the family business in Cults, a suburb of Aberdeen. He sported the red hair, freckles, pale skin and tattoos typical of the males in the family. By dint of being only eighteen, he had less body art than displayed by his father, uncle and grandfather, though the latter was now retired from the trade. His only tattoo to date, in fact, was an 18th birthday present from his parents which he used to decorate his right forearm with the emblem of his beloved Aberdeen Football Club.

He was two years into his apprenticeship and was confident in his abilities though betrayed no sign of arrogance. Along the way, he had accumulated his Diploma for Proficiency in Meat and Poultry Industry Skills along with other accreditations in Food Hygiene and Covid Pandemic related issues, though more important than paper certificates was the practical experience gained using "the tools". The morning trade in the shop, always the briskest, demanded his presence at the main counter, but in the afternoon he was usually delegated to other tasks, and today he was alone preparing offal in a separate room towards the rear of the business. The butcher's apron that he had put on fresh that morning now bore the evidence of his day's toil, and would be confined to the washing basket once more at the end of the afternoon.

The main customer base for offal was high end restaurants, some of the more adventurous local domestic culinary enthusiasts and dog owners, some of whom preferred to feed the canine members of their family raw meat, including offal. His isolation was a bonus as it allowed him to play music at a reasonable volume, while not annoying his father or uncle, neither of whom shared his taste in hip hop. The combination of tiled walls and stainless steel surfaces contributed little to sound absorption which only added to his auditory experience.

He worked away diligently, the offal being no match for his ultra sharp scimitar knife which sliced effortlessly through the soft tissues. He picked up a porcine heart, a particular favourite of their canine customers apparently, and commenced his normal routine of dividing it into more manageable sized pieces which would then be bagged and made available for sale the following day. He was mulling over whether he should save up for a sleeve tattoo for his left arm or a season ticket for Pittodrie, the home of Aberdeen Football Club, when he felt and heard something strange. Very strange.

He muted his Dr Dre playlist, to remove any element of distraction, and tentatively explored the incision he had just made. Sure enough, there was the unmistakable feel of something very hard within the wound. While he was used to the dull firmness of bone that would be transmitted through his knife, on occasion, when working with limbs, joints and ribs, this had a sharp, metallic feel quite unlike anything else he had experienced. He had a sudden feeling of unease, almost like a switch had been turned on; not just because of the novelty of the sensation he had just experienced, but also by the knowledge that there should only be soft tissue in the heart, liver, kidneys, thymus and stomach; the organs which traditionally make up the umbrella term of offal.

He knew his father was currently wrestling with new PAYE software, and would not welcome interruption but, nevertheless, his curiosity, not to mention concern, overcame any lingering reluctance and he knocked with slight trepidation on the office door before entering.

"Dad. Can you come and check something for me please?"

George Mitchell looked up with more than a hint of annoyance, but softened his response when he noted the strained and worried look on the face of his normally placid son. His usual pale skin was even more like alabaster, and he really didn't look his normal self.

“Aye. OK. Give me a couple of minutes son.”
In truth, his limited IT skills frequently led to protracted and frustrating sessions, laced with some choice swear words, in front of the business PC, and he was secretly quite glad of the temporary relief his son offered.

He finished the current line on the spreadsheet he was working on and followed him through to the preparation room where he noted the absence of music, which was quite unusual, and a partially dissected heart on the workbench.

“There’s something funny in this pig’s heart Dad.”

“Let me have a look son.” While he had confidence in his son’s abilities, he was still towards the beginning of his career and was only just starting out on the journey of accumulating experience which would surely follow if he continued on his chosen career path. His own anxiety levels, therefore, did not match those apparently vexing his son. He picked up the nearest knife and a small T-handled boning hook to give him a greater degree of control in parting the edges of the previous excision and inspecting the current darkness of the wound. This matter-of-fact calmness lasted for about another five seconds before he said, with what his son took to be a slight tremor in his voice,“Pass me your phone son”

He rapidly punched in a three digit number, and pressed the send key.

CHAPTER 3

Dr Dexter Brewster swung his feet up onto his desk and sank back into his chair which creaked and groaned, but accepted the challenge of his ample frame. He noticed his blue socks were not an actual match and made a mental note to revisit the mystery that was his underwear drawer. The last hour of his day shift between five and six pm always dragged. Not for the first time he envied others whose work was guaranteed to finish at an appointed hour. As a Police Pathologist employed by Forensic Services SPA (Scottish Police Association), and based in Aberdeen, he nominally finished at six pm but, at the same time, was aware that if a new referral came in before that time he would be morally bound to accept responsibility for the workload that might bring, or break the unwritten rule of keeping the slate clean for the on-call Pathologist based at home after six pm. He would, of course, be the potential beneficiary of the same system at the other end of the night shift before he started next day at eight am.

He pulled out his phone and - for the second time in an hour - checked his e-mail and Whatsapp accounts. Less frequently he would stray onto Facebook in the knowledge that the chance of him gleaning anything useful from such a visit was probably less than 10%...on a good day. This, however, didn't stop him doing it and the occasional nugget was found to reinforce his habit. His wife, Chloe, teased him that he was surgically attached to his phone and he had to admit there was a ring of truth about the spousal observation. At fifty-six, he was somewhat between the Baby Boomer and Generation X cohorts and had arrived slightly later than others to the IT explosion, but had since embraced it, and kept up to date as best he could. He would still admit, however, that such things as memes and Tik

Tok were well out of his comfort zone.

Being closer to sixty than fifty, he now had half an eye on retirement. He still enjoyed the clinical forensic aspects of his work but there had been several management and bureaucratic changes over the years, not least of which the swallowing up of Grampian Police, along with the other regional forces, into the much larger Police Scotland. As ever, change inevitably brought stress and, as he got older, he seemed less able to adapt, especially to what he viewed as at times unnecessary and multilayered management. He reflected sometimes that it was the process of the job rather than the clinical work that was making him visit the SPPA web site more frequently, to calculate when he might reasonably retire, but still maintain an acceptable standard of living. At the moment, the figure was about sixty-two, but he was aware this was likely to change as The Government tried to square the circle of pension payments to a population living ever older.

He looked at his abdomen and was once again reminded that middle age had brought what seemed the inevitable male paunch. At a recent health check with his Practice Nurse, he was told, over the rim of pince-nez glasses, and with a slightly disapproving look, that his weight was 85kg, and his BMI 30. This meant little to the imperial wiring within his brain, but his own personal barometer of his corporation, which hole in his belt he was obliged to use, was not to be ignored, and was currently telling him that he needed to re-focus on his lifestyle efforts. He was mulling over whether he should consider taking Archie, his eight year old Labradoodle, for extended morning walks before work, or perhaps re-engage with his local gym, when the phone rang, making him jump slightly.

"Dr Brewster speaking. How can I help?"

"Hello, Dexter. It's Bob McLeod here," and, with that, Brewster's heart sank a little. This was not likely to bode well.

McLeod was an old school Police Sergeant, who Brewster had known for years, and who was also getting towards the twilight of his career. He was a straightforward, no nonsense officer who

Brewster held in high regard. If he was phoning it was almost always likely to be something significant, unlike some of his younger colleagues. He wasn't everybody's cup of tea but, by common consent, junior officers were likely to learn as much shadowing him for six nights on front line duty as they might glean from six months in the classroom.

"Hi, Bob. How are you? What's up?"

"Fine thanks, Dexter. Listen, I know this is an unusual request but can I trouble you to pop out to Mitchell's butcher in Cults? I'm over here just now. Young Mitchell found something unusual in a pig's heart, and now George Mitchell has called us in as he's got himself convinced this heart is human. I realise it may be a wild goose chase, but I'm not the man to decide that."

Brewster glanced at his watch and noted the 5:50 pm time displayed. He cursed internally but, ever the professional, he hoped his dismay wasn't betrayed in his answer.

"Aye. No problem, Bob. I'll just get tidied up here and should be over in half an hour or so."

He finished the call, picked up his case and coat, and stole a glance out of the window. As it had been a mid December day of leaden skies and wintry showers the city had already been swathed in darkness for the best part of two hours. He could see the latest snow flurry silhouetted against the glow of a nearby street lamp, the individual flakes swirling and dancing on the light breeze, and sometimes even defying gravity, it seemed, by drifting upwards. He searched his pockets and found the reassuring presence of gloves, before heading to the lift for the staff car park.

As he exited the building and made his way towards his car, he was reminded, even though he was near the heart of the city, of the impressive stillness, and quietness, that often accompanies snowfall. It was only about six miles from Police HQ to Cults, but at that time of night, and with the light falls of snow earlier in the afternoon, it wasn't going to be a quick journey. As a Police Pathologist, he wasn't afforded the privilege of a blue light for his car, and would just have to take his place in the evening exodus from the city.

Progress was indeed slow from the city centre to the urban periphery but, after fifteen minutes, he turned his car onto the North Deeside Road to Cults and, with a sigh, noted the long queue of car rear lights snaking into the distance. With spluttering exhausts, and their fumes crystallising in the dropping evening temperatures, it brought an image to Brewster's mind of a vast queue of vaping ex-smokers. Every now and then, a sudden sideways billow of smoke would betray the presence of a real person satisfying an ongoing nicotine requirement prior to getting home for the evening. As a distant ex-smoker himself, he felt their struggle.

He switched on an Ian Dury playlist just in time to hear the declaration "There ain't half been some clever bastards!" to which he felt obliged to respond, at quite high volume, along with the rest of The Blockheads, "Lucky Bleeders. Lucky Bleeders," in his best pseudo Cockney accent.

Brewster actually lived in Maryculter, just off the South Deeside Road, on the other side of the river Dee, one of two rivers that flow through the city, the other being The Don. He calculated that he could do what he had to do in Cults, carry on westwards, cross over the river at Milltimber, and then start heading eastwards back towards Aberdeen; exiting right to Maryculter before he reached the city outskirts again. He glanced at his control panel which dutifully informed him he had 39% battery strength remaining in his Nissan Leaf EV, so his "range anxiety", well known to most EV owners, was at a relatively low level. He gained comfort in the knowledge that he could top up overnight on his home charger.

After what seemed like an eternity, but was probably no more than fifteen minutes, he caught sight of Christmas lights suspended from lampposts, heralding his destination. Cults had previously been a satellite village but had, over the years, been snared by the creeping extension of its bigger urban brother, Aberdeen. It had always been, and still was, seen as a very desirable place to live with high quality housing, good schools, a selection of shops and an excellent golf course, Deeside, which spans Cults and the next westward suburb of Bieldside.

He drove past the ubiquitous Subway and Costa shops, relatively new and seemingly inevitable additions to the Cults high street, before finding a space near Mitchell's Butcher which, in contrast, seemed to have been there forever.

Bob McLeod and a rather sheepish looking PC, who looked about twelve, were waiting for him at the front door. Brewster realised that the latter observation was probably another sign he was getting old.

"Hi, Dexter. Thanks for coming. This is certainly a first for me, and I'm not sure if it's something or nothing to be honest. Apologies if it turns out to be a wild goose chase, but appreciate you being here."

"No problem, Bob. It's more or less on my way home anyway. Let's have a look."

Without exchanging any further words, the unlikely entourage of a police officer, butcher and pathologist squeezed through the narrow corridor toward the back of the shop where Brewster realised he felt somewhat at home amongst the smell of refrigeration, meat and blood. The room was well lit and there was no mistaking the presence of a partially butchered heart on the preparation table. Brewster was aware that human and animal hearts can be very similar, indeed to the point where cardiac valves from animals can be transplanted into humans, so the external anatomy alone was not conclusive.

He donned apron, gloves and mask to protect both himself and any potential crime scene and hefted his bag onto the table where he wasted no time in fitting a head torch and then selecting two cat's paws retractors as the most appropriate exploratory instruments. He carefully applied the retractors to the wound edges to minimise any further tissue damage and gently parted the existing excision allowing light from his head torch to flood the wound. He noted this had been made, presumably completely randomly, at the base of the aorta where it exited the left ventricle and carried oxygenated blood for the entire body.

Even for an experienced police pathologist, what he saw next sent a slight shiver down his spine. Although he had seen many artificial heart valves before, it was the context of this discovery which was making the hairs on his neck stand to attention.

A bi-leaflet mechanical aortic valve, possibly a St Jude's, was staring him in the face. He felt a slight bead of sweat on his brow despite the chilled ambiance. Paradoxically, he also felt a dryness in his mouth and a subtle quickening of his pulse. Although his natural instinct was to explore further, his professionalism ensured he stood back from the table. He realised that he had already established, with that brief glance, that the heart before him was indeed human and therefore, also, a likely crime scene; it was not appropriate for him to advance assessment any further at this stage. That would come the following day at the Police Morgue.

He cleared his throat with a slight cough.

"Right, Bob. I can confirm, from my assessment, that this is very likely to be a human heart. What young Andrew discovered with his knife is an artificial valve and, as far as I am aware, these have never been used in animals, other than human beings. Ergo, this should be considered as a crime scene, and a potential homicide."

"Right you are, Dexter. Leave it to me."

McLeod's experience quickly manifested itself as he immediately set about securing the scene with the help of his junior, somewhat terrified looking, colleague. Several crackly radio interchanges followed with Police control and CID.

"OK. That's the troops on the way. DI Bankhurst and DS MacDonald will be here in about twenty minutes. They've requested you stay on site for a bit, Dexter."

"Aye. OK, Bob."

Brewster used the time to Whatsapp 'Mapleleaf', his wife, to say he was delayed by a potential serious crime, and request she put a hold on tea. Tuesday was usually fresh pasta night. He knew the dough would be made by now, but was also confident his wife, who shared his passion for food, especially Italian food, would put a damp cloth over it to prevent drying out. He doubted, however, she would wait for him before sampling a little Amarone.

Fair enough he thought.

Mapleleaf was the Whatsapp nickname for his wife, Chloe. She was born and raised in Labrador on the east coast of Canada, but moved to Toronto University to study English and art. It was while Brewster was completing a postgraduate doctorate at Toronto that he fell in love with Canada and indeed a Canadian. Their romance survived the subsequent geographical challenge of living on either side of the Atlantic Ocean for two years before Chloe joined him in Edinburgh, where she completed her UK teaching qualifications. Edinburgh proved an ideal city to cement both their relationship and their love of food being adorned with numerous and varied restaurants and hostelries. Their wedding in Canada was followed by several more years of early married life in Edinburgh, spawning two children and developing careers, before the Aberdeen Pathologist vacancy surfaced, and was accepted by Brewster as an opportunity for a first consultant position.

What was seen at the time as a potential career stepping stone for Brewster, actually turned into a career defining role instead as both he and Chloe became increasingly, and happily, entwined in what the Granite City and the North East of Scotland had to offer. Initial rental accommodation was jettisoned for their first house purchase together after three years, and they moved into their current converted steading in Maryculter five years later. This seemed a natural progression at the time, and nothing had happened since then to change that mindset. In recent years, both children had left the family home, their absence having been partially compensated for by the arrival of Archie, a fox red miniature labradoodle, who soon became the new centre of attention in the family.

After receiving a Whatsapp acknowledgement from Chloe, he

turned his mind to the case in hand and how he might proceed in the very unusual circumstances presented to him. Normally at postmortem 99% of the time the exact identity of the corpse would be known to the pathologist along with significant information on the time leading up to the death, and the details of the discovery of the, usually, whole corpse. Occasionally, a body would be dismembered, but most of the time it would be intact. Never before had he been presented with a single organ. While heart tissue would yield a plentiful supply of DNA, and therefore a multitude of information, including gender, it would not give the age of the person, or indeed confirm the identity unless the Police had previously collected and stored a DNA sample from the same person.

Brewster was sitting alone with his thoughts in the office, the PAYE software frozen in time on the PC screen, when a collection of noises, chatter and cold air announced the arrival of the CID team. He had come across both DI Bankhurst and DS MacDonald before ,briefly, on previous cases but did not consider that he knew either of them well.

McLeod facilitated brief introductions and the newly assembled team ducked under the hastily erected crime scene tape into the room where the heart sat in splendid isolation, like it was an exhibit in the museum of the Department of Surgery.

Nobody spoke for a few seconds, as if dumbstruck by the scenario presented. Bankhurst broke the silence.

"OK. Dr Brewster. Can you give me a summary of your findings please?"

"No problem. By the way, Dexter is fine".

"That's grand. I'm Lily and this is Hamish," as she nodded towards DS MacDonald who responded with a nod of his own and barely a glimmer of a smile.

Brewster obliged by stating his conclusion about the presence of the artificial valve and the significance thereof. He expanded somewhat by stating that there are essentially two main types of artificial valves used in humans. Those from animals, principally cows and pigs, and those manufactured by humankind. Of the latter, there were three main types, namely caged-ball, tilting disc and bi-leaflet. The one exposed by Andrew Mitchell's excision was a bi-leaflet variety, possibly a St Jude's. He explained further assessment at postmortem would yield more specific information, and also noted that had it been a porcine or bovine valve, it might never have been discovered as a sharp butcher's knife may well have passed through unhindered.

Brewster also thought to himself that, if Archie was anything to go by, then no self respecting hound would turn their nose up at human flesh either if it had reached that far in the intended journey.

"Obviously my first question, Dexter, is whether an individual can be identified from their valve replacement?" said Bankhurst.

"That was my first thought too. I had a quick check online and it seems it might be dependent on the exact make of valve, when it was fitted and in which country. It's certainly true that for many years every valve has had a unique ID number and this is given to the patient on an ID card but, of course, we don't have that luxury here.

I suppose we might get lucky if he or she is on the Police DNA database, but that seems a long shot. Certainly we will have no shortage of DNA for testing."

"How soon can you do the PM, Dexter?" interjected MacDonald.

"I'm aiming for tomorrow afternoon, I think. If you guys can get the organ over to the morgue this evening, the on-call technician will do the necessary for tonight re security and preservation of the organ. Tomorrow morning, before any further sharp dissection, we'll proceed with a PMCT scan. The idea behind this is to try and help age the victim. Normally, if we get an unknown victim, we usually rely on dental and skeletal analysis to help age a corpse, but clearly these are not available. If we can get a CT calcium score from the walls of the coronary arteries this might help give an approximate age for the victim. It's not an exact science, and can be influenced by other things such as smoking and family history, but it might help place the heart in a particular decade for instance."

"I'll also be able to have a direct look inside the lumen of the arteries myself at postmortem which may also help with informing an age estimate."

"Once the PMCT scan is completed we can proceed with a formal postmortem including sampling of tissue for DNA and toxicology analysis. The latter results will be available in twenty-four hours, but DNA assessment can take another twenty-four hours or so."

"Ok, Dexter. That's great. I'll organise a team meeting at our end for first thing tomorrow morning to agree strategy and priorities, and will also have a word higher up the food chain to see about maximising any available help. I'll have a word with Corporate Communications tonight as we really need to get ahead of this story. The local, not to mention national, media will be all over this soon, so we need to be in the vanguard and not play catch-up."

"OK. Sounds good to me," replied Brewster. "See you at the PM tomorrow; 2pm."

There was a general nodding of heads as Brewster packed his instruments into his bag, doffed his PPE, and put his coat on. He left the CID to do what they had to and excused himself through a small crowd that had gathered outside to find his way back to his car.

He pulled back out on to North Deeside Road and Ian Dury kicked back in, resuming his apparent interest in intelligence, with 'Clever Trevor'.

The snow and the evening traffic had abated and it was only fifteen minutes later that he pulled into his steading driveway noting, as he did, that the usual crunch of gravel under his tyres had been replaced by a much softer and quieter experience, courtesy of the fallen snow. He shivered slightly as the cold evening air contrasted with what had become a cosy temperature inside his car, but his discomfort was only temporary for, as soon as he crossed the house threshold, he was enveloped in both warm air and the enticing smell of a ragu sauce permeating through from the kitchen.

He heard the customary skittering sound of paws trying to gain traction on the stone kitchen floor as Archie, having heard the front door open, attempted to launch himself towards his other human. The welcome offered was as if he hadn't seen him for twelve months, never mind twelve hours.

After negotiating the obligatory enthusiastic canine greeting, which in truth he never tired of, Brewster followed the tantalising smell into the kitchen, where he found Chloe slowly stirring the sauce.

"What time do you call this?" she said, but with a mischievous glint in her eyes. The postponement of dinner had been softened by some Amarone and she knew, in fact, that there would be a good reason for the delay. Although they both mostly enjoyed their jobs, it had become customary over the years to have a debriefing, aka moaning, session while waiting for tea to cook. These had become longer over the years, and often demanded a little more alcohol than previously. Both had to be mindful of confidentiality issues and, in truth, they probably crossed the invisible acceptable line on occasion but only in the complete trust that the other would not take the conversation outside the marital home.

Brewster poured a generous amount of wine into a glass for himself and topped up his wife's at the same time. He took a couple of sips and felt unable to prevent himself offloading an edited version of the extraordinary event which had detained him in Cults.

"Wow!" was the only word Chloe could offer, followed by, "Bloody hell."

"So what happens now?"

"Well, the Police will do what they have to at the scene, and I'll do a PM tomorrow to see what other information can be gleaned from a single organ. DI Bankhurst is SIO and is arranging a team meeting for first thing tomorrow in what will be considered at least a suspicious death, and very possibly a homicide."

By the time Brewster had related the story the pasta had been cooked and the sauce heated up. Chloe strained most of the water from the pasta and then added the pasta along with the remaining water into the ragu. A gentle stirring coated the pasta with the sauce and the steaming contents were soon transferred from pot to waiting plates. Food and drinks were taken to the breakfast bar, and devoured with minimal conversation as their ravenous appetites demanded.

As per usual, Brewster finished slightly before Chloe and he took a generous inhalation of air to address the oxygen debt he had built up by prioritising eating over adequate respiration the previous five minutes. An announcement of, "That was good!" preceded a stifled burp and an, "Excuse me."

Chloe nodded in agreement, but wasn't in a position to answer as she was still eating heartily herself. Archie, meanwhile, looked on with a hopeful expression but he knew, from experience, that the humans rarely gave anything up from their evening meal. He changed position from sitting to the more comfortable lying but kept one beady eye on proceedings, just in case.

The evening threshold for regular coffee had long since been passed, so two decafs were brewed and slowly consumed as Brewster and Chloe flicked through newspaper and website pages respectively.

After coffee, as routine demanded, Archie came looking for any sign that his evening constitutional was about to happen. Although Brewster could have seen it far enough today, Archie's doleful look could not be denied and he began to make his way towards his coat and gloves at the front door, accompanied by an excited hound.

In truth, Brewster enjoyed his evening walk with Archie. Apart from helping digestion and getting some fresh air, having usually been inside most of the day, it was also a chance to think without fear of distraction. This evening his thoughts turned swiftly towards the case of the human heart discovered at the local butcher and what further information the 'testator silens' might yield at postmortem. Several trains of thought were running through his mind when he was interrupted by Archie doing his obligatory revolving manoeuvre heralding a poo. Having settled on a site and commenced proceedings he then, much to Brewster's dismay, started another revolution which produced an end result not unlike the sun and its solar system spreading out in an arc. Brewster sighed and bent down hoping that he had enough room in the one poo bag for all the 'planets' up to and including Neptune.

Having completed the task, Archie looked up. As he was very much a dog of routine, Brewster wasn't sure if the eyeballing was saying *That's what you get for delaying my walk* or if he was on the look out for a treat.

"No chance, mate," was Brewster's reply as he headed off towards the nearest doggie bin, before taking a direct route home to the warmth of the house and an early night. Tomorrow was going to be a big day, he sensed.

CHAPTER 4

Wednesday 11th December

Lily Bankhurst woke slightly before her alarm at 0700. She'd had a fitful sleep which often happened at the start of a big case, especially if she was SIO. Although the postmortem was still to be done, she felt that there were already the hallmarks of a very unusual case, likely to spark interest at a national level. Excitement and trepidation filled her in equal measure. It was still pitch dark outside when she entered the shower to help vitalise her for the day ahead. She'd had a look in at her eight-year-old son, Andrew, who was still fast asleep and she decided to leave him undisturbed a little longer, before attempting the daily challenge of getting him up, dressed, fed and ready for school. He was most certainly not a morning person.

Lily's parents had moved from Southampton to Glasgow when she was a child. She had developed a hybrid accent of Hampshire mixed with Glaswegian, and had not had an easy time at school. She had been easy prey for teasing, if not outright bullying, and hated the way she spoke. Over the years, however, she had grown more proud of the individuality of her accent, and now wore it like a badge of honour, though was still frequently mistaken for North American, Irish or even Indian on one occasion!

Perhaps because of her school years, and ongoing challenges she had faced ascending the Police Scotland career ladder as a single female parent, she had developed into a strong woman. She was fair to colleagues but didn't suffer fools gladly, and at times would tell them so. She was confident she could look after herself in the still, at times, misogynistic world of the Police Force. In truth, she actually identified well with many of her male colleagues at work and quite liked a bit of blokey humour, as long as it didn't go too far. She was not unaware, in fact, that some of her most demanding issues had been generated by her XX bearing female colleagues.

She towel dried her hair before straightening it with her beloved GHD irons.

Thank heavens for GHDs.

She noted her roots were a bit more obvious, and wondered how much more noticeable they would be by the time of her next appointment with her hairdresser. Make up was applied. Enough to still look attractive and professional, but not like she was about to go on a night out. She glanced down at her nails and grinned. As a type 1 diabetic, she had always had short, non-feminine looking nails because of the rigours of multiple daily blood sugar testing which demanded the use of fiddly equipment and nimble fingers. Longer nails were a luxury she had denied herself for the sake of practical expediency. Scientific advances had produced continuous blood sugar monitoring devices which were attached to the skin. A swipe of a reader could produce an instant result, without the necessity for pin prick finger testing. An unexpected, and very welcome, benefit was to allow her to explore the world of local nail bars and she had settled on some quite subtle, but stylish, acrylic nails, the novelty of which still raised a smile from time to time.

A final look in the mirror produced a whisper to herself "Not bad, girl. Not bad." Satisfied that she was ready to face the rigours of the day she went through to Andrew's room to give him his first nudge before heading downstairs to put the kettle on and prepare her first insulin injection of the day.

By 8.30am, Andrew had been dropped off at school and Bankhurst was in the Incident Room of Aberdeen Police Station. The white board on the wall was conspicuously empty of data as the investigation team shuffled in. Some were carrying coffee, the aroma of which did not go unnoticed by Bankhurst, and she

wished that she too had taken the time to visit the machine in the corridor. At that time, because the possible extent of the investigation was not fully established, a team of six officers had been assigned. Bankhust herself as DI and SIO supported by DSs Hamish MacDonald and Zafar Iqbal, along with DCs Alison Fraser, Hugh MacLennan and Michel Babinski (aka "Reflex").
Bankhurst, who already had a reputation for being a stickler for punctuality and a no nonsense approach , wasted no time in focusing the team, even though one of them was still to arrive.
"Ok guys, listen up, we need to hit the ground running on this one."
"As some of you may know, the post mortem isn't until this afternoon, but there's nothing to stop us from cracking in the meantime."
"Hamish. Can you and Reflex go over to Cults? We need to get a list of, and interview, all employees there. Can you also speak to the SOCOs about getting prints from all staff and DNA samples from father, son and anyone else who may have handled the heart. It's mainly for exclusion purposes but we can also check for any records in the PNC."
"Aye, no problem, Boss," replied MacDonald.
The door opened and Alison Fraser tiptoed in five minutes late, with coffee in hand. Bankhurst's eyes glanced at the wall clock for probably less than a second, but that was enough for everyone in the room, including Fraser, to feel the unspoken admonishment. One or two looked slightly uncomfortable and shifted positions in their chairs.
Bankhurst was pleased her subtle gesture had not gone unnoticed as she was thinking *If you've enough time to put makeup on and joust with the (notoriously unreliable) coffee machine you can get your arse to the meeting on time!*

"Now that I think about it, Alison, you go with the guys to Cults too."
The order might normally have been framed in the form of a request but she had lost that privilege as a result of her tardiness,

and the mood had become more imperative.

"I want you to focus on the security of the premises, including any CCTV from Mitchell's or surrounding area. Any recent break-ins? Signs of forced entry? Anybody seen any odd behaviour recently? You know the sort of things."

Fraser nodded her understanding of the delegated task.

"We need to be thinking," continued Bankhurst, "About the potential chain of possession for the heart and opportunities to get it to, or place it at, the butchers."

"Zafar. Can you and Hugh work on this?"

"Which abattoir do they use? Is there more than one in Aberdeen? How is the meat transported? Is it checked on arrival? How is it processed after arrival?"

"Hugh, can you organise a list of missing persons for Grampian, Highland and Tayside for the last three months please? While you're on the PNC can you do a search for any similar MOs in Scotland in the last five years. On second thought, better make it the whole of the UK."

"I've to have a meeting with 'upstairs' this morning but I'll catch up with you at lunch time and we can go to the postmortem this afternoon," she said nodding in Iqbal's direction, who acknowledged the instruction.

"Ok, what else do we need to be thinking about?" she said. addressing the whole group. Training sessions encouraged such inclusiveness, but she actually found brainstorming with colleagues a useful tool and also found it a means to get a handle on the abilities, or not, of her youngest colleagues, and what roles she might entrust to them.

"Motive," said MacDonald, following up with "Why, why why?" with a perplexed look on his face. "It's so bizarre."

"Was it meant to be discovered, or have gone under the radar?" he added.

"Can't really think about the 'Who would gain?' question until we get an ID," added Iqbal, getting dangerously close to stating the bleeding obvious.

"Are there any other body parts lurking around the butcher?"

contributed Fraser trying to recover some lost ground.
"All fair points," admitted Bankhurst, "which will be kept in mind as we move forward."
"The other thing to mention, and I hope it is actually superfluous saying this, but I want strict confidentiality in this case. Nothing goes beyond the immediate team, and a complete blackout on any social media comments no matter how obtuse."
Her tone of voice and body language did not invite any further comment and, if there was any lingering doubt that the meeting was finished, it was dispelled as she stood up and closed her laptop in one swift movement.
"Ok. Everybody on with your tasks."
"Meet back here at 4pm for an update".
And with that she departed, the door slowly swinging closed behind her with a slight creak. A diminuendo of chattering noise from her colleagues followed her as she paced down the corridor.

Feeling the need for coffee, she persuaded the machine to part with something loosely described as a latte, and took it to her office to nurse while she gathered her thoughts for her meeting with DCI Anderson scheduled for mid morning. Bankhurst didn't watch too many TV police dramas but those that she did always seemed to portray the SIO's immediate boss as demanding and unreasonable, who in turn was being squeezed by those further up the police or political food chain. DCI Ken Anderson, however, could not be further from this image, unlike his own boss, Superintendent John MacNiven who, in Bankhurst's opinion deserved his reputation for being slippery, evasive, manipulative and someone who would prioritise personal career progression above everything else. Even good police work.
He wasn't known as Shifty MacNiven for nothing. She was forever grateful that the mild mannered, supportive Anderson frequently acted as a human buffer between herself and what she perceived as her somewhat odious Superintendent.

Half an hour later, she had climbed the three flights of stairs to the DCI's office. She felt slightly sweaty and dizzy as she alighted on the designated landing and, not for the first time, faced the dilemma of deciding if it was due to low blood sugar or the myriad of other states, both physiological and pathological, that unhelpfully mimic hypoglycaemia.

A quick scan of her Freestyle Libre monitor on her arm reassured her, on this occasion, that the latter was not a contributory factor and her symptoms were probably just due to the exertion of climbing the stairs at pace and some anxiety ahead of her meeting with one, or more, of her superiors. A mid morning snack, to help regulate her blood sugar control, could reasonably be delayed until after the meeting, and it would give her a good excuse to accompany it with a second coffee as she felt the need for a further caffeine boost.

She cursed her type A personality for making her rush everywhere and took a few moments to compose herself as she was aware of both her sweaty brow and clinging blouse.

Two knocks on the door were followed by an, " Enter". She obeyed her instruction and within seconds felt more at ease, pleased both by the presence of her smiling DCI and the absence of Shifty MacNiven.

"Hello Lily. Come in. Have a seat," as he gestured to one of the vacant chairs ,which Bankhurst gratefully accepted.

" Well. This is certainly a strange one, is it not?" he asked rhetorically.

"I know it's early days but where are we at?"

Bankhurst outlined the team involved and their agreed plan moving forward, including her and Iqbal attending the afternoon postmortem. She considered requesting an expansion of the team but thought better of it at that point.

Anderson appeared to read her mind.

"We'll stick with six meantime until we get some preliminary results, but I can look into sending you some extra bodies if required in due course."

"Thanks, Sir. That would be appreciated."

"Who's briefing the Communications Team? With the police activity and crime scene tape all over Mitchell's in Cults, the P & J and Northsound Radio will be all over this in no time."

P & J are the widely used initials for the Press and Journal, the local daily newspaper covering NE Scotland and Highland areas, also noted for being Scotland's oldest daily publication, and still read by a significant percentage of the local population, either on-line or in traditional print.

"We need to get ahead of this, as there is likely to be all sorts of speculation."

"Totally agree, Sir. I'm going to liaise with Communications myself. As it happens, it's Alan Zimmerman on today, covering the whole of Police Scotland, but based in Aberdeen. I actually know him quite well. He might have an added sensitivity to a local issue perhaps. At any rate, we'll put our heads together and he'll draft a press release. We'll probably limit it to something like 'investigation of a potentially serious item' or words to that effect and once he's fleshed it out and edited it, he'll proactively publish to the various media outlets with a promise of an update tomorrow."

"OK, sounds good," responded Anderson. "Let's have another face to face tomorrow; same time. Keep me in the loop if there are any significant developments in the meantime."

"Will do. Thanks, Sir."

Bankhurst skipped down the stairs with a slight spring in her step having got the, potentially awkward, meeting with senior staff out of the way, and with the prospect of a coffee and snack on the horizon. Normally she would content herself with a piece of fruit or an oat based bar but today, with the easy excuse of the extra weight of a homicide case, she was going to have an Aberdeen roll, also known as a rowie, from the canteen. To hell with the extra carbohydrate load. She would make an adjustment to her lunchtime insulin to compensate.

The rowie did not disappoint and the salty, fatty treat was exactly what she was hoping for. She took a few minutes, while drinking her coffee, to check her own social media, and then phoned Communications to provide Zimmerman with the necessary information for their particular cog in the Police Scotland machine. Satisfied that she had set appropriate investigative wheels in motion, she decided to spend a couple of hours on other ongoing cases before grabbing some lunch and liaising with DS Iqbal prior to the postmortem.

The walk over to the Police Morgue was a short enough distance not to demand going back to pick up a coat, but long enough to freeze them to the core such that they were both shivering and muttering expletives about how cold it was by the time they entered the morgue foyer.

Brewster, who had already lunched on homemade soup and a sandwich, was donning the last of his PPE when he heard the stamping of feet announcing the arrival of his chilled colleagues. Sensibly they seemed to take a couple of minutes to warm up before entering the deathly coolness of the morgue. Brewster detected a smell of aftershave and perfume and he suspected both detectives had re-charged their scent to help disguise the many noxious smells potentially liberated during an autopsy.

Mind you, he considered, on this occasion there was only one well preserved, non-putrid organ and no gastric contents to worry about, so they probably needn't have bothered.

Having warmed up slightly, Bankhurst knocked on the door as a courtesy but opened it before receiving an answer. Pleasantries were exchanged with Brewster while she and Iqbal moved towards their customary position in the viewing gallery where she was reminded how uncomfortable the wooden seats were. Brewster put on his head piece and mike which would allow him both to dictate to his voice recognition software and communicate with the assembled CID officers.

"Before we start the PM, I had a call from the reporting radiologist on the PMCT scan about fifteen minutes ago. The calcium score of the coronary arteries would be in keeping with someone in their fifties or sixties although, as I mentioned to you before, there are several factors, other than age, which can influence this. Still, it's a small piece in the jigsaw and hopefully we'll get more from the PM, DNA and toxicology."

"Thanks, Dexter. All information is useful. Obviously, our top priority at the moment is to ID who this heart came from. We're assuming foul play is very likely but could it be some kind of sick joke? Could it have come from an anatomy department for instance? Wouldn't be the first time medical students have overstepped the practical joke mark."

A raised eyebrow and a tilt of the head was directed towards Brewster as if to say *No offence Doc.*

"None taken," he responded with a slight smile remembering some of his own undergraduate antics though this, he reflected, would be in a completely different league were it to be so.

"What about diseased hearts that have been removed just prior to transplant?" she continued. "Are they destroyed or kept as specimens? Could someone within the NHS access such organs? What about laboratory grown organs from stem cells? I've read there have been great advances in this area of science."

"Just trying to keep our minds open at this stage," she continued.

"All very good questions," conceded Brewster, "two of which are easily put to bed very soon. I can rule out a stem cell grown heart, though, with rapid advances in medicine, perhaps I wouldn't be able to do so in a few years. As far as an explant heart is concerned, that should be immediately obvious when I start the PM as, by definition, the heart will be severely diseased."

Bankhurst made a mental note to delegate one of her team to contact the Departments of Anatomy and Surgery at Aberdeen University.

"Ok. Let's get started then," he continued.

"I've actually already weighed and measured the heart. The first thing to say is that this is a bigger than average heart. Now, that could just be it is a normal heart proportionate to the size of a large human, and therefore more likely to be male, or it is cardiomegaly, that means an abnormally large heart that could have come from a normal sized human but was abnormally large because of some pathological process. In the latter case, it's as likely to be from a female as a male. Having handled the heart as I measured it, I would say it is likely to be unhealthy.

The heart is basically a very efficient, and thankfully reliable, pump. It's approximately 90% cardiac muscle and a healthy heart feels just like toned muscle. This heart felt a bit floppy to my hand. Imagine the difference between the six pack of a gym bunny and what I've got under my scrubs."

The detectives appreciated Brewster's attempt to lighten the mood.

He continued, "I'm just opening up the two ventricles now, that's the larger lower chambers of the heart, and I can confirm as I'm doing that that these are indeed abnormal in that they are dilated and floppy but, beyond that, I see no further abnormality."

There were no comments at this stage from the gallery as Brewster expertly and efficiently dissected the heart and within twenty minutes he had completed his examination. He checked to see if his ongoing commentary, at times edited for the lay detectives present, had been recorded by the speech recognition software and, once confirmed, he logged out of the programme but kept the mike on for discussion purposes.

"So, in summary, this was a diseased heart showing evidence of three different coronary pathologies affecting the valves, coronary arteries and coronary muscle. The presumed valve disease was confined to the Aortic valve and had already been treated by a St Jude mechanical valve. There was no serial number on the valve."

The last sentence was slow and deliberate accompanied by a knowing look above his mask in the direction of Bankhurst and Iqbal as if to say *That would have been too easy!*

"The coronary arteries showed evidence of nascent coronary artery disease which may or may not have been causing symptoms in the form of angina at the time of death. The coronary musculature showed evidence of significant cardiomyopathy which would very likely have been causing symptoms, in the form of exercise related breathlessness, at the time of death. Despite the pathologies present, I don't think the extent of the coronary disease would have warranted transplantation so we can exclude that theory."

"I've taken samples for histology, DNA and toxicology," he added.

"Thanks, Dexter. Remind me what Histology is again please?" said Bankhurst.

"That's where we look at the tissue under the microscope."

"Of course," muttered Bankhurst, annoyed with herself for having to ask the question.

"When can we expect some results?" enquired Iqbal.

"Histology in the next twenty four hours and DNA/toxicology in about forty eight hours," replied Brewster.

There was a slight pause before Bankhurst added, "What could have caused the...what did you call it again?"

"Cardiomyopathy?"

"Yes."

"There's actually many different potential causes of cardiomyopathy, including such things as prolonged high blood pressure, genetic susceptibility, metabolic conditions and certain poor lifestyle choices.

It may be difficult to say without the Past Medical History, not to mention the rest of the body, being available to assist the diagnostic process but the histology may throw some light on the issue."

"Lifestyle choices?" repeated Bankhurst with a slight inflection at the end to indicate a question.

"Mainly prolonged significant alcohol and cigarette consumption," he replied, "though the latter is more likely to be related to the coronary artery disease."

Bankhurst inwardly wondered what constituted *prolonged significant alcohol consumption* as she considered her own lifestyle choices, especially during her training years at Tulliallan Police College. As a teetotaller and non-smoker, Iqbal required no such self examination.

"OK. Thanks, Brewster. Can you let us know as soon as you have anything?"

"No problem. Will do," he replied before switching the mike off and beginning the process of doffing his PPE.

Both detectives were content that the postmortem had been relatively brief and, thankfully, odourless but slightly deflated that it hadn't generated any immediate signpost, such as a serial number on the valve, to establish the much desired ID. The cool ambiance of the morgue did not encourage unnecessary lingering, and they promptly took their leave and walked briskly back to the main station making a bee line for the potential warmth to be had from a coffee machine offering.

Bankhurst had nipped into the toilet and, when she came out, she noted Iqbal seemed to be rehearsing some kind of defensive looking cricket shot while he waited for his coffee. He had his left elbow at a right angle, and the back of his left hand pointing diagonally towards the floor as he had fended the imaginary delivery.

He didn't see her coming and jumped slightly when she observed, "I think that one may have got through between bat and pad."

"Ha ha," he said, looking slightly embarrassed. "See you, Boss, you're dead right! A often get bowled through the gate, so I do."

"Never knew you were interested in cricket, Boss."

"Don't worry. I'm not. Could never understand a game you can play for five days and end up with a draw! Or even a tie, I believe, which is different again!"

"Och, a tie is very rare, Boss, by the way...but it is dead exciting!"

"For someone not interested you seem to know quite a bit about cricket," he continued.

"Oh my ex was into it; I guess I absorbed some stuff by osmosis."

"Well, you'd be very welcome anytime at Mannofield if we've a home match. We still put on a pretty good tea, you know."

"No thanks, I'd rather spend my free Saturdays on something that interests me a wee bit more...watching paint dry, for instance."

"Ooh, below the belt, Boss, below the belt," as he flashed her a handsome grin.

Not for the first time, she felt a slight rise in her heartbeat in response to his smile. She did her best to ignore it this time but in the past she had considered what it might be like to get Zafir *under the covers.* Other more salacious cricketing innuendos came to mind, involving his middle stump, but she tried not to entertain them and cheapen her thought process. She satisfied herself with a grin of her own and a gentle shove to get him out of the way of the machine.

Two hundred metres away in a different building a different hobby was being enacted. After Brewster had finished his mini postmortem, he was having a few minutes to himself in his office before editing and correcting his dictation. He looked around for the most appropriate prop; in the end he picked up a pencil from his desk-tidy and held it in both hands at waist level. He then proceeded to 'play' *The Rose of Kelvingrove* on the pencil, in lieu of the chanter on his Great Highland bagpipes, at the same time as puffing out his cheeks in a mock inflation of the same. He had been a member of the Grampian Police Pipe Band for fifteen years, and Wednesday was rehearsal night during the winter. A wee reminder of the current tune being practised seemed like a good idea. At the height of the summer season, the band would often rehearse twice a week as well as compete at weekends, sometimes at the expense of a little marital harmony. While Chloe supported his continuing membership of the band, he was aware that she sometimes begrudged the commitment required particularly during the short summers that NE Scotland tends to be granted.

In truth he had, himself, found the commitment latterly more onerous than previously but each year the lure of the camaraderie, musicianship, teamwork and humour proved too alluring to resist. It was still a thrill to be part of a well-rehearsed, perfectly in tune, moving musical ensemble.

Indeed, when multiple bands contributed to a massed pipe band, at a Highland Games or specific Pipe Band competition, the collective result was as powerful and glorious as ever, and still made the hairs on the back of his neck stand to attention.

Having acquitted himself, he thought, reasonably well on the pencil, he returned it to the desk-tidy and spent the next few minutes editing and saving his dictation. Having used the voice recognition software for some time, it was now well attuned to his accent and was probably 95% accurate. However, in his occupation, 100% accuracy was required, so he always had to edit and correct his work to achieve the necessary benchmark. Having satisfied himself that all appropriate corrections had been made, he saved the document and moved over to an adjacent desk where the slide he had prepared earlier sat in readiness on the stage of the microscope awaiting further assessment. He made himself comfortable in the seat, settled his left eye into the eyepiece and adjusted the focus. He spent a few minutes moving the slide around on the stage, then paused to refer to Muir's Textbook of Pathology, before returning to the slide for a further assessment.

"Interesting," he muttered to himself as he stretched over to pick up the phone. He glanced at his noticeboard to check his list of "useful numbers", and dialled in the sequence for the Incident Room.

CHAPTER 5

"Incident Room," was stated in the unmistakable Western Isles accent of DS MacDonald.

"Hi, Hamish (Brewster felt he knew him well enough to call him by his first name) this is Dexter Brewster here. Is your boss around at the moment?"

"Aye, she is that. I'll just go and get her for you."

A few moments later, Bankhurst picked up the phone.

"Hi, Dexter, I wasn't expecting to hear from you so soon."

"Something of interest has turned up in the initial histology assessment, and I wanted to let you know before your afternoon team meeting. I've found extensive extracellular spaces and shrunken cells in the sample of cardiac muscle."

When no further explanation was forthcoming, Bankhurst ventured, " Sorry to sound like a cliché, Dexter, but could I have that in English please?"

"Apologies!" he stated as he realised that he wasn't speaking to a Pathology colleague.

"What this is highly suggestive of is that the heart has been frozen and subsequently thawed."

He paused for a few seconds to let this sink in.

"This is significant for two reasons. Firstly it could significantly affect the time frame when the presumed victim met their fate, and it will potentially adversely affect the accuracy of our examination of the tissue in our attempt to diagnose the underlying cause of the cardiomyopathy."

He continued,"I think I overheard you discussing earlier with Zafar that you'd delegated someone to generate a missing persons list for the last three months..."

He let the sentence trail off but Bankhurst joined the dots and finished it herself with, "So we'll have to extend that search period significantly," she said with a sigh.

"OK, Dexter, that's good to know. Appreciate the heads-up. Let me know when anything else turns up."

"Of course," he replied. "bye for now."

She put the phone down and whispered, "What the fuck?" to herself.

MacDonald, who was still relatively nearby, raised an eyebrow as if to say *What?*

Bankhurst duly explained the content of the call.

"I'll explain it to the rest at the briefing."

Those who weren't already in the Incident Room started to drift in from about 3.30pm and all were present and correct at 4pm, with no repeat of the morning tardiness.

"OK. Let's get started. I'll kick off by bringing you up to date with the result of the postmortem," said Bankhurst.

She then proceeded to present what was essentially Brewster's summary and subsequent phone call along with the likely time frame for getting toxicology and DNA results.

"I've also had a meeting with 'upstairs'- we've to continue with our current team meantime but may get reinforcements depending on how things pan out," to which there was some general mumbling of discontent.

"I know. I know," she continued, "but it is what it is meantime."

"How did you guys get on at Cults?" she asked while looking in the direction of MacDonald, Babinski and Fraser.

"Fine so far, Boss," replied MacDonald as the senior officer who had been to Cults. We've established there are a total of seven staff at Mitchells; three butchers, a baker who does their pies, two counter staff and a cleaner. It's a very stable staff and there have been no recent changes. We've done home interviews on three who lived locally and, as the SOCOs will hopefully be finished by close of play today, we thought we might get the rest of the staff into the premises tomorrow to finish the interviews, and spare them the trip to the station."

"Sounds reasonable," agreed Bankhurst. "Any surprises so far?"

"No. Not really. We've PNC'd all the names. Apart from a couple of minor traffic offences, there's nothing to report. The interviews thus far have been unremarkable."

"Alison?" Bankhurst enquired of her DC with a look in her direction inviting a contribution.

"Same with me really. Nothing out of the ordinary. Premises were secure and no history of recent break-ins. Security cameras at the back of premises and in the main shop. I've arranged downloads of footage but haven't had a chance to view yet. Nobody in or around Mitchells itself has noticed any suspicious behaviour that they can recall. I'm also arranging to get data from four nearby businesses, and a house across the road, who have CCTV. Unfortunately most of the business cameras are focussed internally on their clientele, and the till, but you never know, we might get lucky."

"OK. Have you anything to add, Reflex?" Bankhurst enquired.

"No. Not really...except to say the pies look A-MAZ-ING!" Bankhurst allowed herself a subtle facial acknowledgement of the humour. She wasn't averse to some wit and sometimes it was essential to get you through some of the grimmest days that police work threw at you.

"Zafar?"

"Ok. We've established there's only one main abattoir servicing Aberdeen. Wilson's. It's on the outskirts of the city in Dyce. Actually, quite a big concern and employs forty-four people. We've been over there earlier and talked to management."

"How much did you tell them?"

"To be honest, Boss, I gave them a fair idea as we noticed on the way that Aberdeen Live had picked up the story, and were already posting significant details on-line. Must have been some leakage from the butcher's staff or nearby businesses. Inevitable, I suppose."

"Damn. I was hoping to keep it under wraps for another twenty-four hours or so. You know what's going to happen now?"

Bankhurst asked rhetorically.

The team all nodded as most of them had previous experience, either first hand or by proxy, of the added challenge that a case with high press interest would bring.

"OK. We need to try and keep ahead of this. I'll speak to Alan Zimmerman in Comms about putting out another press release. We should also proactively contact all butchers, or businesses that have butchery departments, in the North East, and ask them to have a low threshold for reporting anything suspicious in their meat and organ stocks."

Iqbal continued, "We've asked the Abattoir to pause their operation meantime and have a thorough inspection of all their stock to see if there are any more suspicious organs identifiable. We've also set up interviews for tomorrow and Friday though, to be honest, we could do with a bit more manpower, by the way."

He hesitated slightly after using the gender specific noun.

As an east end Glaswegian Asian who played cricket and also happened to support Partick Thistle, he was well placed to know what it was like to be in a minority group. A thick skin, a prerequisite of his childhood, and a sense of humour, had helped. He was not easily offended.

Nevertheless, he was aware of, though didn't necessarily agree with, woke driven societal changes, and was still getting his head around gender neutrality and political correctness.

He needn't have worried. A quick scan of the room showed no eyelids batting, far less any other signs of offence.

He pressed on.

"That's a lot of interviews to get through."

"It is," agreed Bankhurst. "I can give you a hand while we're waiting on the lab results."

"Thanks, Boss."

"Right , a plan moving forward," said Bankhurst. "Hamish, you and Reflex can continue at Cults and, Alison, you can start trawling through the CCTV footage. Hugh, in light of what we now know from the postmortem, can you extend the mispers list to the last twelve months please? We may have to extend beyond that in due course, but let's see how many names that search generates in the first instance. Obviously, we're only interested in those that are still actively missing. Might be interesting to see how many are in the fifties to sixties age bracket."

"Ok. We'll meet again tomorrow first thing; unless there are any significant changes between now and then we'll go with the current plan."

While Bankhurst, in her own mind, had been formulating the team's schedule for the following day, she was keeping in mind that she also had to accommodate a personal commitment she could not break - the Primary Four Nativity play. Andrew had been "super excited" to get the part of one of the wise men, and was impatient to perform his role to his Mum and other parents. She knew it would break his heart if she didn't go so she vowed, despite the gravity of the current case, to take an hour and a half personal time the following day. She was, after all, she argued to herself, significantly in credit with Police Scotland in terms of the many extra unpaid hours she had contributed over the years. She made a mental note to speak to Iqbal the following day about covering her as she drew the meeting to a close.

"OK. Good work, everybody. See you tomorrow at 8-30."

The team shuffled out of the Incident Room and, as they left, Zafar and Reflex were in an animated debate about whether mince pies or steak pies were best and the virtues of short crust versus hot water pastry.

"I'm telling you, Reflex, the best pies **ever** are Glasgow spiced mutton Scotch pies, so they are," was the last audible contribution to the debate as they left the room.

As predicted, that evening the media interest accelerated exponentially across all platforms. Even the local Cults Neighbourhood app had almost gone into meltdown. While a lot of people expressed concern about having something so apparently gruesome in their midst, probably at least as many were worried that they wouldn't get their pre-ordered Festive bird in time for the big day. At least it made a change from reporting an unsolicited dog poo on the corner of Quarry Road and Hillview Crescent.

It was a general rule in police work that the amount of press interest in a case was directly proportional to the pressure and expectation placed upon the SIO by more senior staff. This case was no exception and, in addition to an evening call from Anderson, she also received a text from MacNiven demanding an early morning briefing the next day. *Bang goes the school run* Bankhurst thought as she resigned herself to phone round some of the other parents she knew to arrange a lift for Andrew. At times like this, she really missed living close to her family who remained in the central belt of Scotland. While it was only a two and a half hour drive door to door, and her parents were very willing, it was far enough to exclude them from babysitting, helping out with the school run and other typical grandparental tasks. Still, she had built up a good number of friends who generally were happy to help out, as indeed she was happy to reciprocate when her own commitments permitted.

After moving to Aberdeen, she had applied, as part of the flexible working scheme, to move away from the typical 2-2-2 Police Scotland shift pattern (equally divided between earlies, lates and nights) to a more favourable rota befitting a single parent living away from her nuclear family. She felt, if necessary, she could also have played the diabetic card though she was reluctant to do that as, most of the time, she tried to play down her condition at work.

She needn't have worried as Police Scotland seemed, along with most national organisations, to have embraced anti-discrimination and other modern occupational pro-employee work practices and her application, which would have been unthinkable ten to fifteen years earlier, went through without hindrance. Truth be told, A Division of Police Scotland were glad to have a DI move up from the central belt. Local recruitment and retention, particularly due to artificially high house prices secondary to the oil industry, was challenging. There were only so many officers who could be housed in the dwindling Police accommodation stock. Thus, she had been granted a more or less day shift pattern involving one weekend in four and a week of nights every eight weeks, albeit with an acceptable reduction in salary. Her mother quickly agreed to live-in for the week of night shifts as she enjoyed the break from the, at times, claustrophobic extended family in Glasgow, and she could watch what she liked on the TV away from her husband's dominant remote control behaviour.

In addition to family and friend support, Bankhurst also employed a retired lady for two hours Monday to Friday after school for the afternoon pick-up and to look after Andrew until she got home. He was usually starving after school so Olive would often give him tea and toast to keep him going until his evening meal, which Bankhurst liked to share with him. Olive was a gem and Andrew was very close to her. She had come to realise the unpredictable nature of her employer's job and was happy to stay on for a few hours, or even have him for a sleepover on occasion, which Andrew thoroughly enjoyed as he got the double bonus of more screen time and a later bedtime than was granted him at home.

Bankhurst attended to administrative necessities, but made sure she left in good time to get back to her terraced house on the Countesswells estate on the west edge of Aberdeen by 6pm to relieve Olive of her duties. They had the customary exchange of pleasantries and chit-chat before she bade her farewell.

Bankhurst was desperate for a glass of wine, but thought it wasn't a good optic to immediately head for the half drunk bottle of Sauvignon Blanc in the fridge as soon as Olive had closed the door.

She could see that Andrew was very excited about the prospect of the Nativity Play and she let him vent about that, ending in a promise she would go over his lines after tea. Her earlier temperance could not be sustained and she enjoyed two large gulps of wine as she started busying herself with food preparation. She continued her chat with Andrew who had meanwhile picked up an ipad and was increasingly drawn to the attraction of the tablet at the expense of conversation with his Mum. It was near the end of term and homework was minimal so she let it go while deciding a top up of wine was warranted.

Tea was easy as she had taken out a homemade chilli aliquot from the freezer in the morning which had dutifully defrosted during the day and just had to be heated through. Andrew liked a mildly spiced chilli but was not keen on kidney beans, so Bankhurst always substituted them with baked beans which, in truth, kept both mother and child happy. She put the rice on to cook knowing that by the time it had done so the chilli would be more than ready to serve, and she would also have time to check her blood sugar and calculate her evening dose of fast acting insulin.

Mother and son were soon enthusiastically devouring the evening's fare as Andrew discussed both his playground football exploits and the much anticipated Christmas Day. He was just on the cusp of being a non-believer of Santa Claus but couldn't quite allow himself to join that camp lest it somehow adversely affected the flow of presents. Bankhurst was in no hurry to enlighten him and was happy she would have at least one more Xmas with Santa's legend largely intact.

Having completed the meal, washed up and rehearsed the Nativity Play there wasn't much of joint interest on TV so Bankhurst allowed Andrew a little more screen time while she surfed the internet. She would aim to get Andrew up to bed and settled by 9pm so she could watch some sort of post watershed TV; anything but a police drama.

Thursday 12th December

"Come on, Andrew!"

"I'm coming."

"What are you **doing?"**

"I can't find my gym top."

"It's been washed...it's drying in the utility room...might still be a bit wet."
"Awh, Muuum!"
"It won't kill you."
"I'll get pneumonia...or something."
"No you won't."
"Gran said that's what happens if you wear wet clothes."
"Well Gran's a diddy then," she said in a low voice.
"What did you say?"
"Nothing. Come on! We're going to be late."

Andrew, who was capable of nursing a grievance, was still muttering about 'double pneumonia' when Bankhurst closed the car door behind him. She felt a pang of guilt and, not for the first time, questioned her credentials as a mother. She climbed into the driver's seat, promised to return to some self reproach later, and switched on the radio seeking some diversion. Reinforcing a recent trend, she opted for Radio 2 instead of Radio 1.
OMG, I'm turning into my mother!

Despite the slight altercation, Bankhurst managed to arrive reasonably promptly at the Nelson Street station to give herself ten minutes preparation time ahead of her meeting with her superintendent. After knocking on the door and entering, MacNiven eyed her up and down from behind his alpha male desk.
"Ah, it's you, Bankhurst. Sit." as he beckoned to the one available seat.
"Thank you, Sir."
MacNiven made a point of finishing the documents he was signing before re-engaging with his subordinate.
"Now, bring me up to speed with where we are on this Cults matter."
Bankhurst had anticipated the question and, in her mind, had prepared a summary of where the investigation had reached to that point. Before she could finish, he interrupted her.

"The thing is, I had old man Mitchell on the phone to me last evening. I play golf with him on occasion at Deeside and know him quite well. The family are very keen to get this sorted out ASAP, as this is their busy time of year. The last thing they want is another William Low type scandal."

Bankhurst had no idea what he was speaking about, and it must have shown on her face.

"Of course, you're not from this area, and neither are you old enough to know about the William Low food poisoning outbreak. There was a significant cluster of typhoid cases in Aberdeen in the 1960s. Eventually, it was traced to some corn beef that had been through a meat slicing machine in a family chain of grocers called William Low. Unfortunately, many people became unwell and there were several fatalities. Aberdeen was quarantined from the rest of the country for weeks, and there were daily health bulletins quite similar to what we had recently during the Covid pandemic. There was a stigma attached to coming from Aberdeen for months, if not years, afterwards and the William Low shop never recovered, eventually closing its doors permanently."

"Although this is a completely different situation, people of a certain age still remember the notorious typhoid outbreak, and old man Mitchell's point is that mud sticks; they want to get back to business as usual as soon as possible with their reputation untarnished."

Bankhurst felt herself bristling.

"You'll appreciate, Sir, that SOCO will take as long as they need to do the job properly," she retorted in the knowledge that if things went south in the future, and any shortcuts were identified in a subsequent investigation, it would be her neck, and not MacNiven's, that would be on the proverbial chopping block.

"Of course. Of course," he muttered.

"But let's keep this thing moving along at good speed nevertheless." Bankhurst recognised this was an opportunity to press for extra help so she countered.

"To do that, Sir, I could really do with some extra bodies to help, as there's a lot of work to get through as you can imagine."

"Very well," he replied in an almost begrudging tone. "I'll see about organising a few more officers for your team."

"Thank you, Sir," Bankhurst replied.

That's the least you can do if you want to keep your golf buddy happy.

As she closed the door behind her, she felt a slight flush of success.

"Yes!" she uttered, while balling her right hand into a fist to give a small celebratory air punch. It felt like a positive start to the day.

She was still on a slight high when the morning briefing started and wasted no time in breaking the good news to her colleagues, whose facial responses suggested they were grateful recipients.

"Right," she said, "Today's about carrying on the groundwork while we're waiting for toxicology and genetics. We need to continue trawling through the Cults CCTV footage, and I also want every scrap of CCTV in and around the abattoir. I can't help thinking that the overall size of that building, and the significant number of staff coming in and out, offer a better opportunity of placing a nefarious object in the food chain there. Check their own cameras first obviously."

"Also, I know it's more an industrial than residential area but, as I understand it, there are a few houses nearby. See if any of them have CCTV, and don't forget to check for doorbell cameras. When you're over there watch out for any cyclists who may use that street as part of a regular journey. Some of them have cameras on their helmets. Long shot, I realise, but you never know."

"Hugh, can you ring toxicology just now and see if they have any provisional results?"

"Will do, Boss."

"What sort of tack are we going to take on the interviews, Boss? It's a bit tricky not knowing the ID of the deceased. Can't really ask what was their knowledge or relationship to the victim and other such questions," enquired Iqbal.

"Fair point, Zafar. Guess we have to concentrate meantime

on general questions about suspicious behaviour, security concerns, disaffected colleagues etc. Make sure we PNC the entire staff and start with any that have a sniff of a record. There may well be foreign nationals working there, so don't forget to check Interpol."

At the latter, Iqbal frowned and tilted his head a little as if to say *Really*?

"Sorry, Zafar. I know. Granny...sucking eggs...teaching," as she realised her slightly less than diplomatic error.

"It's just such an important case, and may turn out to be the biggest I have been SIO on, so just want to get everything right."

Zafar raised his right hand with fingers spread slightly to signify *I get it, don't worry.*

"As soon as we get extra bodies, I'll get them to help out with interviews and CCTV research, while we wait for some more concrete lines of inquiry."

"Let's see if we can get something....anything...on that white board. I don't like it being blank."

At which point MacLennan, who had been phoning Toxicology in the corner of the room, interjected.

"I may be able to help you with that. The lab has found Benzodiazepines and alcohol in the sample. They're working on trying to identify a specific drug."

"Ok. Thanks, Hugh. That's a start! Put it on the board please."

"Benzos can be prescription or non-prescription, self-administered or covertly administered so, I guess, we have to keep an open mind meantime," to which there was general nodding of agreement within the room despite the fact that one junior officer present wasn't exactly sure what covert administration was and made a mental note to google it afterwards.

"OK, thanks everybody. Afternoon briefing is a bit earlier today at 3pm. See you then."

As the team shuffled out she added, "Can I have a quick word please, Zafar?"

The DS duly obliged and hung back while the room emptied.

Bankhurst explained the festive parental commitment she was very keen to honour that afternoon, and asked if Iqbal would cover for her for an hour or two. Of the two DSs she had on the team, she had more faith in Iqbal. She found MacDonald to be slower and less conscientious than she would like. His soft, lilting, almost musical, Hebridean accent perhaps didn't help but there had been a few occasions when she had felt like lighting the proverbial fire under him. She had been on enough courses to know that you can't expect everybody in a group to have the same personality trait as herself, in her case type A, and that groups work well with a personality mix. She couldn't make up her mind if he was a type B or just, in fact, lazy. Either way, she preferred to entrust Iqbal with the investigative reins, and could live with the possibility that MacDonald's nose might be out of joint, if indeed he ever found out.

"No problem, Boss. You go and see your waen in the play," was the predictable response from the affable DS.

"You could put your phone on silent and if there's something that comes in which can't wait, I could always text you."

"Thanks, Zafar. Appreciate that'

Iqbal left the room and, while Bankhurst was in child cover arrangement mode, she dialled her mother's mobile number. She explained she was SIO on the case, which her Mum had actually seen in the national media, and, although she was rostered to be off that weekend, the gravity of the case demanded at least the part time on-site presence of the SIO on Saturday and Sunday. Her Mum, who had no commitments she couldn't extricate herself from, was quick to agree a trip north for the weekend as she hadn't seen either her daughter or grandson for a few weeks. Besides, with her over sixty travel card, it would only cost a 50p booking fee for the very comfortable express bus journey to Aberdeen, where she could browse the internet to her heart's content and perhaps even treat herself to an on board snack.

In the Pathology department Brewster was slightly frustrated at a lack of histological progress in establishing the cause of the cardiomyopathy identified at postmortem. Although it had been useful to establish that the organ had been frozen and thawed, this process had in turn made further microscopic tissue analysis challenging, and none of the usual staining techniques had yielded a specific diagnosis. Although, to some, this may have appeared somewhat academic, he felt a professional dissatisfaction at what he perceived as an incomplete analysis and, in addition, sometimes a clinical detail, no matter how small, might make a difference in an investigation, especially when the ID of the victim was unknown.

He recognised the limits of his own expertise in the area, and decided to send some of the sample to the national cardiomyopathy reference lab for their opinion. He explained the situation on the electronic request form, marked it urgent and requested the bar code for the sample bottle be printed. After what seemed like a long time, but was probably only a few seconds, the mini desktop printer stuttered into life and spat out the desired bar code, much to his relief; it had been temperamental the previous few days. He made a mental note to raise an issue with the IT help desk, though suspected it would take an outright failure of the device to prompt him to actually do it.

He considered, at that stage, there was nothing more for him to do to progress the case, and he switched his attention to the morning postmortem, a sudden death in a twenty-four-year-old male with needle marks on his arms. Although his training strongly discouraged any form of pre-judgement, it looked like this would follow a fairly predictable, and sadly well worn, path. Time would tell.

Just before lunch, Bankhurst received an e-mail from MacNiven who honoured his promise by confirming another four officers had been assigned to the case. This was more than she anticipated and she reflected that the power of golf cronyism was indeed significant. She e-mailed back expressing her gratitude, and suggested they attend the 3pm afternoon briefing to be brought up to speed, not realising at the time that there would be a further piece of valuable information available to share with her colleagues by that time.

CHAPTER 6

Bankhurst had a light lunch of cold chicken and pasta salad in the police canteen. She was quite relieved to find herself sitting with a dining companion who was both a friend and not on her own team. There was a bit of "non job" chat for a while but, inevitably perhaps, the conversation swung to what was currently the most high profile and intriguing case in the building.

DS Sharon Baxter had already heard the grapevine version of events but couldn't resist getting a more accurate account straight from the horse's mouth.

"Bloody hell, Lily, that's a case and a half!"

Bankhurst nodded her agreement as she had just taken another generous mouthful of what had turned out to be quite a tasty canteen offering and was unable to verbalise anything at that point. She finished her mouthful and drained the last few drops from her Diet Fanta in preparation for re-joining the conversation, but was interrupted by the noise of an incoming text from MacLennan: *Toxicology phoned. Have identified benzodiazepine as flunitrazepam. HMacL.*

Bankhurst raised her eyebrows and tilted the phone to enable her colleague to see the message. They both immediately knew the significance of the result. Flunitrazepam, otherwise known as Rohypnol or, in lay parlance, the "date rape" drug was not licensed for medical use and was invariably used for illicit purposes. This finally removed any vestige of doubt that the extraordinary discovery of a human heart in a suburban family butcher was the product of a homicide.

Bankhurst felt a slight flush of adrenalin and, with it, a renewed determination to get on with it. With a nod to her dining companion, she tidied up her rubbish and headed for the recycling bins.

"Good luck," Baxter shouted after her. Without turning round Bankhurst raised her right hand to acknowledge her colleague's good wishes.

Bankhurst got to the Incident Room early to prepare for the meeting, and took the opportunity to update the white board. The previous comments relating to the discovery of a generic benzodiazepine were removed and replaced with *Toxicology: Flunitrazepam (Rohypnol).*

A steady influx of detectives, including the newly seconded, gathered in the room producing a gradual swell of noise which respectfully faded to silence when Bankhurst got to her feet. She started the meeting with a welcome to the new members of the team, another DS and three DCs. She followed with a summary of the investigation to date, excluding the latest toxicology information.

"For those of the existing team that haven't already noticed I have updated the white board following a recent phone call from the Toxicology lab. They have identified the drug as Flunitrazepam, which I'm sure you will know is the generic name for Rohypnol. Clearly, this case must now be considered as a homicide."

Although, in some ways, she felt she was stating the obvious, she let it sink in for a few seconds. The annual homicide rate for the whole of the NE of Scotland, including Aberdeen, with a total population of about 500,000, could often be counted on the fingers of one hand. Any homicide, therefore, was "a big deal" in terms of the gravity of the crime itself, the amount of press interest it was likely to generate, and the opportunity for officers to gain valuable experience as part of a homicide team. A slight hum returned to the room.

After a brief pause, she continued by inviting feedback from the officers who had been scrutinising CCTV footage of the Abattoir

and surrounding area.
"Nothing significant to report so far, Boss. Just the usual. Staff coming and going, local residents, dog walkers, postie, Prime deliveries and a Deliveroo cyclist last Friday. I checked with the Abattoir and they say they get a Deliveroo at lunchtime once a week for 'Fun Friday', when they also have their staff meeting, so that all checks out. Very quiet at night with just a lone jogger and a taxi driver coming off shift. Oh, and there was also a skulk of foxes around the large waste bins at the back of the abattoir at one point."
"Gaun yersel, Alison," said Iqbal, " [1]*skulk* of foxes," he repeated with heavy emphasis on the word skulk. "Your English degree wasnae a complete waste of time then," he said with a broad smile.
There were those fantastic teeth again, thought Bankhurst before castigating herself.
Stop it. Stop it. It can never happen! I'm his senior officer.
Murray felt like raising her middle finger to Iqbal but contented herself instead with, "Ha bloody ha," and then, after a delay of a few seconds, "Sir!"
"Any doorbell cameras?" enquired Bankhurst.
"Yes, just the one. A couple who live more or less opposite. He's a taxi driver and was in his bed asleep. He works the night shift, but his wife showed us the footage, and all it showed was a good view of his porch and the back of his taxi, which was parked right in front of the door!"
"Typical," muttered Bankhurst with a tut, and slight extension of her neck.
"What about the staff interviews so far?" she continued, directing her attention to those officers charged with that task.
Iqbal, as senior officer involved, took on the responsibility of replying. "We had four PNC hits but nothing major. Breach of the peace, shoplifting, possession of cannabis and drink driving. We've interviewed all of them early on, and don't really have any concerns about any of them. We're making reasonable progress with the other interviews, but will appreciate the extra help,"

as he nodded to the additional officers who had congregated together near to the only heater in the room.

"Ok. Now that we've got extra pairs of hands let's accelerate the interviews, and also start door to door in Cults and Dyce. So far we've just concentrated on houses with some form of CCTV, but time to widen the net and see what it brings in," said Bankhurst. "Mispers update, Hugh?"

"There's about fifty in the last year from the North East that might fit the postmortem projected age but, I guess, with the knowledge the organ had been frozen, and also the relatively small size of the heart itself, making it much more portable than a body, there's really no telling when and where it came from."

"Fair point, Hugh but, for the meantime, let's assume it's relatively local," responded Bankhurst, "While keeping an open mind about other possibilities."

"Any other questions?" she added as she swept the room with her eyes looking for a response.

One of the new DCs raised a hand. Bankhurst was glad when he prefixed his comment by identifying himself, as remembering names was not her forte.

"DC Grant Donaldson, Ma'am. Did you check to see if there was any CCTV available from the taxi?"

"No, we didn't think it would have any because it's always parked with the engine off when the driver's at home," replied Fraser.

"I was just asking as my Dad's a taxi driver. Almost all the cabs have CCTV these days, both internal and external looking. The cameras are powered by the car engine, but they also have small internal batteries which are charged by the same process. The cameras keep recording for quite a while after the engine is switched off until the battery is exhausted. A lot of them also upload images automatically to the cloud."

"OK. That's good information, DC Donaldson," replied Bankhurst, who was both slightly annoyed at not thinking about this herself, and also grateful for the added problem solving ability that a larger team brought. Fraser was also looking a bit sheepish, as clearly it hadn't crossed her mind either, but Bankhurst couldn't hold that against her as they had both been equally unimaginative in their thinking.

"We'll follow that up," as she nodded at Fraser to do the necessary.

The PC understood the non-verbal communication.

"With a bit of luck we should get the DNA result tomorrow which hopefully will be a big help, but meantime let's carry on with the current plan. Probably no need for a briefing tomorrow morning, but let's get together at 4pm. Let me know 'as soon as' if you think you've got anything important in the meantime."

There were a few general mumblings of, "Yes, Boss" and "Yes, Ma'am," from the team. Bankhurst wondered if the new arrivals were a little less enthusiastic in their vocal contributions but perhaps, she reflected, she was being a little paranoid.

Maybe she still had to earn their respect.

She realised the importance of integrating the new members of the team as soon as possible, and trusted that her pragmatic, no-nonsense but fair, approach would suffice in winning them over. *Too bad if it doesn't!*

At 3-40pm she slipped out of the back door of the station towards the car park carrying her handbag, a thick scarf and a sense of guilt. It didn't take long for the biting wind to persuade her to actually wear the scarf, and she enjoyed the warm embrace it offered as she coiled it round her neck.

Although she thought she had left plenty of time for the journey, she found herself rushing through the school hall door and taking her seat near the back with only a couple of minutes to spare. She had felt increasingly uncomfortable at the prospect of being late, and felt a sense of relief as she glanced at her i-watch, after sitting down, to see that she was still within the deadline. She switched her device to theatre mode and waited, with anticipation, for the performance to begin.

The next hour proved a welcome distraction from the weight of the case. Although Andrew didn't have many appearances, with each one Bankhurst felt pride swell within her. She was aware that she was miming his words and doing micro versions of his actions, willing their rehearsals to transform into an accomplished performance. She had considered that this might look slightly strange to anyone behind her. Thankfully, she was in the second last row and, in any case, she wasn't the only person in the audience performing the *anxious parent seat dance.* As the play ended and the house lights came on, there was the obligatory, but actually thoroughly merited, standing ovation. With house lights up it was the first time Andrew had seen the audience, and his sheepish grin broadened into an ear-to-ear smile as he spotted his mother in the audience. The applause finally died away, and the children were ushered off stage to be replaced by the Head Teacher in an effusive and grateful mood. Bankhurst noted that the ever reliable Olive was standing at the back of the hall ready to take her charge home. She went over to share their enthusiasm and appreciation for the play, particularly Andrew's contribution of course, before making a quick exit to extract herself from the car park before it became gridlocked.

The teatime traffic had picked up a bit and it took her slightly longer to return to the station during which time she had tuned the car radio to Northsound for the hourly bulletin. She was relieved to find no surprises in the coverage of the case and retuned back to Radio 2 for the remainder of the journey hoping to catch Sarah Cox's *half wower* spot.
After hanging up her scarf and coat, she checked in with Iqbal who confirmed that she hadn't missed anything of note. In the privacy of her own office, she tidied her hair before ascending the stairs to bring DCI Anderson up to date. She couldn't bear the thought of Shifty MacNiven face to face so decided she would send him an update by e- mail instead, and also inform him that his golf buddy had been told he could re-open his business the following day.
By 5-40 pm she decided that all she could usefully do on case

for the time being had been done and she had no appetite, at that time of day, to look at any of her other ongoing cases. She decided to leave in good time and, for once, meet her 6pm target for getting home.

Andrew was genuinely pleased to see her and was obviously still on a post performance high. An upbeat tripartite dissection of the play followed between Andrew, his mother and Olive before the latter bade her farewells and disappeared into the cold of the evening. Bankhurst made a favourite of Andrew's for tea; sausage beans and chips. In truth it was also one of her own secret guilty pleasures, but she chose not to share that with her son as it might dilute the effect of making a fuss over him on any given occasion.

Such subterfuge but, hey ho, that's what parenthood does to you.

Mother and son spent a pleasant evening together. Andrew even went off to bed without a fight leaving Bankhurst with a couple of priceless hours to herself. She made sure her Lovehoney Ignite 20 was on charge and went back to browsing the net looking for some new trainers.

Her two most favourite battery devices were her electric toothbrush and Lovehoney Ignite vibrator. While nothing could replace the physical and emotional experience of "a good shag" (as her best friend would put it) she was ever the pragmatist. After some initial hesitation, she had grown to like, and even rely upon, her *little pink device*, especially as the length of time between the "shags" was without doubt increasing. The only problem, with both devices, was the lack of a low battery warning. It was not uncommon to have a feeling of exasperation when pressing the 'on' button failed to induce a response. Occasionally, indeed, both devices would be unresponsive on the same night sending her to bed in a somewhat less than convivial mood.

Friday 13th December

Brewster finished the last dregs of his breakfast cup of tea and tossed the toast crust in the general direction of Archie. It never had a chance to reach the floor as the ever alert hound intercepted it in midair. He crunched and swallowed it in an instant, all the while keeping a watchful eye on the human in case any further edible missiles winged their way towards him. Brewster brushed a few crumbs from his trousers onto the floor which Archie looked at disdainfully and decided he wasn't quite that desperate before trotting off to the comfort of the nearest heater. He slumped down somewhat over dramatically and followed up with a big sigh.

Brewster had chosen a good quality suit for the day as he had a court appearance as an expert witness in the afternoon. As was typical of the family routine, Chloe had already taken Archie for his morning walk, with the evening canine exercise responsibility likely to fall to him. He made a mental note to change his trousers when he came home as *Archie's First Law* would likely come into play. As with many cats, and some dogs, Archie had developed the routine of covering any of his pees with surrounding dirt, leaves etc. He only did this when they were walking through the wooded part of their daily route and not, for obvious reasons, on the harder road and pavement surfaces. This would involve fairly aggressive back-pawing of the forest floor debris in an arc of about 120 degrees.

Archies First Law: The likelihood of hitting the human's trousers with post pee debris scatter was directly proportional to the quality and expense of the trousers, or skirt, worn.

This had proven a very reliable law over the years, and one that was unwise to ignore. He hoped he would remember to take appropriate action after being released from the stresses of the day, including a court appearance, and with the lure of something nice in a glass ahead of him.

There had been no further snow overnight but the roads remained treacherous. A slight thaw had been followed by a drop in temperature, creating widespread icy patches on the roads and pavements. He recalled that in a six month spell in Accident and Emergency, during the early part of his career, icy days would inevitably precipitate a surge in fractures from relatively low height falls, in particular those involving the wrist and neck of femur. The department would be packed to the rafters but, on the plus side, it had been an excellent opportunity to practice application of Plasters of Paris... if the plaster technician was in agreement. An offer of coffee and a packet of biscuits would often suffice.

After taking a considerable amount of care, at the cost of being a little late, he arrived unscathed at the small, dedicated car park reserved for the Pathology Department. He swung his car into the duty Pathologist slot wondering, as he did, if his night shift colleague had cause to use the same space overnight. He hoped not. He stamped his feet at the doorway to rid himself of any residual frozen snow on his shoes, and made his way towards his office, exchanging pleasantries with Moira at reception. He hoped he would get the chance to remove his winter overclothes and put the kettle on for his first coffee before anyone came tapping on his door, or calling his phone, with the first demands on his time.

He switched on his desktop computer and navigated through the ever-increasing number of start-up and password screens before finally opening his Police Scotland e-mail account as his normal starting point for the day. He noticed, along with the usual suspects, a recently arrived e-mail from his Pathology colleague in the cardiomyopathy reference laboratory in Glasgow.

Morning, Dexter. Just thought I'd give you a heads up that the cardiac biopsy you sent is staining heavily with Prussian blue. Will probably have more information for you in due course, but thought you'd like to know. All the best, James.

"Ah," Brewster muttered to himself, "another[2] piece in the jigsaw!"

He immediately knew the significance of this information. Prussian blue is a very specific stain for iron, and a significant reaction implies abnormally high levels of the element present in the tissue. This both explained the likely cause of the malfunctioning heart tissue, and also pointed the diagnostic finger towards a small number of rare causal conditions. These were often genetically mediated and he hoped the DNA result expected later that day would give a definitive diagnosis. While not identifying the individual per se, the presence of an unusual illness would perhaps narrow the search significantly. Also, from a clinical point of view, he hated not being able to supply a specific diagnosis for a postmortem abnormality, and this would help salve any sense of his own professional dissatisfaction. He considered contacting Bankhurst, but decided to wait for the DNA result which might yield a more comprehensive answer. Indeed, if the heart belonged to someone "in the system" a specific ID would be available. If not, then other pieces of information, such as relatively rare genetic illness, would likely play an important role in establishing identity.

He briefly looked at the remaining unread e-mails to ensure none looked like they needed his immediate attention before opening his workload screen to see how his day was shaping up. The departmental manager had booked in two morning postmortems for him and a few other relatively light tasks, being mindful of the fact that he was due in court at 2pm. Being late wasn't really an option.

Good for her, thought an appreciative Brewster as he rose from his desk and headed towards the changing room to swap his civilian clothes for the uniform of a pathologist; namely scrubs, mask and gloves. The e-mail from his Glaswegian colleague had piqued both his clinical interest and enthusiasm for the day ahead. He found himself whistling *We didn't start the fire* by Billy Joel, one of his go-to upbeat songs when encouraged by an elevated mood.

By mid morning, after the first postmortem and some admin work, he was more than ready for his second cup of coffee but this time he sought the camaraderie of the staff room where the conversation was more likely to be about TV programmes and restaurant experiences than matters pathological. This suited him just fine. After fifteen minutes of chit chat, he excused himself from the group, topped up his coffee from the cafetière, and returned to his office to check on the Clinical Results Gateway before his next postmortem. Sure enough, as he had hoped for, there was a result waiting from the Genetics department. He opened the report, which ran to two pages, and quickly scanned the text. The main points of interest for Brewster were that the DNA belonged to a male, of likely Viking descent (and therefore caucasian) and there was an abnormality of the HFE gene. Specifically, the unknown male was a C282Y homozygote which implied that he was very likely to have Hereditary Haemochromatosis. This is an abnormality of how the body processes iron resulting in a gradual build up of tissue levels over many years eventually resulting in potential damage to several different organs, including the heart. He smiled as some of the clinical pieces of the cardiac conundrum began to come together. As he didn't have full access to the PNC himself, he forwarded the result to Bankhurst, and also texted her to request she check her in-box.

From the moment Bankhurst was alerted to an incoming text by her watch to her reading and digesting the e-mail took less than ten minutes. She fed the information into the PNC and waited impatiently for a result. It only took about two minutes, but felt a lot longer, before the result was displayed in the middle of the screen.

NO MATCH FOUND.

"Damn it," she said with a ferocity that even surprised herself. She was glad no-one else was in the room to witness what might have been construed as a slight overreaction.

Having been denied the express route to identifying the unknown victim, she nevertheless was aware that they now knew he was a caucasian male, likely to be in his fifties or sixties, with a Past Medical History of an aortic valve replacement and a rare genetic illness. She felt the need to pick Brewster's brain about how they could best use the medical information to narrow down the field. She phoned Pathology but was told he had already started the next postmortem and could not be interrupted. The receptionist agreed to forward a request that he phone her ASAP after the postmortem was completed, and Bankhurst left it at that. She put the phone down and went on to Wikipedia on her PC to see what haemochromatosis was all about.

About an hour later, Bankhurst was busy injecting herself with her midday dose of insulin in anticipation of dealing with the glucose load that lunch would bring. Although not planning to eat anything overtly sweet, she was well aware that many foodstuffs, while being broken down by the body after eating, release glucose into the blood stream thereby requiring insulin assistance. She was literally in the act of injecting when her phone rang. She rolled her eyes as if to say *bloody typical!* However, many years of practice allowed her to swiftly complete the injection and put the needle in her sinbin.

"Bankhurst," she stated, if not in a bark then certainly somewhat clipped.

"Hello, Lily. It's Dexter...Brewster. Just returning your call."

He added the Brewster as an afterthought, though it was unlikely she knew too many Dexters he thought.

"Ah. Dexter," she continued in a much softer tone, "thanks for getting back. I got your earlier message. I've PNC'd the DNA but he's not in the system."

"Ah. Shame," replied Brewster.

"We've got a list of local mispers, but rather than having to organise DNA sampling from all of their houses and/or interviews with potential relatives, I was wondering if we could use the extra information the DNA has supplied to narrow the search. Assuming he is relatively local that is," she added.

"Sure," replied Brewster. "I've been thinking about that in the event he wasn't in the system. The best place to start will be medical databases. Unfortunately, Primary and Secondary

Care IT systems are not that great at communicating with one another. Information held in one is not automatically shared with another, despite the fact they are all under the same NHS umbrella. Their IT systems basically have evolved independently from each other, and it's only in recent years that efforts have been made to make one *talk* with the other."

"Would he not be known to the cardiac department if he had a history of a valve replacement?" enquired Bankhurst.

"Possibly, but not necessarily. He could have been discharged years ago or moved into the area from elsewhere in the UK, or even from abroad," replied Brewster.

"I think the best place to search would be the Primary Care record. In theory GPs are encouraged to have a medical summary for all their patients and, to be fair, the vast majority have. As always, *the data you get out is only as good as the data you put in and*, I guess, some coders are better than others. Nevertheless, you would hope that Haemochromatosis and Aortic Valve Replacement would both be included in Category 1 problems, and, therefore, be more easily identified in a targeted search."

"So, how can we extract this information?" enquired Bankhurst.

"Ah, now there's the rub," responded Brewster. "I've a GP mate in Aberdeen who I was at medical school with. I know he's into IT. I could get in touch with him sometime for advice."

Just as the words were leaving his mouth he grimaced silently as he realised he had just potentially opened a workload door that he could have done without in a busy day, including an unpredictable court appearance. He also had a dinner reservation at 7pm in his favourite Italian restaurant for which his wife would not thank him if it had to be delayed. Spousal understanding only extended so far. Bankhurst did not disappoint in taking her opportunity and walked through the door that had been opened.

"That would be great, Dexter. Obviously, speed is of the essence. Are you able to try and speak to him today? It would be ideal if I had a bit more information for our 4pm team update."

She realised he would have his own existing workload, though was unaware of the court case, and that she was pushing it a bit. Sometimes, you just had to ask.

"Er...I can try. I've a court case to attend this afternoon and I know how busy GPs are. Might be easier to get a hold of The King!" he said half in jest, and half not. He stole a glance at his watch to see what added time pressure he was now under, but also felt a pang of guilt that he was potentially prioritising his stomach over a murder investigation.

Mind you, they do make a particularly good Cotoletta alla Milanese at Giuseppe's he mused.

He made a snap decision.

"Listen, Lily, leave it with me. I'll try and get hold of him just now."

"That would be great. Thanks." she responded, "hopefully speak to you again soon."

Respective phones were hung up. Brewster reached for the directory of GP phone numbers.

His fears were unfounded as he found the receptionist very pleasant, and helpful, and within a couple of minutes he was speaking to his old friend from his alma mater.

"Is that you, Rooster?" enquired Gavin Donald in an upbeat voice.

"It is indeed, Gav," replied Brewster, with a smile creasing his face at the mention of his university nickname.

"How are you doing?"

"Good, mate. And yourself?"

"Yeh. Good too."

"It's not often I get a phone call from a Police Pathologist. Hope I haven't buggered up a death certificate, or something."

"No. No. Nothing like that Gavin. I was actually looking for some advice."

Brewster outlined the details of the case and, after mulling it over for a few seconds, Donald responded.

"I'm thinking out loud here Rooster, but the best plan may be to use the SCI-Diabetes platform as a search tool."

Brewster, who was more familiar with the dead than the living, did not recognise this clinical platform, and hesitated slightly.

"Of course, you've probably not come across this, Rooster, in your line of work!"

"Indeed," agreed Brewster.

"The IT team in Dundee developed a system called SCI-Diabetes and, as the name suggests, it's primarily for diabetic care. It's a clever web-based system that interrogates both Primary and Secondary Care data systems every night, and extracts diabetes related data which is stored on the web and can be accessed by all members of the wider diabetic team, no matter where they work. The searches are done every night, so as not to slow down the clinical systems being used during the day. I know the Tayside IT team love a challenge, and I bet they could bolt on a search looking for anyone with a coded history of haemochromatosis and Aortic Valve Replacement."

"Sounds good," responded Brewster who was impressed with his colleague's quick grasp of the situation and problem solving abilities. *No doubt important skills for a GP to have in their job* he thought.

"Just as I'm speaking about this," continued Donald, "there's a couple of things that come to mind. There's a possibility his haemochromatosis is undiagnosed, and therefore not coded as a problem in his record. Clearly, he has significant cardiac effects secondary to his iron overload, but it can be an elusive diagnosis that goes under the radar for many years. So, just worth thinking about."

"The other thing that's crossed my mind is that all patients with Aortic Valve Replacement should be on an anticoagulant. Even if for some reason his AVR hasn't been coded, and therefore won't appear on a search, we might pick him up on an anticoagulation register. The good thing about that is that the majority of people requiring anticoagulation for things like Atrial Fibrillation or Deep Venous Thrombosis are now on DOAC* drugs, as opposed to warfarin, which don't require any blood testing. Warfarin is still recommended for most AVR patients so he should be having regular venipuncture to check his INR* level. The other thing, which is potentially helpful, is that AVR patients have a higher INR reference range than other patients on warfarin for different clinical reasons so that should help narrow the field further."

"Thanks, Gav. That's really good information. Do you know the Dundee team well enough to approach them?"

"Oh, aye. No problem. I know most of them down there." After a slight pause to collect his thoughts he continued, "OK, so what I think I'm saying is that we ask if it's possible to do a search on the parameters of male, haemochromatosis, Aortic Valve Replacement and INR target range 3-4.5. To be honest, Rooster, I think that would be a fairly small list."

"Sounds great, Gavin. Could be extremely helpful...as long as he's from the North East!"

"Indeed," replied Donald, "though it would be easy enough to extend the search from NHS Grampian to NHS Scotland, if necessary, as it's a national system."

"No such system south of the border though," he added as an afterthought, in case Brewster was wondering if the search could be rolled out UK wide.

"If I give you DI Bankhurst's contact details to pass on to Dundee and they could perhaps liaise directly with her?" enquired Brewster. "I know she's going to be in over the weekend."

"Aye. No problem. I'll let you know if there's any issue."

"Thanks, Gav. That's a big help. I owe you a pint for that."

"I'll hold you to that, Rooster!" promised Donald as he finished the call.

*DOAC Direct Oral Anticoagulant

*INR International Normalised Ratio (assessment of blood clotting)

Satisfied at how the call had gone, Brewster relaxed back into his chair and ran a hand through his slightly thinning hair. He texted Bankhurst an update and risked a quick look at his

Whatsapp account, where he had three unread messages, but didn't feel the authors merited immediate attention. He felt his stomach rumble and began to be aware of being hungry. Time to grab some food he thought before heading over to court where he hoped the sheriff would be as keen as he was for a prompt Friday finish.

Not for the first time, he was glad of the proximity of the police station, pathology department and court, not to mention a few coffee houses and eateries. Sometimes he felt the need for a freshly ground coffee instead of the instant brew available at work, and he had several local options available. Also, on a cold day like this, especially if wearing a suit, he could jog the short distance to the court without having to put on any additional layers.

A ping on his phone signified an incoming message and a brief glance confirmed his suspicion that it was an acknowledgement and thanks from Bankhurst.

A further gurgle in his abdomen preceded some wind being passed. *Better out than in* he reassured himself as he set off for the canteen.

CHAPTER 7

Saturday 14th December

As it turned out the medical networking between colleagues in Aberdeen, and subsequently between Aberdeen and Dundee, had, within a few hours, produced a bolt-on search to the nighttime SCI-Diabetes data mining programme. This was due in no small part to a willingness to go the extra mile for colleagues, a positive attitude to a challenge and having the technical abilities to find a solution to that challenge.

On the Saturday morning the on-call technician, as she had been primed to do, forwarded the result by secure e-mail to the Police Scotland address of DI Lily Bankhurst, and within a fraction of a second it had dropped into her in-box.

Bankhurst had allowed herself the luxury of a small lie-in on the Saturday before making her way to the station, leaving behind her mother and son, who were planning a trip to the swimming pool. She was dressed a little less formally than usual, though not casually, which seemed appropriate to her for someone "going in" on their day off. A reasonably generous application of makeup complemented a more casual hair arrangement.

After the usual pleasantries, and coffee collection, she powered up her computer and, within a few minutes, had opened her e-mail. She was a little surprised, but delighted, to see the unread e-mail from Tayside NHS IT. Two clicks later she was looking at a list of three men. One name looked familiar and, after opening another screen, the same name leapt out at her from the mispers list.

Danny McRobert was a fifty-seven-year-old man from the

Tillydrone area of Aberdeen who had been reported missing two weeks previously. He was also 'in the system', though had not pinged as a DNA match as his, fairly impressive, list of misdemeanours and charges were historical, and predated routine DNA testing. They did have his fingerprints on record, but these were of no help given the unique presentation of the case.

He had disappeared on the walk home from his regular public house, The River View, which overlooked The Don. Bankhurst vaguely remembered the standard Police Scotland appeal for information that had been issued but couldn't recall if it had generated any response. She opened his file and found that, with a complete absence of any information or witness statements, his death was thought most likely an accident. The winding path to his home in Tillydrone, at times, abuts close to the river edge and it was assumed, when no body was found, he had fallen into the river in a semi-inebriated state, and been washed out to sea by the incessant movement, and easy power, of the northernmost of the two rivers that flow through Aberdeen.

Although not as well known as its sister river The Dee, courtesy of it being incorporated into the city name and also its link with the Royal Family, The Don is a significant river in its own right. At one hundred and thirty two kilometres from rise to sea, it is only eight kilometres less in length than that boasted by its more illustrious neighbour. Both discharge a significant amount of water into the North Sea, two miles apart, bookending the original city of Aberdeen in the process.

Indeed, the power of The Don has supported several paper mills over the years (though only one remains) and has a maximum depth of nineteen feet at the ebb tide. It is entirely capable of sweeping a body out to sea, never to be seen again.

Bankhurst left the file open on her screen and picked up the phone. She had already noted Hamish MacDonald in the building and indeed, for once, he was quick to answer. She explained that they now knew, with a reasonable degree of certainty, the ID of the deceased. After tasking him to assemble those of the team on duty for a meeting in thirty minutes, she e-mailed both Anderson and MacNiven to keep them in the loop.

As she got up from her desk to head to the Incident Room, she felt a twinge of pain in her lower abdomen on her left side. Experience had taught her what this might herald, but she decided to ignore it anyway. If it was going to happen, there wasn't a lot she could do about it.

After arriving at the Incident Room she added Danny McRobert's name to the whiteboard and a photograph from the recent mispers investigation. Underneath she created two columns, one headed **What we know** and the other **What we need to know/do.** Under the first heading she added the bullet points:

57 year old male
Married
Labourer. On long term sick
Lived in Aberdeen all his life
Most recent address Baron Court (high-rise) in Tillydrone (10 years)
Convictions for breach of the peace, theft, drunk and disorderly, assault, drink driving and driving without a licence/insurance. Last conviction 20 years ago
History of likely domestic abuse
Reported missing 2 weeks ago after visit to The River View. No suspicious circumstances
Other family members (brothers Jimmy McRobert and Alex McRobert) with similar records. Well known family especially to older officers

Under the **What we need to know/do** heading she added:
Inform spouse
Get Medical records to confirm illness profile
Get DNA samples from home
Mobile phone data
Did he have a PC/Laptop?
Timeline of whereabouts for 24 hours before disappearance

Witness statements- staff/patrons of The River View, circle of associates
CCTV at/near The River View and any on route home
Recent changes in behaviour
ANPR vicinity night of disappearance
Any known current threats/enemies
Finances/Debts
Drugs and/or alcohol abuse
Identify site of abduction/murder
Where is rest of the body?
Will need large search group and canine unit
Identify potential motives

[3]
Consider Criminal Psychology input as a very unusual MO. Possible once off crime, or any chance of repetition?

As Bankhurst was writing the bullet points she realised, with increasing certainty, that the current number of personnel assigned to the case, even if the majority were on weekend duty, was woefully inadequate. Her first priority, even before the proposed team meeting, was to speak to senior staff to rapidly, and significantly, augment the investigative effort. She consulted the senior duty rota and found that DCI Anderson was off the weekend.

That would have been too easy, she thought.

The second realisation to hit her was that the previous twinges of pain in the left side of her pelvis had now developed into a continual nagging pain, essentially in the same region but also now radiating to the left groin and top of left thigh. She recognised the now familiar calling card of an endometriosis flare, a group of symptoms likely to last two to three days and range from relatively mild to fairly crippling, requiring absence from work and even potential hospitalisation.

She had been bothered with bouts of symptomatic endometriosis since she was a late teenager and couldn't deny the pattern currently evolving. It initially developed around the same time as her Type 1 diabetes; she sometimes cursed her bad health luck in having two long term conditions.

For Fuck's sake she thought, *Not today of all days!*

She had a regular monthly cycle and knew her period wasn't due for three days.

Perfect timing for Endometriosis.

Having had the condition for many years, she was well versed in its pathophysiology producing islands of endometrium, the lining of the uterus, in sites out with the uterus itself. These can be anywhere around the pelvis, sometimes around the lower bowel and even, rarely, at the umbilicus. Unlike dysmenorrhoea, period pain, the pain of endometriosis typically builds up in the days before a period is due, and indeed the onset of menstruation may be a harbinger of impending symptom relief. The endometrial islands swell, driven by the monthly hormonal cycle, but have no natural outlet, so tend to "bleed" within themselves, causing pain and often scarring. This in turn can lead to reduced fertility, and Bankhurst appreciated that she had at least once managed to fall pregnant, both from the fact that the end product was a beautiful baby boy, but also that she had enjoyed nine glorious symptom free months.

Although she had tried various treatments in the past, her current management consisted of ascending an analgesic ladder until the pain was tolerable, and then toughing out the two to three days it might last. She found that preferable to taking regular medication on a daily basis, to stop something which may or may not happen towards the end of the month. Step one would normally be Paracetamol followed, if necessary, by Ibuprofen. Today she decided to accelerate the process and took 1g Paracetamol along with 600mg Ibuprofen to try and gain control, without having to consider the most powerful tool in her box, Dihydrocodeine, which often left her nauseated and constipated. The 600mg Ibuprofen, discovered during a trip to Spain and 50% stronger than the typical UK strength, had proven a godsend before, and she hoped her Iberian ally would once again be her saviour. It really was the last thing she needed at the moment, she lamented internally.

She quickly diverted to her locker to access her bag and, equally quickly, located and swallowed her chosen regimen, before turning her attention to contacting the duty DCI, Tony Simpson. Originally from England, he had moved to Scotland years previously and risen up the ranks steadily, without necessarily setting the heather on fire. He was respected and well regarded and probably, at fifty-three, had one eye on retirement. He was interested in, and receptive to, how the investigation was developing, and what extra resources were required. To Bankhurst's relief he immediately promised to second all available detectives to the case and, as Aberdeen were not playing at home, a sizable contingent of uniformed officers for detailed searches. He also thought it a very reasonable use of resource to involve the Canine Department and had no objection to Bankhurst pursuing this.

By 10am MacDonald had assembled, as requested, those of the existing team on duty, namely DCs Fraser, Babinski and MacLennan. A steady stream of extra CID personnel squeezed through the single door to the Incident Room and soon the number had swollen to an impressive twenty, including representatives from Uniform and Canine departments. Most had already spotted the whiteboard and a buzz of conversation filled the room.

Although Bankhurst could still feel some discomfort, the combined effect of the analgesics and a caffeine hit had put her in a better place than she had been forty-five minutes previously. She rose to her feet and waited for the room to quieten for possibly the most challenging meeting of her career. There were now some seriously experienced, some would say gnarled, detectives in the room. While she was glad of her improved resource, she was also acutely aware that some in the audience might question her SIO abilities, and she was damned if she would give them the slightest fuel for their cause.

"Good Morning everyone," she began formally, "Thanks for coming at short notice. I'm sure most of you will have been aware, on the station grapevine, about the discovery of a human heart in the butcher at Cults."

A general nodding of heads suggested her assumption was not far wide of the mark.

"As of this morning, we have what is very likely to be a positive ID for the deceased. We will need DNA confirmation but, for the meantime, we are assuming it is Danny McRobert," finishing her sentence with a point to the whiteboard, followed dutifully by everyone in the room.

"We obviously need to know as much as possible about McRobert, and the timeline leading up to his disappearance. Was this random or targeted? Possible motives?"

"As you can see, I've made a list of the immediate areas I'd like to cover, and I'll delegate you into groups to pursue this."

"Uniform and Canine are also primed to do a detailed search of the route between The River View and Tillydrone. As most of you will know, while there are urban sections at the beginning and end, there is a long semi-wooded path in the middle that runs along the bank of The Don."

"Ideal place for an abduction," contributed one of the audience.

"Absolutely," agreed Bankhurst.

The team, under Bankhurst's firm direction, then spent about an hour prioritising and agreeing mini-groups to tackle the workload. The first task was to get a ranking officer and a Family Liaison Officer (FLO) to break the news to the

widow, followed by a tech team visit for DNA sampling and collection of mobile and other IT devices.

Bankhurst made it clear she wished to do the widow's interview herself but would wait until the FLO and technical team had visited. She had calculated that she could complete the interview in the early afternoon, and still have time to honour her promise to Andrew to take him to a Marvel movie and Nandos afterwards. In the meantime, she would need to factor in five minutes to phone her mother and brief her on her likely ETA.

"Needless to say, we need to pull out all the stops on this one," she continued. "Reach out to your snitches. I want to know if there's any chat on the street about McRobert being involved in anything currently. Right, let's get on with it. Keep me up to date with any developments."

Bankhurst and Babinski drove the two miles to Barron Court in an awkward silence, the gulf between rank being hard to bridge. Bankhurst eventually broke the silence.

"So, Reflex. How do you come by that nickname?"

"It was one of the GP Police Surgeons, Ma'am," he responded quite enthusiastically, glad to have a question well within his purview.

"To be honest, I'm not quite sure why he coined it, but it's stuck anyway. I've noticed it usually raises a wee smile when I come across someone medical, if that's any help."

"Can't say it is, Reflex!," Bankhurst responded. "Guess we'll both have to remain in the dark."

"What about you, Ma'am? Ever had a nickname?"

Bankhurst could think of a couple, but not any she was going to share with Babinski, in the sure knowledge they would be all round the station before the end of the day. She was recalling one of the less flattering ones from her school days when she rounded a corner and Barron Court came into view to the slight relief of both parties.

It was a typical high-rise accommodation block so beloved of city planners in the 1960s and 1970s but looked as if it had had a fairly recent facelift. Bankhurst wondered if this had been driven by post Grenfell cladding legislation. She noted, with relief, the lack of a barrier, and found a parking space with ease. It wouldn't have been the first time she had become trapped in a residential car park, and had to go, tail between legs, to try and find someone to release her.

Babinski, head down into the biting wind, picked up his pace slightly to arrive at the door first, and held it open for his DI.

"That's not necessary, Reflex," before adding, after a few seconds, "but the effort is appreciated."

The foyer of the high rise was typical of many similar buildings in Aberdeen. A notice board, advertising local services including discounted fish suppers on a Friday, separated two lifts: one for odd and one for even floors. She knew McRobert lived on the 10th of twelve floors, and was approaching the buttons of the appropriate lift when the door opened and a diminutive lady carrying a washing basket eyed up the couple before her. Bankhurst presumed she had come from the basement laundry.

"You'll be needing the tenth floor I suppose," she sneered, as she reached for the buttons within the lift.

"We are indeed," concurred Bankhurst as she managed to force a small smile onto her face while, at the same time, marvelling at the ability of certain people to spot 'The Polis'.

Following the door closure there was, what felt to Bankhurst, a prolonged pause, during which time she noticed the surprising lack of graffiti, and only a very faint smell of marijuana. This was in contrast to many high-rise lifts she had been in before in the central belt.

Finally, the lift jolted into action with a lurch, which did nothing for her elevator phobia. She focussed firmly at a spot on the ceiling, both as a tool against her phobia, and to avoid any eye contact with the woman which might have precipitated a conversation she could do without. Another unwelcome jolt heralded their arrival on the tenth floor and a few seconds later they were alone in a landing servicing four apartments.

Bankhurst felt her pulse slowing appreciably.

The door bearing the name 'McRobert' was fronted by a brush mat and to the side was an occasional table supporting a vase and a collection of colourful plastic flowers coated in a fine layer of dust.

The ringing bell was greeted by a somewhat gruff and distant, "Come in," and the officers duly obeyed their instruction. The apartment was oppressively hot, compared with the landing temperature, and a pall of cigarette smoke hung in the air. A narrow, poorly lit corridor led to the living room, where Helen McRobert sat in an easy chair. A grunt and nod of her head suggested she was both expecting them and indicating they should sit on the sofa opposite her.

Bankhurst took in her surroundings as she skirted the back of the sofa to get to the far end. A small living room with a three-piece suite, sideboard and oversized TV competing for space. One generous sized window supplied ample daylight, and also afforded a spectacular view of the north and east of the city, including The Don estuary. With the eye of faith, she thought she could see the roof of The River View and wondered to herself *What happened to you Danny McRobert between there and here. And why?*

She returned her focus to the room, in particular to Helen McRobert, who sat slumped, and bleary eyed, in her chair. The years had not been kind to her, as she looked more like she was in her late sixties rather than the late fifties which Bankhurst knew her to be. She was at least moderately overweight, had an impressively lined face for her age and the nicotine staining on her hands and teeth was only marginally less than the yellow hue of the cigarette tainted walls and ceiling. She had done the detectives the courtesy of stubbing out her current cigarette which lay in an ashtray on a small table beside her seat, still leaking the last few trails of smoke, as it died a slow death.

Bankhurst noticed numerous burns on the table and one side of the seat suggesting perhaps that she was a right-handed, and at times, careless smoker. She wondered if her neighbours knew how much a fire risk they lived beside, especially in a high-rise building.

As the smoke began to subside, Bankhurst noticed an aroma, of what she thought was probably soup, escaping from the adjoining kitchen. Perhaps she had sought some comfort in a familiar task since the earlier visit from the FLO and technical team. Perhaps she just needed to feed herself.

Bankhurst didn't want to open the interview with the customary, *"Sorry for your loss,"* as it was premature until DNA confirmation, so she contented herself with an introduction of who they were, and went over her understanding of what had been discussed with the FLO to ascertain that she had at least a reasonable grasp of the current situation. Having done so, to her satisfaction, she proceeded with the interview.

"We are treating your husband's disappearance as a likely murder, Mrs McRobert. We'll need to find out as much as we can about him, his recent movements and his behaviour."

"My first two questions are 'Can you think of anyone who would want to harm your husband?' and, 'Have you noticed any change in his personality or behaviour recently?'"

"That's easy," she replied, "No and no…it's been the *same old same old* here for the last few years. Nothing much ever changes, ken." She added, "You'll ken fine well I'm sure, from your records, that he was a rogue back in the day, but he's nae been involved in any o' that stuff for years."

"Ken this, when he's nae asleep in that chair, he's either at the bookie, The River View…or the doctor. There might have been a few in the past who would have punched his lights oot. But nae murder; and certainly nae these days. I just cannae figure it oot." She continued, "He turned into a lazy bastard to be honest. Either that or he was doon in the moo*. Couldnae even be bothered giving me a hidin' the last few years. Not that I wasnae grateful for that mind you, ken."

The two detectives exchanged a brief glance, but the spousal assault was hardly an unexpected revelation given what they already knew about McRobert.

"Did he have any significant debts that you know about?" continued Bankhurst.

"Nae that I ken o," replied McRobert, "sure, he liked a gamble, but that was one thing aboot him. He never spent what he didnae have."

"What about his brothers? Does he have much to do with

them now? Could they be mixed up in something?" continued Bankhurst.

"Na. One of them bides in Peterheed, and the other in Kincorth. He disnae see much of them these days."

"Does he use the internet much?"

"No. We havnae even got a computer, or one of them tablet thingies. He had a mobile phone, but it was right auld fashioned. I kept telling him to get a smart phone but he widnae listen, ken. He didnae even carry it with him most of the time. Your guy took it away with him earlier."

Bankhurst's heart sank a little. Mobile phones, particularly smart phones, are a source of invaluable information for every police force up and down the country. More old-fashioned devices were likely to yield significantly less data and, as it wasn't being carried on the night of his disappearance, there would be no useful triangulation information around the time of the likely abduction and/or murder.

After a further ten minutes, Bankhurst began to feel, with half an eye on her personal commitments, that there was little to be gained by extending the widow's interview, and was content to see what the other lines of enquiry would bring in.

*down in the mouth (depressed)

She drew it to a close and, after getting permission, she and Babinski had a look round the apartment, but neither found anything remarkable.

She noted a two-week-old Daily Record, opened at the racing page, lying folded with a pen and some gathering dust, on top. She presumed Helen McRobert had been unable to throw it away while her husband was missing, in the hope he might return and resume where he left off perhaps. The 3:30 at Chepstow by the look of the circled entry in the paper.

Bankhurst left her card with the usual reminder of 'Phone me if you think of anything else. Anything at all', said her condolences, and nodded to Babinski that they should take their leave. As McRobert wasn't showing any sign of movement, they made their own way out of the apartment and closed the door behind them.

As they approached the lift door on the landing there was a low growl of wind which built to a crescendo and sent a shudder up the lift shaft. The wires and mechanics groaned in response.

"Bugger that," said Bankhurst as she about turned and opened the door into the unheated stairwell, being met with the smell of cold stone and Jeye's fluid. Babinski, who needed no further invitation himself, was hard on her heels.

While rapidly assuaging her phobic symptoms, every step she took down the ten flights of stairs reminded her there was something inflammatory going on in the left side of her pelvis, and that she would need to top up her analgesia soon. It also occurred to her that she had missed both her lunch, and linked insulin dose, neither of which were consistent with good diabetes management.

Bugger it.

CHAPTER 8

Sunday 15th December

The Aberdeen streets were virtually deserted when Bankhurst drove to the station on Sunday morning at 0800. The wind from the previous day had proven reluctant to settle and still had sufficient energy to propel the remnants of the previous night's revelry around the city centre.

Municipal Christmas lights strung across streets were buffeted mercilessly, but most remained safely tethered. One or two had broken loose from their anchor point and dangled down like some giant illuminated trailing plant. An anthracite sky of low cloud was preventing the proper expression of dawn, and the city remained in a grey half-light.

Two joggers, and one of the earlier dog walkers of the day, braved the bitingly cold wind. The dog tried to stop to sniff a lamp post but was immediately yanked back into forward momentum by the human who, with head down and a forwardly angulated body, gave the impression of someone who was on an express route home.

Having grabbed a coffee and walked along to the Incident Room, Bankhurst was greeted by a buzz of noise from those colleagues already assembled. The various teams had been busy, and seemed purposeful, and ready to feed back.

She organised her bag and laptop on the desk, and then brought the room to order.

"Right, let's make a start."

"DS Brown, Ma'am. I can report from The River View. They do have CCTV cameras, but unfortunately only keep recordings for one week, and we have nothing for the date in question. We've interviewed most of the staff and the regular punters. McRobert was a well-known customer. Not a big spender, unless it was his GIRO day, when he drank a bit more. Usually nursed a pint for two to three hours and played dominoes or darts with his mates."

"The owner said he used to be a handful a few years ago, and was temporarily barred on two or three occasions, but has been no trouble the last few years. They almost seemed fond of him as the current staff didn't know him from his bad boy days, and he's a bit of a fixture in the bar apparently."

"Yes, there seems to be a lot of commonality about the various descriptions of McRobert," agreed Bankhurst. "A pretty nasty piece of work, and a habitual criminal in his earlier years, but very little involvement with ourselves for many years. He had a caution for possible abuse of his dog three years ago, but it was not proven and he was never charged, so didn't have his DNA taken. According to his wife, he used to beat her up too, but again not in recent years."

Bankhurst nodded at Brown inviting him to continue.

"Nobody remembers any unusual incidents recently, including the night of his disappearance. We've got him on a camera a couple of streets from The River View at 10-30pm, but then he disappears towards the riverside path, where there are no cameras. There are a couple of cameras on the far side of the river walk, but he doesn't appear on either."

"So," Bankhurst joined in, "we can assume there is a high chance the abduction or murder happened not long after 10-30pm in the riverside area. Good. That's helpful."

"What about ANPR that night?" she said, directing her gaze to the officer she had delegated the task to, but couldn't quite, for the life of her, remember her name.

"We've got over one hundred vehicles picked up in the area on the night in question. The most interesting one is a dark, medium sized van… whose plates should be on a Nissan Micra in Wrexham. We've contacted the owner who stated they have not had their plates stolen, and the car was parked outside their house."

"Excellent," purred Bankhurst who had a feeling they were beginning to get somewhere. "I presume the vehicle experts are working on trying to give us a make and model?"

"They are, Ma'am. We also wondered if it might be worth checking local garages, just in case he got fuel. A lot of them use number plate capture technology to discourage their 'fill up and flee' customers."

"Sounds good," agreed Bankhurst.

"Finances, Hugh?"

"Nothing out of the ordinary, Ma'am. A few hundred in his account. No unusual activity. Also checked with his bookie and The River View, and no change in his spending pattern at either place. I've also got his medical records now, Ma'am, which I've shown to the duty police surgeon, who confirms they very much fit the profile of our man."

"Where are we with his phone?" enquired Bankhurst knowing not to enquire about PC or laptop.

"Old fashioned Nokia phone, Ma'am. Digital Forensics looking at it but doesn't look like it's going to be too useful."

"What about the riverside search?" Bankhurst directed her question to the representatives of Uniform and Canine.

"No material finds, Ma'am, but the dogs did get quite excited a couple of hundred yards into the path, and we suspect that may have been the site of the crime as there seems to be a bit of residual scent there, but not elsewhere. It's not that far from a lane that's accessible by a vehicle, so would potentially be an attractive option for the perpetrator as good cover, but also wouldn't be far to take an abductee or body to a van."

"Ok. Good work. Let's get a SOCO team over there. I know it's a wee bit 'horse after cart', and there might not be much left after two weeks of winter weather, but worth checking for any trace. At the very least, we can get some soil samples in case we find the vehicle in due course."

"What about the snitches?" she continued but was met with a

collective shaking of heads and negative murmurings.

"No whispers on the street, Ma'am," said an anonymous voice.

"Ok. Anybody got anything else to highlight?"

There was a pause for a few seconds before Fraser rather hesitatingly raised her hand.

"I might have something on the CCTV from the taxi across the road from Wilson's."

Bankhurst could hear the stress in her voice, and recalled how she herself had felt when contributing to her first large Incident Room meeting. *Bricking it* would just about cover it.

"Go on," she said, in as encouraging a voice as she could muster.

"It's just that I was checking the video this morning, and I noticed something strange about the Deliveroo cyclist last Friday. I thought, on Wilson's own CCTV, he went in the main entrance at 12-30pm, but on the taxi footage he went in a side entrance. When I checked the timing on the taxi recording, it was at 12-40pm, and when I re-checked the original Wilson's footage there is no Deliveroo recorded at that time. I wondered if he'd maybe forgotten something, and taken a shortcut back in, but in the last half hour I've had footage from both cameras on adjacent screens, and I'm beginning to wonder if there are some subtle differences between the images of the cyclists."

"OK. Let's have a look," said Bankhurst enthusiastically, and the entire room bunched up together behind the dual screens to watch the recordings. Fraser pressed both start buttons. Fourteen pairs of eyes flitted from one screen to the other and back again like they were watching a tense rally at Wimbledon.

Although both images of the cyclist showed similar apparel including helmet, face covering, dark clothes, Deliveroo backpack and gloves, there did seem to be an appreciable difference in their build, and also subtle differences in the shape of the bikes themselves. While most observers were slowly coming round to the opinion that they were in fact two different people, the clincher was delivered by MacDonald who pointing at one screen and then the other before announcing, with a slightly triumphant note in his voice, "He's got a bicycle pump and water bottle, and he hasn't!"

"BINGO!" announced Bankhurst, before immediately regretting her somewhat tasteless choice of word.

"That's a great spot, Alison, and thanks also to DC Donaldson (*at least I remember his surname* she thought) for pointing us in the direction of the taxi CCTV."

"That's what you call hiding in plain sight," observed MacDonald, with perhaps a hint of admiration.

"Indeed," agreed Bankhurst.

"Deliveroo, and all the other delivery companies for that matter, are so ubiquitous these days that they are just seen as part of the background of a cityscape. Very clever way of going under the radar, especially as nobody would blink an eye if you had a helmet and face covering on. Perfect disguise."

"And the timing is spot on if you think about it," contributed MacLennan.

"After the proper Deliveroo cyclist has been, most of the staff will be congregated in the boardroom to get their take-out, and would not see the arrival of the second cyclist. That would also mean it would be potentially easier to move about the rest of the building. For any other staff that perhaps were still scattered here and there, if they were to look up and see a Deliveroo cyclist, especially at that time on a Friday, they probably wouldn't think anything about it."

"This surely implies an inside job, or at least inside help," contributed MacDonald. "He obviously has fairly detailed knowledge of the routines of Wilson's but also, presumably, the layout of the building, in that he was able to place the heart in a suitable site that wouldn't arouse immediate suspicion. He also knew coming in the side entrance would evade Wilson's own CCTV."

"Fair point," agreed Bankhurst as she turned towards the whiteboard. "Time for an update."

Likely time of abduction/murder 10.30 to 11.00 pm on 30th November

Likely that drink spiked in the pub. Where was flunitrazepam sourced from? Local? Dark web?
Likely site 200 yards from entrance to riverside path
Vehicle of high interest -dark van with false plates
No recent ANPR images since 30th November. Plates removed ? Vehicle hidden?
No obvious motive. Random?
Likely site of entry into food industry - Abattoir
Likely disguised as Deliveroo cyclist
Why take such a big risk?
Inside job or inside help?

"Just as I'm writing this," she continued, "it strikes me that a large number of staff will effectively be alibied by being in the boardroom at the time of the second Deliveroo. Wouldn't stop them being an accomplice I suppose, but they obviously couldn't be the cyclist." Bankhurst's observation was greeted with several heads being nodded, and the realisation that they could be dealing with the rare scenario of two murderers working in tandem.

"OK, we need to change focus slightly. I want any remaining stragglers of the current staff to be interviewed and get a list of any that have left in the last five years. They need to be traced, PNC'd and interviewed. We also need to get in touch with Deliveroo and get a list of all current staff, and anyone who has left them in the last, say, two years. Let's start with the authentic Deliveroo cyclist last Friday, and any others who have ever delivered to Wilson's. After that, concentrate on males who have bikes and not mopeds."

"Also, keep pressure on our vehicle recognition guy. I want a specific vehicle to look for ASAP."

"Might not be anyone available at Wilson's today, Ma'am, with it being Sunday," suggested MacLennan.

"Too bad," she said, "get in touch with the owners and drag them down to the office if you have to. This is a murder investigation". As she was saying it, she realised she rolled the r in *murder* a bit longer than was necessary creating an unintentional echo of Taggart from the eponymous TV series. It wasn't unnoticed by a few in the room and generated a raised eyebrow and a slight snigger.

"OK. Thanks everybody. Good work. Let's keep the foot on the pedal. I'll be at home, or on my mobile after lunch. The DNA result should be available this afternoon. Let me know when that comes in, and if anything else significant happens."

There were a few responses of "Yes, Ma'am" as she stood up and collected her bag and laptop. She felt the room was energised and responsive to her leadership, which felt good inside.

Looks like you CAN lead a murder investigation she said to herself as she left the room with her head held high, and a flicker of a smile appearing on her face.

Two years previously, Zafar Iqbal had been considering a DS post in Aberdeen as a means of distancing himself from his well-meaning, but sometimes claustrophobic, family. When he received a phone call from a friend saying there was a vacancy for a decent all rounder at Aberdeenshire Cricket Club, the South African incumbent having returned home and there being no obvious local successor, he needed no further encouragement. His application was e-mailed the following day and three months later he, and his cricketing abilities, moved to North East Scotland to the benefit of both A Division and the top local cricket team.

Iqbal was a morning person. Always had been. Although arriving home quite late on Sunday evening from a trip to Glasgow, he was up early on Monday morning. Behind him a weekend of too much mother's food, and the usual interrogation about when he was going to settle down with a "Nice Bangladeshi girl."

He lived in The Hardgate, not far from the city centre and a two minute walk from the local Puregym. As per his usual routine, he was at the gym at 06:15 for a forty-five minute cardio session, where he would either listen to music or a cricket related podcast. He would leave enough time to get back home, shower, grab a light breakfast and get to work. He had three reasonable quality suits from Slaters which he used in rotation for work purposes, but outside of his job, with the possible exception of weddings and funerals, he rarely wore a tie or a suit. He did, however, quite like the sharp look a suit and tie combination offered him at work and took time to get the selection correct each morning. Having satisfied himself that a grey suit with blue and grey tie was hitting the sartorial mark, he put on his winter coat, inserted his ear buds and headed off to the station.

After a fifteen minute walk down Union Street, the main thoroughfare of Aberdeen city, he was struck by how many businesses he passed that had failed to re-open after the Covid pandemic. Probably not an unfamiliar site up and down the country, he considered, and not doing anything to enhance the look of the city centre.

Energised by the walk in the cool morning air, he took the steps at the front of the station two at a time, and walked briskly to his desk while removing and storing his earbuds, nodding at colleagues as he went. He booted up his computer and went to pick up a coffee en route to the Incident Room, the noise from which he could hear well along the corridor. When he entered the room, he was taken aback both by the size of the contingent assembled, and the amount of detail on the whiteboard. After taking a minute to digest the information on the board, including the fact that McRobert's DNA was now a proven match for the heart, he said to no-one in particular, in his Glaswegian brogue, "Gaun yersels guys. A man has a weekend off and comes back to find the case half solved!"

As was often the case, his observation was delivered with a generous smile and was well received. His arrival was noted by Bankhurst but she focused on her laptop screen rather than track his progress through the room which might not have been a good optic. Even without looking she couldn't help but marvel how the arrival of his effortless upbeat personality had already boosted the feeling in the room.

A good presence in the changing room, to use a football analogy.

He was a Glaswegian through and through. A second generation, Asian subcontinent Glaswegian, but a Glaswegian none-the-less, reflecting the modern cosmopolitan nature of Scotland's largest city. She had missed him over the weekend.

With her eyes still on her screen, she heard a slight diminuendo of the background noise in the room and looked up to see the cause in the shape of DCI Anderson, and Superintendent MacNiven, slipping into the back of the room to hear the briefing.

"Fuck," she said softly to herself in the expectation that no-one could hear her, but the nearest DC turned and gave her a knowing grin after hearing the expletive and understanding the source of its generation.

I could do without this today, she thought.

Her endometriosis pain, and therefore her need for regular analgesia, were ongoing, and she hadn't had the best night's sleep. She had definitely felt better before, but she resolved to power through the briefing, giving no hint of her discomfort, with the incentive of a painkiller and caffeine afterwards.

As was her custom, she stood up to attract the attention of the room and convey the unspoken invitation for conversations to end in anticipation of starting the briefing.

"Good morning. Thanks for all attending promptly, and welcome to DCI Anderson and Superintendent MacNiven."

Those who hadn't noticed their arrival swept the room to see their senior officers hugging the back wall and were awarded with a slight nod. Attention returned to Bankhurst.

"As you may have seen from the whiteboard we now have DNA confirmation that the heart came from Danny McRobert. The FLO will break the news to Mrs McRobert this morning."

"Hamish. Where are we on the Deliveroo staff?"

"Ma'am, so far we've identified two-hundred and fifty-four past and present staff in the Aberdeen area. We're confident from CCTV images that the person in question is a male, so after excluding female staff and those with motorised vehicles, we're left with one hundred and sixty-two. Of course, it wouldn't be that hard to manufacture your own Deliveroo livery, but for the meantime we'll go with known staff."

"Ok. Good. They'll all have to be traced, statements taken and alibis checked for last Friday at midday."

"Yes, Ma'am."

"What about the vehicle analysts? Any progress there?"

"Yes, Ma'am," replied one of the fresh-faced DCs, "they're saying, with over 90 % confidence, it's a Ford Transit Custom."

Bankhurst's satisfaction at knowing the likely make of the van was tempered with the realisation that, even with her relatively limited knowledge of vehicles, this was the most common van on UK roads.

The DC continued, "We're working on producing a list of owners in the North East but it is likely to be a lengthy one. Two have been reported stolen in recent months, and have not been recovered at this point."

"OK, that's good," replied Bankhurst as she took a moment to update the whiteboard.

"Now, what about the interviewing of Wilson's staff?"

"Still ongoing, Ma'am, but nothing of note meantime."

"OK. Keep on it and let me know if anything turns up."

Satisfied that appropriate lines of enquiry were being followed, she invited comment from the floor, but none was forthcoming, so she directed the team to meet again at 4pm. Accompanied by the noise of chairs being moved, and people gathering their belongings, she noticed MacNiven speaking to Anderson before the senior officer departed the room. Anderson hung back and attracted her attention indicating he wanted to speak to her. As some of the detectives left the room and congestion eased, Anderson made his way over to speak with Bankhurst.

"Hello, Lily. Hope you don't mind us gatecrashing your meeting? We should have given you a heads-up."

"No problem, Sir."

"The Super thinks we need to give a press statement today and would like you to lead it. No need to parade relatives at this stage, but we do need to keep the media briefed."

"That's fine," replied Bankhurst, although internally she knew that standing up in front of the press was not something she relished. She gained some comfort from the use of the word *statement* rather than conference which implied, perhaps, more a one-way flow of information than a question and answer session. She had actually noted, with a sense of relief, that the Comms officer, Alan Zimmerman, had squeezed into the busy room at the last minute to take in the briefing, so he should be up to date.

That's a bit of luck.

After exchanging relatively banal pleasantries about how the investigation was going, she excused herself from DCI Anderson and headed towards Zimmerman's office. Police Scotland only have a relatively small Comms network and they are scattered around the country. With modern communication systems, and with the nature of the work involved, it was a fairly easy transition to home working for Comms staff during the Covid pandemic. Some had chosen to continue their domiciliary base while others, including Zimmerman, had elected to return to the hub of the station. Bankhurst knew from a previous conversation that he missed the workplace camaraderie, and also the chance to ride his Kawasaki 500 to work.

She tapped on his door and was invited to enter. She was immediately aware of the subtle, but unmistakable smell of tannin and noted his motorbike leathers on the back of the door as she swung it to closure. His helmet lay on a chair alongside an impressive desk containing three different computer screens, and various other pieces of electronic equipment. His framed degree hung on the wall beside a liberally adorned noticeboard and a duty roster. A photo of a timid looking greyhound formed the screensaver for one of his screens.

"Hey, Lily, what brings you to the dark side?" he joked.

"Hi, Alan, the Brass want me to do a press statement today, and I

wouldn't mind a bit of help drafting it."
"Ah, I did wonder when that was going to happen. No problem. That's one of the reasons I dropped by this morning."
"Yes, I did see you there. Anything else I can add for you?" she continued.
"No, I don't think so. I'll get something drafted now and e-mail it to you in the next half hour or so. We can ping it back and forth until you're happy with it."
"That would be great, Alan. Appreciate it."
"Have you thought where you're going to deliver it?"
"I was wondering about the steps of the station rather than the press conference room," she responded.
"Fair enough," he replied with a knowing smile. Bankhurst knew he could see right through her attempt to minimise the length of the Q and A session. He had probably seen the tactic many times before, but he also seemed to appreciate that some officers were less comfortable than others in dealing with the fourth estate which was, after all, the very raison d'être for his own position.
"I'll get back to you ASAP," he continued. When you're happy with the content, I can arrange the time and place and let the media know. Just be aware, for a case like this, there may well be TV presence. You might want to add some more makeup, if you don't want to look like a ghost on the 6 o'clock news."
"Understood," said Bankhurst as she got up from her chair and prepared to leave.
"Thanks, Alan, appreciate it."
"No problem. Any time," he replied.
Before she reached the door, his phone rang and he answered it promptly. After listening for a few seconds, he raised his other hand beckoning Bankhurst not to leave and, although the room was quite dark, Bankhurst thought she noticed him turning a bit pale.
"You may want to take this. The enquiries desk has been looking for you. There's a butcher from Inverurie on the phone. They think they have a suspicious heart.

CHAPTER 9

Seconds after the words came out of Zimmerman's mouth, Bankhurst felt a chill in the pit of her stomach and a dryness of her mouth. She took a few steps towards the Comms officer to accept the phone being offered by her slightly ashen faced colleague. Although she had considered the possibility of a second murder with the same modus operandi, and therefore introducing the concept of a serial killer, the arrival of the phone call that might herald that development triggered an immediate physiological response in her body which could not be denied. The only external evidence, as far as she was aware, was a subtle quiver in her voice when she spoke, which she hoped wasn't audible to Zimmerman.

"This is DI Bankhurst."

"Morning, Ma'am. This is Sergeant Duncan from the General Enquiries desk. I'll patch you through to Ian Bowman, who's a butcher in Inverurie. I've already checked out his credentials and phoned him back at the business to make sure he's not a crank caller."

"OK. Thanks, Sergeant Duncan. Put him through please."

"Good Morning," she continued, "this is DI Bankhurst from Homicide. To whom am I speaking?"

"Aye...hello," Bowman responded in a somewhat uncertain voice. "I'm Ian Bowman, and I'm the manager at Lawrie's butcher in Inverurie."

Bankhurst let the silence hang, inviting him to continue.

"I think you might have to come and have a look at something we've found today. We'd already had a look at our stock following your e- mail the other day, and didn't find anything of concern, so never thought any more about it. But, to be honest, we forgot that three weeks ago we were short staffed for a couple of days, and froze the offal part of the abattoir delivery. We didn't have enough bodies on the ground to deal with everything, and it was the lowest priority. We got round to de-frosting the stock overnight, and when we were sorting it out this morning we found a heart we're suspicious of. On any other week we might not have given it a second glance, but one of my guys brought it to my attention, and I'm concerned it could be the right size and shape to be human."

"OK," Bankhurst interjected, "thanks Mr Bowman. I need you to segregate the area where the heart is, and close the shop immediately," she continued with some authority.

"Close the shop?" he repeated in a slightly incredulous tone, "This is one of the busiest weeks of the year."

"That's as maybe, Mr Bowman, but, given what has happened recently in Cults, we need to exclude a potential homicide. That means no more stock must leave your shop and, as a potential crime scene, we need to limit any contamination. We'll get out to you shortly and try to make sure any closure is as brief as possible."

Even as Bankhurst was saying the words, she knew that it might be a couple of days before the business could be cleared to restart trading.

"One last question, Mr Bowman."

"Aye."

"Who supplies your meat?"

"We get most of it from Wilson's Abattoir."

She finished the call impressing on Bowman the action required of him, and then phoned the police substation in Inverurie to get local officers to attend immediately to secure the scene.

She returned the phone to Zimmerman who, although the call had not been on speakerphone, made it obvious he had understood the nature of it.

"Not a word to anyone about this at the moment, Alan. It might be something or nothing," though in her own heart she had an ominous feeling about the new development.

"Can we maybe organise a press conference for about 3pm, and work on a draft, but keep this out of it meantime?"

"Of course," he replied.

Bankhurst returned to the Investigation Room and, although most of the team had dispersed, she was glad to find Iqbal still there discussing a T20 cricket match that had been played at the weekend. It wasn't often he found someone willing, and able, to converse about cricket and he was obviously making the most of it. He looked a little guilty as she approached, and hastily wound up the conversation.

"Zafar. I want you to come with me to Inverurie."

He looked a little puzzled and she continued, "We've had a report of a possible human heart being found at a butcher."

"Of course, no problem. Let me grab my coat and I'll be right there," he replied.

"Give me ten minutes," she replied, "I'm going to phone Pathology to see if Dexter Brewster's available to attend the scene."

It took Bankhurst a couple of minutes to firstly be told that Brewster wasn't the duty pathologist, and secondly to convince the department receptionist, nevertheless, to track him down and put her through.

" Hi, Dexter, it's Lily Bankhurst here."

"Hi Lily. How're you doing?" he enquired.

"Good," she said somewhat automatically though, in truth, her endometriosis symptoms had all but settled and the morning's developments, with their associated adrenalin rush, had indeed facilitated a feeling of better health.

"Listen, Dexter, I know you're not actually on-call today, but we've got another possible heart discovery in an Inverurie butcher; I was wondering, as you've already been involved in the case, if you might visit the scene and take a look. There was a slight pause as Brewster considered his quandary.

Although an acute referral would normally be handled by the duty pathologist, he or she would not mind if a colleague took ownership of some workload. In addition, he already felt invested, and indeed interested, in the case. He had two postmortems scheduled, but the dead were not impatient and could possibly wait. He would have to officially run it past his duty Pathologist colleague, and make some rearrangements with the mortuary staff, but generally he felt in credit with them and that a request to reschedule would be looked on favourably.

"OK," he said, "let's do it. I take it you just want me to say if it's a human heart or not and clear off until I can do a formal postmortem?"

"Yes, that would be great," Bankhurst replied. She gave him the address and postcode of Lawrie's, although as it was on West High Street, it sounded like it wouldn't be hard to find.

Bankhurst relocated Iqbal and they negotiated the necessary steps to get a vehicle from the carpool. She was aware that, as the morning had worn on, her blood sugars were likely to be getting low, and she hadn't had a chance to have a morning snack. Normally, if she was going to drive in such circumstances, especially at speed, she would take the time to check her blood glucose level and take any appropriate action. She also considered that her handheld glucose reader might not pick up the signal from her Freestyle Libre monitor through several layers of clothing, including a thick coat, therefore requiring a degree of undressing to facilitate testing. *Bugger it* she thought, and chucked the keys to Iqbal who quickly snared them one handed, like the good slip fielder he was.

"Blue light run?" he enquired.

They both knew it wasn't exactly an emergency. After all, the heart had been in a butcher's freezer for three weeks. Nevertheless, with Monday morning traffic likely to be quite busy, and with half an eye on her afternoon press conference, Bankhurst nodded an assent but added, "Don't go daft."

Iqbal sent her a boyish grin.

With the extra heat generated by the city itself, the heavier traffic, and, most importantly, the proximity to the relatively warm North Sea, Aberdeen had lost most of the evidence of the recent snowfall. Only small banks of graphite grey, almost black, roadside slush remained where once fresh snow had been marshalled sideways by council ploughs, and remorselessly stained by the dirty spray of urban traffic.

Bankhurst wished that the first snow of winter could have come a week or two later bringing with it the possibility of a white Christmas. Even in North East Scotland such an event remains somewhat of a novelty, and only once before, when he was aged two, and living in the central belt in fact, had Andrew experienced festive snow. At the time, he was more interested in his new toy digger and had no recollection of the white blanket that had obligingly settled over most of Scotland on Christmas Eve.

On the furthest outskirt of the city, where brown and green belts collide, there remained a smattering of snow, and for every few miles driven north-west towards Inverurie, there was extra snow depth evident in the surrounding countryside.

Indeed, by the time Bankhurst and Iqbal took the Inverurie exit from the A96, the snow was about four inches deep, and closer to a foot in drifts nestling in shaded field corners. The sun had come out and the winterscape of glistening snow, bowed trees and a white capped hill, Benachie, in the distance could have been taken straight from a Christmas card.

An added bonus for Bankhurst to having Iqbal drive was to enable her to do a little research on Inverurie. As an incomer to the area, she was aware of the town, and might even have been to its Garden Centre coffee shop on one occasion, but she didn't feel she *knew* it in any detail. Wikipedia was quick to inform her that Inverurie is a centuries old traditional market town some sixteen miles north-west of Aberdeen, situated where the river Urie joins and swells the size of The Don, as it continues inexorably towards the North Sea and its final destination. The largest single employer, traditionally, was a family run paper mill which typically would have about five hundred men and women on the payroll, but the business, along with numerous other Donside mills, had become a victim of reduced demand and cheaper foreign labour. It closed its doors for the final time in 2009. However, the flourishing oil industry from the early 1970s onwards had led to a steady expansion as Inverurie became an important satellite town for Aberdeen, such that its population, and that of a few adjacent small villages, grew to over twenty thousand. It remains a vibrant town, and an important regional hub for trading livestock and farming equipment.

She felt better informed by the time the two detectives passed through the small village of Port Elphinstone, about one mile from Inverurie, and then the re-developed site of the former mill, before crossing the bridge spanning The Don, and into Inverurie itself.

Bankhurst was aware, from investigations into the occupational history of McRobert, that he had worked at the Donside paper mill, near Tillydrone, for four years in his thirties before being dismissed for reasons unknown. She was also aware that Wilson's abattoir, in Dyce, lay less than a quarter of a mile from the river. Like most detectives she had a natural distrust of coincidences, and asked herself if there could be any link, no matter how tenuous, between the unfolding case and either paper mills or The Don itself. She acknowledged, however, that the Cults connection, in the western suburbs of Aberdeen, and closer to the River Dee, was an obvious outlier to that theory.

Even though there was a reasonable amount of snow in the Inverurie area, Bankhurst was impressed how clear the streets and pavements were of their winter covering. Both types of surface had been well cleared and gritted, and encouraged smooth flow of cars and pedestrians alike. Looking at the latter, she thought she could see signs that they were more used to hardy weather than their coastal cousins. Exposed faces appeared generally more weather beaten, and their choice of winter clothing much more appropriate than she would see in Aberdeen, especially in the younger generation on weekend nights when all common sense was completely abandoned on the altar of peer pressure.

All in all, it appeared that the Aberdeenshire councils and citizens were more adept at dealing with winter than those of Aberdeen city.

Not surprising perhaps she considered.

The well cleared streets and light traffic encouraged Iqbal to abandon the blue lights. They were, by now, largely redundant and the detectives had no wish to attract unnecessary attention as, at this point, they didn't know the significance, or not, of the discovery. They made swift progress through the town, and a left turn at the imposing Town Hall took them from High Street to West High Street. Less than a minute later, they had pulled up behind a patrol car parked on double yellow lines, with blue lights still flashing.

So much for keeping it discrete thought Bankhurst.

The two detectives bustled into the building with their heads partially down, though not without noticing a small gaggle of onlookers who, no doubt aware of recent developments in another North-East butcher, were taking a keen interest in the police presence at one of their own such shops.

They were greeted by a local PC and, after showing their IDs, were ushered from the front shop along a corridor. Bankhurst noted the staff sequestered in a side room as she went down the corridor. They appeared to be having some sort of hot beverage and were talking in hushed tones, though the volume audibly went up a notch after the CID officers passed their door.

It was impossible not to have a sense of deja vu. Another butcher; another corridor; another back room. The now familiar smell of raw meat, accompanied by the hum of fridges and freezers in the background, with an array of intimidating looking saws, knives and hooks hanging on the wall.

She felt her pulse quicken and wondered if Iqbal had any similar physiological changes going on, or if he was as calm and collected inside as he seemed to be on the outside. They stole a glance at each other as they surveyed the scene and tried to establish *first impressions,* using all available senses, as drummed into them on many training courses.

Unlike in Mitchell's butcher where, by the time CID had arrived, the heart was displayed in splendid isolation on a clean metal table, there was a sizeable bloody, visceral conglomerate sprawled across two different tables. A chainmail apron, splattered with blood and tissue, had been thrown over a nearby chair, and two different looking knives had been abandoned within what seemed to Bankhurst's inexpert eye to be various kidneys, livers, stomachs, something she didn't recognise...and a heart. Roughly the same size as the one she had seen in Cults, and then subsequently on Brewster's postmortem table. Somebody had obviously made a hasty retreat when the disentanglement of the frozen offal had delivered something alarming enough to trigger an immediate withdrawal, and a subsequent phone call to Police HQ in Nelson Street.

Although the bloody scene before Bankhurst and Iqbal was unappealing, at least it meant there had been minimal interaction with the suspect organ, and its surroundings, since discovery and, for that, Bankhurst was grateful.

"Let's hope Dexter Brewster will be here soon," she voiced.

"Can't argue with that, Boss."

"Can you go and have a preliminary word with the butchers please, Zafar, especially the one who raised the alarm?"

"No problem, Boss."

Bankhurst thought she could detect both a slight pallor to Iqbal's face, and a ready acceptance to take his leave of the somewhat gory anatomical scene laid out on the tables before them. Literally *blood and guts,* and a few other things besides.

Perhaps he was affected after all? No harm in that, though he obviously was trying not to show it.

*Typical male s*he thought.

"I'll phone the Path department and see if he's left," she called after him but he had already made a speedy exit and she was

left alone in the chilly room with only the bloody organs and her thoughts for company. She shivered slightly and felt glad of the warmth offered by her thick Mint Velvet coat that she had bought in an on-line sale at the end of the previous winter but hadn't really had a need for it until the previous week.
Where is this all going? she thought as she reached into a pocket and located her i-phone.

Dr Dexter Brewster was indeed on his way to Inverurie, but not before he had popped out to Costa to get a medium sized extra hot latte. If he had to disrupt his day, he was going to make it a reasonably pleasurable sojourn into the countryside, with coffee and music of his choice. While he was waiting for the barista to weave her magic, he checked the EV app on his phone. As he was not duty pathologist, he had anticipated predictable journeys to and from work, and hadn't bothered to charge his car above the 40% he knew he had when he got home the previous evening. He punched in the Inverurie postcode and was immediately informed what percentage car battery charge he could expect when he got to Inverurie, and when he arrived back in Aberdeen. From that he was reassured he would have enough to get home without going into the unchartered waters of single figure charge percentages, which he had never had the confidence to explore before. Content with his freshly made coffee and car status, he had set off for Inverurie, but the speed of his travel was determined by fellow motorists, and speed limits, and it took him forty minutes to make the journey. He had enjoyed an Elvis Costello playlist which even raised a smile as he was passing the turn off for Kemnay, not far from Inverurie, when *Watching the Detectives* began to play.

The track was just coming to a close when he entered Inverurie, and he killed the music to re-focus on the job in hand. That lasted for about thirty seconds because, as he was moving at a fairly low speed along High Street, he saw a dog, very like Archie, approaching on the pavement.

Hello boy he mouthed while smiling broadly towards the dog through the windscreen but the gesture, perhaps not surprisingly, was not reciprocated. It did, however, raise a strange look from his owner. The dog and the moment passed and he resumed his professional game face in time to draw up behind the two police cars in West High Street, where Bankhurst was pacing the pavement like an anxious parent waiting for a teenager to return home at night.

Although not entitled to emergency lights, Brewster did have a Duty Pathologist sign which he retrieved from the glove compartment, and placed in a prominent spot on top of the dashboard. He trusted this would protect him from receiving a parking ticket from an overzealous attendant. In the same movement, after seeing Bankhurst, he deftly stashed away the empty Costa cup out of sight. No need to advertise he had had a pit stop on the way.

"Hi, Dexter. Thanks for agreeing to come."

"No problem. Not every day we get a case like this…if indeed it is related to the Cults one."

He opened the boot and extracted his bag before following Bankhurst's lead into the butcher past the ever increasing group of onlookers.

"Zafar's had a word with the butcher who called it in. Quite an experienced guy. They've all been on a heightened state of alert since the publicity around the Cults case, and our own e-mails, and there was something about the size, shape and type of incisions made around the heart that aroused suspicion."

"Ok. I'll take a look."

Brewster donned appropriate protection for his shoes, body, hands and head before crossing the room threshold. He quickly scanned the space and noted the typical white tiled walls and ceiling strip lights bathing the windowless room in bright, naked light. The blue glow of an Insect-O-Cutor displayed the remains of its prey on a metal grill, lured to their premature and abrupt death.

A radio lay muted on a work surface near a giant-sized Belfast sink equipped with a long, flexible and very capable looking tap. Unlike paint splatter often seen on a tradesman's Makita radio, it bore the effects of being proximal to an area of active animal dissection, with the dried-in accompanying micro-spray of carcass fluids and tissues.

For some obtuse reason, Brewster briefly wondered if it would be tuned to Northsound, or even NECR in this area of rural Aberdeenshire, but quickly dismissed the thought to focus on the matter in hand.

He strode over to the bloody tableau and placed his bag on an unaffected area of worktop. He removed some equipment and, without hesitation or further conversation, went purposefully to work. He quickly weighed and measured the heart, noting the dimensions as he went. He then proceeded to careful inspection, followed by palpation and finally, after fitting a size fifteen blade to a scalpel handle, made a two centimetre longitudinal incision in the right coronary artery, and parted the tissue to look inside. The whole examination took less than ten minutes and was obviously finished when Brewster peeled off his gloves, inverting one inside the other. He tugged at his plastic apron until the neck and back straps parted, bundled his protective clothing together, and dropped it into a nearby bin. He unhooked one side of his face mask so that it hung vertically from the other ear which Bankhurst presumed was a prelude to his verbal report.

"Lily. I can confirm that I am 99% certain this is another human heart."

"I'll be able to make absolute confirmation, or not, once I've done a postmortem with tissue and DNA testing, but I think you can assume this is another murder."

CHAPTER 10

Bankhurst found herself temporarily lost for words. Within seconds, numerous thoughts had collided within her brain and were fighting for superiority. Several more were threatening to crowd in. It felt distinctly unsettling. Normally, one of her strengths was to process information and take decisive action so what appeared to be a cerebral traffic jam was as puzzling as it was unwelcome.

Fuck. Fuck. Fuck she thought.

Although it hadn't been going on for long, the pregnant pause had not gone unnoticed by Brewster who felt obliged to fill it with more detail of his analysis.

"The dimensions, weight and anatomy are all consistent with a human heart, but the clincher is the presence of visible atherosclerotic change in the coronary artery. Not bad enough to cause the owner any symptoms at the moment but could have been a cause of angina in later years, had they lived longer. Animals, at least the sort we have in this country, with their plant-based diet, shorter life expectancy and non-smoking status, are not afflicted by this pathological change. Ergo, this is a human heart."

"The one other thing to mention is that the incisions made around this heart, to free it from its anatomical connections to the great blood vessels and other surrounding tissues, seem very clean and precise. Almost surgical I would say."

Bankhurst was grateful for the time afforded by Brewster's intervention and forced herself to regain a measure of cognitive control. She formed a strategy in her mind.

Step 1. Exclude a hypo.
Step 2. Prioritise.
Step 3. Pull yourself the fuck together!

Much to the surprise of her colleagues, she swiftly removed her overcoat and then swiped the glucose reader over her upper arm. The penny dropped with Brewster but, by the look on his face, Iqbal was still processing his loose change.

"Just checking my blood sugar," she said by way of explanation.

"Didn't even know you were diabetic, Boss."

"Not many people in The Job do," she replied while giving him a knowing look.

"Understood," he said, "you can count on me."

"How's the reading?" enquired Brewster.

"Fine," she said, though at 5.1 it was getting on the low side of acceptable. She rooted around in her bag and finally located a snack bar that had been hidden in the lower recesses for months. She deftly peeled back the wrapper and began to chomp in a somewhat noisy and ungainly manner. Expediency trumping aesthetics.

Not unlike Archie eating a bit of toast mused Brewster, though he kept that particular thought to himself.

Whether it was the fact she was within her comfort zone of diabetic management, or it was just the passage of time, Bankhurst began to feel a measure of control returning.

The coldness of the room might also have helped sharpen her focus, but it had fairly quickly penetrated her blouse and jumper and she began to shiver slightly. Iqbal held out her coat which she gratefully accepted and hoped it wouldn't be too long before she felt its warmth.

"Right," she said, signalling to herself as much as to her audience that a line had been drawn under something, and it was time to move on.

"At best we are facing a double murderer, and at worst a serial killer." Brewster and Iqbal had already drawn the same conclusion, of course, but to hear it verbalised only increased the magnitude of what lay before them.

Beyond the imagination of local crime authors, multiple homicides in North East Scotland are virtually unheard of, and were likely to bring a public interest and professional scrutiny the likes of which few, if any, on the case would have experienced before.

"Zafar, can you mobilise the team and get SOCO out here ASAP?"

"On it."

"I need to get back to Aberdeen for the press conference, so hopefully Dexter might allow me to cadge a lift," she said inflecting the end of the sentence to make a question, while looking hopefully towards the pathologist.

"Of course. As long as you don't mind the faint smell of dog, and the not so faint sound of David Bowie, who I had a mind to play on the way back to Aberdeen."

"Either him or The Royal Scots Dragoon Guards pipe band!" he added.

"Four wheels and a heater would do right now to be honest. You can choose the music."

"OK. Give me ten minutes to clear up here and give the department a heads-up as to what's happening. I'll want all these other organs bagged and tagged for further assessment, though to my eye none of them look human."

"That's fine. I've got some e-mails I need to check, and I'll need to let the top floor know about the development."

The main e-mail, in fact, that she wanted to check was from Zimmerman. The press conference would have been arranged and the clock was ticking. She needed to check his suggested script. Any inclusion, or not, of the Inverurie development was for someone well above her pay grade to decide. As it was, she had very few edits to make as Zimmerman had done what he normally did, producing a polished and eloquent narrative:succinct and accurate divulging just the right amount of information. Not for the first time, she was grateful to have him as a colleague.

She returned the edited draft for him to check her tweaks made sense, but didn't mention, for the meantime, what had developed in Inverurie, although she realised he would be desperate to know as he had been party to the alerting phone call.

Brewster finished tidying up, and noticed Bankhurst was still actively engaged with her i-phone screen. He took the opportunity to quickly leave the building to make the front of his car respectable but was stopped in his tracks at the front door. In the relatively short time they had been in the butcher's, the weather had changed. A winter shower was sweeping across the town, but seemed undecided whether it was rain, sleet or hailstones as all three were represented. Parallel diagonal rods were driving across his field of vision. He pulled his coat zip up to its full extent and held the edges of his collar together in the midline, before dashing for his car through a much diminished group of onlookers. All but the most committed had been dispersed by the unpleasant squall. He pulled the passenger door open and removed sweet papers and parking receipts from the central well, and a few dog hairs from the seat itself.

How the hell does Archie's hair get in the front seat anyway?

He hadn't been expecting to give the DI a lift and didn't want his car to look like it was halfway to a pig sty. He hoped she wouldn't look in the back where she might see anything from half eaten canine toys to an abandoned, hollowed out marrow bone.

He finished just in time to see Bankhurst leave the butcher and scan the parked cars looking for her lift. He held up his hand both to identify himself, and thereby his car, but also to encourage her to go back under the cover of the doorway. He retrieved an old umbrella from his boot. It was brightly coloured and bore the insignia of a company who manufactured disposable surgical instruments. It had been a 'gift' from a rep about fifteen years previously, back in the day when such gifts were allowed. As he extended the somewhat grubby umbrella, he noted the obligatory broken spoke, but the device managed to open out regardless and he scurried back to the shop to offer some protection against the elements.

Bankhurst gratefully accepted, and they huddled together to

make the most of the moderate protection while making their way to the car. He was so close to her he could smell her perfume. It seemed quite familiar, and he wondered if Chloe may have worn it before, though he was unable to put a name to it. Just before reaching the car, a gust of wind inverted the part of the umbrella unsupported by the broken spoke and they both received an unpleasant, icy blast to the face. Expletives were muttered as they ducked into the protection of the car.

By now the hailstones were winning the meteorological battle for superiority, and were drumming hard on the roof and windscreen of the car, turning it into a kind of oversized percussion instrument. The noise was deafening for about twenty seconds, and then, almost as quickly as it had built to a crescendo, the hailstones, and with it the noise, disappeared abruptly, leaving behind the *thwack, thwack* of the windscreen wipers to break the ensuing silence.

Brewster pulled out onto a freshly lain, crunching carpet of hailstones and made steady progress to the edge of the town. Even as he passed the *end of the speed limit* sign, a wintery sun was edging out from the retreating cloud, and beginning to melt the latest winter offering.

Despite the previous discussion about a playlist, Brewster and Bankhurst quickly settled in to a conversation about the case and its ramifications, followed by polite enquiries about each other's families such that, before they knew it, they were heading along Great Northern Road in Aberdeen, only a few minutes short of Nelson Street . Realising that the journey would end soon, Brewster returned to their previous conversation.

"If you can put the hurry on SOCO to do their thing and get the heart to me in three to four hours, I'll try and get the postmortem done today. I'll ask for urgent DNA analysis and try to get a result by late tomorrow."

"Thanks, Dexter. That would be great, and at least would give me something to offer the top floor."

She was not looking forward to the afternoon which promised challenging encounters with the media and her own superiors.

When she had phoned earlier to break the news to DCI Anderson, he said, as expected, that he would have to escalate it higher up the chain of command, and she had received a text only about fifteen minutes later summoning her to a meeting before the press conference.

On the way to grabbing some lunch, and giving herself some short acting insulin, Bankhurst slipped into the Incident Room where she found a scattering of detectives mostly engrossed in their computer screens.

She picked up a marker pen and with a few squeaky strokes on the white board changed the narrative of the case, and possibly her career. While it was possible, given the potential for a serial killer being at large, she might have to relinquish control of the case to a higher rank, she also imagined that those above her might be quite happy with a middle layer between them and the sharp end of proceedings. A type of insurance, perhaps, if things didn't go according to plan. Time would tell.

As she was writing, she was aware of less tapping on nearby keyboards, and the swivelling of seats, as she was slowly grabbing the attention of the, by now largely hushed, room.

POSSIBLE SECOND VICTIM
INVERURIE 16/12/22

She turned to face the room and several people spoke at once, contributing to an unintelligible noise. Holding up her right hand with fingers spread, she beckoned patience and silence, which were gradually granted.

"DS Iqbal and I have just come back from Lawrie's butcher in Inverurie where we attended with Dr Brewster. He has confirmed that the heart they discovered is 99% likely to be human. Formal postmortem will hopefully be later today, but it looks very like we have a second victim."

"Not a word of this must get out until we get confirmation. I've got a meeting shortly with senior staff, and then a press conference at 3pm." "Hamish, can you organise our team to

meet at 4pm for a general update please?"
"Will do."
"I'm off to grab a bite to eat before my first meeting. Anything good on in the canteen today?"
"There's a half decent lasagne, but I would avoid the garlic bread. Bit like a brick," suggested MacLennan.
"Duly noted," she replied.

As it turned out, Bankhurst did indeed enjoy the pasta and even, contrary to advice, ran the gauntlet of the garlic bread. She survived with her fillings intact and actually enjoyed the flavour of the herb which, as ever, was well suited to partner lasagne.
She attended to her midday diabetic housekeeping, checked her e-mails, had a quick squint at Whatsapp and, mindful of Zimmerman's advice, applied a little fresh, but still fairly subtle, makeup along with a small top-up spray of eau de toilette. She was determined to look at her best for the meeting with senior staff and, more importantly, the press.
At 2pm she knocked on the door of MacNiven's office and entered as invited. On this occasion, Superintendent MacNiven and DCI Anderson had been joined by Chief Superintendent Grant McCulloch. An impressive gathering of high-ranking officers indeed, thought Bankhurst.
Almost immediately she became aware of the earliest flutterings of disquiet in her stomach. She wasn't averse to a little situational anxiety, as historically she had often been able to harness and utilise it to energise her performance in any given stressful situation. What she didn't want was a repeat of what appeared to have happened earlier in the day when, for a brief period at least, her physiological response threatened to be more foe than friend.
Perhaps in order to feel in control, and not give any nascent anxiety a chance to gain a foothold, she decided to take the initiative.
"Good afternoon, Sirs. Thanks for arranging the meeting."
She wasn't sure if handshakes were in order or not, especially

with Chief Superintendent McCulloch who she hadn't actually met before, but the body language of the senior officers did not appear to invite it.

Although MacNiven was playing at home, by hosting the meeting, the senior officer McCulloch clearly had the air of the person in charge.

"Hello, DI Bankhurst. Thanks for coming. I don't think we've met. I'm Grant McCulloch," as he stretched out his hand and gave a firm, but not intimidating, handshake accompanied by a generous smile.

So a handshake was in order! thought Bankhurst.

"Please. Have a seat."

Facing so many uniforms, Bankhurst couldn't help but feel she was in an interview situation. McCulloch sat behind the desk, a serious looking Anderson was to one side and Shifty MacNiven sat more towards the corner looking…well…shifty.

"Thanks for letting us know of the possible double homicide. That's obviously why we called this meeting, especially with the press conference timetabled for this afternoon."

"We appreciate all the efforts you and your team have made already but, and I'm sure this won't come as much of a surprise, we will be setting up a Major Investigation Team, with immediate effect. DCI Anderson will head up the team, and you will be second in the command structure."

"As you're already prepped for the press, it would make sense if you take the conference (*I thought as much,* mused Bankhurst), though we may have to speak about what should, and should not, be disclosed at this stage."

"Yes, Sir," replied Bankhurst, automatically.

"Where are we at the moment with the investigation?" continued McCulloch.

"The team is working hard, but progress is relatively slow I'm afraid. As you can appreciate, we don't have our usual sources of information.

No body…just an organ.

No clothing.

No forensics.
No definite crime scene.
No murder weapon...if indeed a weapon was used.
No useful information from the victim's phone.
No idea of motive.
No suspects."

She continued, "As you know, with some help from Dr Brewster, along with his medical and IT colleagues, we managed to identify the owner of the first heart discovered."

She was careful to avoid saying *first victim* as she had no idea, especially with the involvement of deep freezing, where he stood chronologically in the event of two or more victims being discovered.

"In the absence of other evidence, we're digging deep into Mr McRobert's life to see if we can unearth any possible motive, but nothing obvious so far."

"We're also fairly sure the suspect is posing as a Deliveroo cyclist to introduce the hearts into the food industry, and we plan to have a surveillance team at Wilson's Abattoir every Friday meantime."

"Interviewing with staff at Mitchell's in Cults, and Wilson's in Dyce, is complete; we'll start on Lawrie's ASAP, but no red flags so far. Deliveroo staff are proving harder to track down. They are often students, or other types of transient worker, and quite a few have gone home for the Christmas break. This is obviously a major area of interest, and we've targeted our efforts focusing on males with non-motorised transport. No joy so far, I'm afraid."

Bankhurst was into her stride now, and any initial anxiety had settled. It felt good to have a feeling of self-confidence returning, and she had lost any sense of being intimidated by the situation.

Perhaps I might be on the other side of the table in future years.

"Are you considering any Criminal Psychology input?" contributed MacNiven

"Yes. I believe Dr Louise McEwan is very good. We plan to get her opinion ASAP."

"Good."

"Any progress with the van?"

"Not really, though the whole force is on alert for blue Ford Customs, and ANPR will alert us if it picks up the false number plate."

"What's your own feeling, Lily, about whether to include any reference to Inverurie in today's press conference?" The question came from Anderson who was the only one likely to address Bankhurst by her christian name.

"My gut feeling is not to, Sir, as we don't yet have 100% confirmation. I realise that, with social media and Aberdeen Live being what they are, there's a risk that information may well be out there already, but I think we just have to accept that."

"Very well. That's more or less what we were thinking too."

"Assuming a second case is confirmed, our top priority will be to identify and research the victim to see if there is any commonality with McRobert, which might help us establish some kind of motive."

"Dr Brewster's hopeful of doing the postmortem today, with a view to getting the DNA result tomorrow."

"OK. Good," replied McCulloch, "it goes without saying that the eyes of the whole of Police Scotland, and further afield, will be on us with this case. The press, especially the red tops, will have a field day. You can just imagine the headlines! We need to play everything by the book."

"Understood, Sir."

"OK. Good. I'm sure you and DCI Anderson will keep Superintendent MacNiven and myself up to date."

"Yes, Sir. Of course."

McCulloch stood up and offered a handshake to finish the meeting in the same way he had started it. Three of the quartet exited the room, leaving a slightly brooding MacNiven to reclaim ownership of his territory. Bankhurst was walking down the corridor and heard some brisk footsteps approaching from behind.

"I'll walk with you, Lily," said Anderson.

"No problem, Sir."
"Lily, I'm very pleased to be the SIO on this MIT but I want you to know that you have my full confidence, and I'm very happy for you to run the show. I'll take responsibility, and deal with upstairs, and allow you to focus on the job in hand."
Bankhurst thought it was odd for Anderson to use the term *upstairs* as she already imagined him as one who had already ascended the metaphorical staircase.
I guess it's all relative, she thought.
The piece of good news was very welcome to Bankhurst in a day of challenges. She liked and respected Anderson, and she could trust him to be true to his word. She would be able to continue leading the case safe in the knowledge that her back was covered. It put her in a good mood to face the fourth estate.

The press briefing had been moved inside at the last minute, due to the threat of another winter squall, and therefore had the feel more of a conference than a statement. Bankhurst and Anderson, stony faced, sat facing the assembled journalists.
A fairly motley looking crew thought Bankhurst, though she knew appearances could be deceptive, as there would be many sharp minds amongst them, not to mention those with interrogation skills she wished some of her CID officers possessed. She noted a variety of recording devices on show, and it even looked like one or two of the older hacks had a pencil and notepad. Old habits…
Anderson began with a welcome and introductions before handing over to Bankhurst, who followed her agreed script without interruption as had been requested. Some of it had been a little vague.
"A locus in Cults…human remains…following lines of enquiry."
After she had finished, and with a little trepidation, she invited questions from the floor. A forest of raised hands duly obliged, and she picked one at random.
"Steve Smith. The Herald. Is it true the only remains found were a heart?"
"Yes."

"Peter Davies. P and J. Have you identified the deceased?"
"Yes. I can confirm that we have."
"What is their name?"
"Sorry. I'm unable to share that with you at this time."
"Susie Gilmore. Daily Telegraph."
Bloody hell. The Telegraph! thought Bankhurst.
"Do you have any suspects yet?"
"Not at this stage, though we are following several lines of enquiry."
"Peter Davies, again. P and J. What **are** the lines of enquiry being followed?
As if I'm going to tell you that! thought Bankhurst but instead said "As I'm sure you'll understand I am unable to share that," while trying to keep any note of sarcasm out of her voice. She didn't particularly like the look of Davies, or the tone in which he asked his questions, so searched the room for another eager face.
"David McKerral. The Scotsman. Are you getting any help from outwith Grampian to investigate the case?"
Bankhurst bristled at the less than subtle implication that A Division was somehow not up to the task.
Keep calm, she told herself.
"No," said with a subtle inflection as if to say "Why *would we do that?*
"Peter Davies. P and J."
Not him again!
"What about the second heart found at Inverurie this morning?"

And there it was.
The intervention Bankhurst had hoped to avoid. She always thought if the information had begun to leak from the Aberdeenshire market town it would most likely be picked up by local journalists in the first instance.
Had Davies known about it since the beginning of the meeting, and had saved it until this moment for maximal effect, or had he just received a text from his news desk or Aberdeen Live?
Either way, it had an immediate effect on the room and he

was now very much the centre of attention. Perhaps that was his game? There was an immediate buzz within the journalists as they seemed divided between those shouting questions and those looking quizzically at their phones, puzzled as to why they were not in this particular information loop.

Anderson's intervention was clear and firm.

"Can I **please** request a degree of order in the room?" It was said with sufficient authority to change the question to an instruction and, with a little reluctance, the audience acquiesced.

Anderson nodded at Bankhurst inviting her to continue.

"I can confirm that we were pursuing a line of enquiry at a locus in Inverurie this morning, but it is too early to say if there is any connection with this case."

"Was there another heart discovered?" was shouted anonymously from the press.

"I'm afraid we are at a very early stage with this enquiry, and I am unable to give further details."

"Were there any human remains?"

"Was it another butcher?"

"Is there a serial killer loose?"

The questions were coming thick and fast, and without any identification from the questioner. The more experienced Anderson recognised the signs of potential loss of control of the conference, and decided a strategic retreat was the best tactical option.

"OK. We'd like to thank you for coming today but we have no further information to share at this time. This meeting will now be closed."

A torrent of raised hands and voices followed which the two detectives ignored. They stood up and, a bit like newscasters at the end of a bulletin, shuffled their papers together in another visual clue that the briefing was over.

CHAPTER 11

Bankhurst looked out at her third audience in as many hours. She saw a sea of serious faces, and an equal number of black Police Scotland lanyards tapering down to IDs showing the same serious, if somewhat younger, faces. The formation of an MIT had led to a further allocation of detectives, and had formed the largest investigative team in living memory in Aberdeen. As in the press conference, Anderson made himself conspicuous, but also made it clear who was leading the meeting.

"Welcome, everybody," began Bankhurst.

Whether it was practise making perfect, or she was more comfortable with her, albeit expanded, team she felt in control; it felt good; it felt empowering.

"As most of you will know, we attended Lawrie's butcher in Inverurie this morning. It appears highly likely that the heart they discovered is human. Dr Dexter Brewster is doing a postmortem as we speak and, with luck, we should have DNA results by tomorrow. Sergeant MacDonald is representing us at the postmortem."

"This is obviously a very serious development, and we are now in a Major Investigation. It really goes without saying, but we'll be looking for 100% commitment until we resolve this."

"There's going to be intense media interest. The **only** people who will liaise with the press are either myself or Alan Zimmerman and his Comms colleagues. I don't want **any** leaks. I trust that's understood."

There was a general nodding of heads and audible expressions of agreement.

"As well as following our current lines of enquiry, our top priority now is to ID and research the Inverurie victim. We need to find any potential connections between him/her and McRobert which might help inform our search for motive."

"We need to redouble our efforts to interview all Deliveroo staff, though we also need to be aware that the suspect may be masquerading as one of their employees...you can buy almost anything on the internet these days."

More nodding of heads.

"I want the surveillance team to do a site visit to Wilson's before Friday. Look for good vantage points which don't advertise our presence. I want units inside and out. Make sure Wilsons place their usual order as we don't want any deviation from normal to put our guy off - if he's planning a visit."

"Moving forward, I want to emphasis the importance of timely and accurate communication. This is a big team now. The right hand needs to know what the left is doing. Due to the very unusual nature of the case, and the dearth of physical evidence, any small piece of information may turn out to be vitally important. Don't keep concerns to yourself. Speak up. I don't bite!"

One or two in the audience weren't sure that was entirely true, but it seemed well intentioned, and raised some muted laughter. Bankhurst fielded a few questions, and then closed the meeting with a commitment to re-gather as a full team the following afternoon.

As she was closing her laptop, she noticed MacDonald entering the room at a brisk pace and making a beeline for her.

"PM's over. Dr Brewster is convinced the organ is a fairly healthy, but definitely human, heart. He estimates that it might belong to someone in their fifties or sixties."

"Same age range as McRobert. Might be something or nothing," mused Bankhurst.

"He's done the usual tests and sent them off as VERY URGENT samples. Expects results by tomorrow."

"OK. Good. Thanks, Hamish."

Four hours later, Bankhurst was sitting at her breakfast bar finishing off the family Christmas cards. A few days later than she had planned, but with good reason. She had survived the annual battle with the computer to print out the correct labels for her Christmas list and had enrolled Andrew to help with the envelopes and stamps. He was justifiably proud of his improving language skills and was delighted at being allowed to add a few of his own words to selected cards. Bankhurst imagined the smile it would produce from the chosen few when they opened their cards.

Sitting by the Christmas tree, complete with lights and baubles, Bankhurst was struck by the contrast between the fairy-tale-like scenes much beloved by Christmas card designers and the bloody evil she was currently embroiled in by day. She was doing her best to shut it out, but it wasn't easy. A decent sized glass of sauvignon blanc was certainly helping. She doubted it would be her last.

Eight miles away in Maryculter, another glass of wine had just been poured. Two in fact.

Dexter and Chloe Brewster were halfway through a half decent bottle of merlot[4]. Dexter had, unwittingly, monopolised the majority of the post work de-brief with a recounting of his trip to Inverurie and subsequent postmortem. Chloe was happy to let him offload as it was, in fact, an extraordinary tale and, by now, the first glass of wine had crossed the blood-brain barrier and was working its cerebral magic. She felt the warm embrace of the alcohol and was content for it to carry her towards a state of relaxation. She had temporarily zoned out of the conversation.

"...might even be a paper in it for me in the MSL journal."

Dexter read the signs of his wife's disengagement and went to give Archie a pat on the head instead.

He noted his bowl in the middle of the kitchen floor.

Must have been quite a tasty tea mused Dexter.

Archie's 2nd Law declares: *the distance a dog's bowl travels is directly proportional to the tastiness of the meal offered.*

This could vary from minimal, if any, movement during the consumption of a standard supermarket offering to a major journey if high-end food products were involved.

The ultimate epicurean temptation, for Archie, was the leftovers from the human's Sunday lunch. His bowl would be propelled relentlessly until it became snared in the corner of the kitchen, the perpendicular skirting boards allowing no further retreat from the ongoing lingual assault. Once satisfied that both bowl and beard were cleaned to within an inch of their lives, and there were no further morsels forthcoming from the humans, Archie would slink off to a suitable piece of floor and walk round in a circle four times to satisfy the pre-historic part of his brain which still demanded that any tall grass be flattened before lying down.

Not usually a problem on laminate flooring, but that didn't stop him.

He was already fast asleep on the floor, and Dexter assumed all dog routines had already been completed to Archie's satisfaction.

CHAPTER 12

Tuesday 17th December

Bankhurst was deep in thought. Although Christmas Day was still over a week away, as a single parent, she needed to be organised. There were the practicalities of Christmas Day itself, and last minute presents to be bought, not to mention the scrum that would be the pre-festive supermarket shop. Such domestic responsibilities didn't stop even though she was in the middle of the biggest case of her career. A definite bonus had been the offer from her parents to come to Aberdeen for the Festive break, which she had gratefully accepted. The plan was for them to arrive on Christmas Eve, and stay for three nights, which seemed long enough to be enjoyable, and certainly very helpful, but not long enough for them to tire of each other's company.

She jumped when the phone rang.

"DI Bankhurst."

"Hi, Lily. It's Dexter Brewster. Can you speak just now?"

"Sure, Dexter."

"I've got some results."

"Firstly, one of your colleagues was over in the department on another matter and she kindly ran the DNA through your system. No match I'm afraid."

Somehow that didn't come as a surprise to Bankhurst.

"Histology confirms the naked eye appearance of a healthy heart.

DNA confirms it is a human heart. Female. European ancestry. Viking and Neanderthal influences. Very likely caucasian. Genomic assessment indicates she was likely to have blue eyes and red hair. She had a gene putting her at higher risk of dementia, but it is likely she would have been too young for this to have manifested yet."

"The other main abnormalities were in fact in her Brca1 and Brca2 genes. She had abnormal mutations in both genes, putting her at significantly higher risk of breast cancer."

"Unlike McRobert, whose genetics placed him in a relatively small group, these abnormalities could put her in the very significant group of ladies, and indeed some men, in North East Scotland, who have had breast cancer. Many thousands. Also, she may not yet have developed the condition or, indeed, she might never, as it's not a guarantee, even if you have been dealt the most unfavourable genetic hand."

Bankhurst's heart sank a little. The investigation really needed the ID of the Inverurie victim, and she had hoped that Brewster's phone call might have provided the answer.

Brewster could feel her disappointment on the other end of the phone. He was in two minds whether to say anything or not, but eventually filled the silence that was developing.

"It's not really my place to say this perhaps, but have you considered IGG testing?"

"As in Investigative Genetic Genealogy?"

"Yes. It pops up from time to time in Forensic journals and definitely seems to be on the rise. I know there are some legal and confidentiality issues, and that not all Ancestry companies cooperate, but there have been some quite high profile crimes solved as a result."

"I am aware of it but have no personal experience. As I understand it, people who get their DNA checked, as part of an investigation into their ancestry, often accede to it being made available on-line for the greater good of genealogical investigation."

"That's correct," confirmed Brewster, "and by consenting effectively sign away their most personal information for others to access. There is now a vast amount of DNA posted online. Normally access would be restricted to other interested parties on a genealogy site, but Law Enforcement agencies in several countries have been applying, with some success, on a case by case basis, to Genealogy sites for DNA comparisons."

"Even if the perpetrators themselves haven't, and presumably any self-respecting criminal wouldn't, upload their genetic profile, it sometimes only takes a relative with an interest in Genealogy to post their similar, but not identical, DNA, to snare the perpetrator."

"OK. Thanks, Dexter. Appreciate you highlighting that. It may have been something we might have considered in due course, but I think, particularly in view of today's results, I'll advance it right to the top of the pile. Can't see any harm in it, and I've got a big team at my disposal now, so may as well give them something to get their teeth into."

Bankhurst hung the phone up and opened her laptop to search for the latest IGG information, and any possible guideline on the Police Scotland intranet and Google.

"Worth a shot," she confirmed to herself.

At the afternoon MIT meeting, Bankhurst highlighted the postmortem and DNA results, which generated a few groans from the team. The disappointment in the room was palpable.

She then, with an appropriate acknowledgement to Brewster's involvement, outlined the plan to explore IGG as an investigative option. Mixed emotions were evident in body language and facial expression.

To be expected she thought.

There would always be rapid adopters and dinosaurs in any large group faced with a change or initiative. Too bad.

She felt like saying: *If anyone has a better idea at this stage, I'd like to hear it* but thought better of it.

CHAPTER 13

Wednesday 18th December

It was midafternoon when the breakthrough came. There had been a flurry of activity late Tuesday and Wednesday morning as the collective power of an MIT rolled into concerted action focusing on IGG and Genealogy sites.
DS Sharon Baxter was working on a different website when she received notification of an e-mail arrival from YouandYours, a genealogy site she had approached earlier in the morning.

Dear DS Baxter,
Further to our phone call and your subsequent secure e-mail/ attachment, I can confirm that we have a partial match for your DNA profile. It is highly likely this belongs to a close relative. It seems the individual was interested in her ancestry and also her strong family history of breast cancer. Her details are:
Shona Rennie 4/5/70 Westhill, Aberdeenshire.

Get in there! thought Baxter.

Baxter called over to Bankhurst who was in a different area of the MIT room.
"Boss, you need to have a look at this."
Although she was good friends with Bankhurst, and would normally address her by her first name, she chose to retain the hierarchy of rank within the context of the MIT.
Several heads turned, while others peered above the rims of their glasses, seduced by her promising statement.
Bankhurst read the e-mail and gave a low-five to Baxter. This was

potentially the boost the investigation required.

After a few failed attempts to call Rennie, they managed to find her by late afternoon. It seemed likely she had been at work.
"Is that Shona Rennie?" began Baxter.
The usual hesitation followed as Rennie assessed whether it was a genuine call, or yet another unsolicited contact.
"This is DS Baxter phoning from Aberdeen."
"Have you found her?"
"Excuse me?"
"Have you found my **sister**?"

Jean Munro had been reported as a missing person four weeks previously. She was a fifty-five year old farmer's widow who still lived, along with her twenty-eight year old son Angus, on the family farm just north of Turriff, a small town thirty four miles from Aberdeen on the A947 road to Banff.
She had gone missing on the way home from an evening yoga class in Turriff on the 20th November. It was very unusual for her to be late home, especially without making contact, and her son had reported her missing by midnight on the same night.
Her yoga teacher recounted that Munro appeared her usual quiet, somewhat introverted self and that the class itself was unremarkable. CCTV footage in Turriff town centre, and the Aberdeen to Banff bus, documented her, apparently uneventful, journey homewards up to the point she alighted from the bus some two hundred yards from the road-end to her farm. She either never arrived home, or she did and some incident at home was responsible for her disappearance. There was no suicide note and nothing in her pre-disappearance behaviour to suggest she would have either self-harmed, or arranged her own disappearance. It was acknowledged that neither of the two possibilities could be entirely dismissed, especially as it was subsequently found that the farm was in financial difficulty, and that Munro carried significant life insurance.
It was noted that this detail could also provide possible motive

for matricide, but it appeared the son was genuinely devastated by her disappearance, and there was no sign of a disturbance, or unexpected forensics, at the farm. Assessment of his phone data suggested he, or his phone at least, had not left the farm that night. His mother's phone had never been recovered; the last signal placed her near the drive to her farm.

Overall, the original investigation team thought a domestic murder unlikely, and more plausible theories included abduction or self-managed disappearance, but their minds and the file remained open.

Bankhurst disseminated the file to the MIT, with a directive to familiarise themselves with every last detail. A FLO was organised to visit the son that evening, and to sow the seeds for a formal interview on Thursday morning. Bankhurst wanted to do the interview in person and thought, on this occasion, she would take DS Baxter with her, partially as she had established the ID and partially as she would be an easy companion in the forty-five minute journey it might take to reach Turriff. She also didn't want tongues wagging if she persistently chose Iqbal as her preferred partner though, in truth, it wasn't unusual for a DI to have a go-to sergeant that they favoured.

Thursday 19th December

At 10:30am Bankhurst, behind the wheel this time, drove past the country bus stop, and the site of Munro's last mobile signal, before turning right into the quarter mile drive that would deliver them into the farm courtyard. The previously tarred drive had long since lost its integrity and was studded with potholes, many of which were filled with water. It was an uncomfortable and slow journey which made Bankhurst glad her endometriosis flare had completely settled, as any inflammatory focus in the pelvis would have been found out immediately with such a bumpy ride.

She was reminded of a doctor friend, who worked in Accident and Emergency, who often said one of her diagnostic criteria for acute appendicitis was whether the pain flared up while crossing the speed bump on the way into the A and E car park. The wire fencing on either side of the drive had been breached in several locations, without evidence of attempted repair, and the sign indicating they had reached Fairlieknowe Farm looked like it hadn't been troubled by a paint brush for many years.

If the road into the estate suggested underinvestment, if not outright neglect, the farm itself, and associated outbuildings, did nothing to dispel the notion. Everywhere there were signs of poor maintenance and apparent disinterest from the owners. Several of the outbuildings had slates missing from roofs. Some had gone a stage further and water ingress, with subsequent damage, had exposed underlying rafters. Wooden doors with blistered, peeling paint appeared to be rotting from the bottom up giving the impression of an upside down game of Tetris. Rusting gates hung at odd angles from their hinges and there were several leaking gutters. One had become detached from the down pipe and there was a weed growing down through the gap. A dirty, old-looking Massey Ferguson tractor was parked in the corner of the yard. The bald tyres looked like they should have been changed years previously.

"*Bleak* doesn't even cover it," ventured Bankhurst.

"You see, this is why I'm a city girl," muttered Baxter, as she looked right and left to survey the scene.

Bankhurst parked the car in an area of the yard that looked relatively uncluttered and free of puddles. Taking care not to step in anything they might regret, the two detectives, with trousers hitched up and a slightly high stepping gait, made their way to what appeared to be the entrance to the kitchen. Angus Munro had seen them coming and had opened the door in anticipation.

His face was pale and tired looking. Bloodshot, sunken eyes looked the detectives up and down as he motioned to them to take a seat at the large, wooden table which dominated the kitchen. It looked like he hadn't shaved for several days, his body odour was unpleasant and he had numerous stains on his clothes.

"Good morning, Mr Munro. I'm DI Bankhurst and this is DS Baxter. We're really sorry to meet you in such circumstances."

"Thanks," replied Munro in a quiet, expressionless voice.

As with the interview with McRobert's widow, Bankhurst went through the formalities of checking Munro's understanding of what the FLO had told him and gave him time to vent his grief.

As was common, he expressed bewilderment about how this could have happened to one of his family, and what his mother could possibly have done to deserve it.

Bankhurst went over the history of the night of the disappearance but didn't glean anything that hadn't already been documented in the initial investigation. Further general questioning informed her that George Munro, Angus's father, had died in an RTA eight years previously and, by the sound of it, the farm had more or less died with him. Wife and son, with additional seasonal help, had laboured to maintain the arable and poultry farm but it had always been an uphill battle, and financial pressures inevitably followed. The resultant underinvestment in maintenance, and competitiveness, had created a downward spiral.

It seemed that mother and son kept themselves largely to themselves. Jean Munro's weekly yoga class was one of the few times, apart from shopping, they would leave the farm. She had, to his knowledge, not fallen out with anyone or had any "enemies". She was not, and had not been, in any relationship. In short, the whole situation had been a mystery to son and Police alike.

Up to this point.

Now there was a body, or at least part of one.

Now there was a strong link to another serious crime.

Now she could be the victim of a serial killer.

Bankhurst didn't think there was too much to be gained by prolonging the interview, but she informed Munro that they would need to take all phones, tablets and computers for analysis, and there would be an in-depth assessment of all

aspects of their lives including farm accounts, banking, social media etc.
Munro didn't seem particularly bothered, even at the thought of parting with his own mobile for a few days, usually anathema to a young adult in Bankhurst's experience.
Although not explicitly stated, both detectives were glad to leave the sad, degenerating farm behind as they made their way back to Aberdeen. As befitting friends comfortable in each other's company, conversation flowed easily between professional and social topics which Bankhurst, in particular, found therapeutic. A problem shared...
By the time they arrived back at Nelson Street, she felt a renewed strength of purpose and clarity of thought for how the investigation should move forward.

By early afternoon, the MIT whiteboards had been updated with as much useful information on the two victims as the team could muster, but obvious parallels remained elusive.
"So," stated Iqbal ,beginning his sentence with a conjunction that seemed to be almost obligatory in modern conversation, "what does a fifty-seven year old, overweight, urban, burnt out, recidivist male have in common with a fifty-five year old, fit, rural female with no criminal record?"
Iqbal had voiced the question that was on everyone's mind.
"There **has** to be some connection," Bankhurst added.
"We just haven't found it yet."
"Let's keep looking. I want their past history, and current lives, turned upside down. We must be missing something!"
"Hamish. Is the surveillance team fully prepped for tomorrow?"
"Yes, Boss, all good."
"Alan, can I have a word about another press release please?"
"Be glad to, Boss. There's a real sense of fear in the population of Aberdeen and the Shire since news of the second victim got out. My phone and e-mail in-box have almost gone into meltdown today. I've had to draft in another Comms Officer to help. This thing's gone viral. We've had media enquiries from all over the

country, and abroad.

A statement should take some of the heat out of the situation for the time being at least."

Bankhurst and Zimmerman grabbed a coffee and sought out a spare desk in the corner of the MIT room where they put their heads together for half an hour to hammer out a statement. Zimmerman committed to publish it across multiple media outlets within the hour. Meanwhile, the rest of the room continued extensive research into every aspect of the lives of McRobert and Munro, hoping to unearth something to link the two together, there being a natural reluctance to consider the murders as being random, and therefore harder to solve. Connections, however, might inform motive and opportunity, which, in turn, might lead to a suspect.

CHAPTER 14

Thirty year old Sergeant Hamish MacDonald was born and bred on the Island of Lewis and Harris in the Outer Hebrides. Educated at the Nicolson Institute in Stornoway he completed basic Police training at Tulliallan College before spending his informative Police Scotland years in Inverness. Having passed his sergeant exams he decided he had reached the possible limit of his abilities, and definite limit of his ambitions. He had no desire to climb the ladder any further. Not for him extra unpaid hours to show commitment or, what he saw as, brown-nosing senior colleagues.

He often said he was *quite happy* where he was if asked but, in truth, that wasn't accurate either, as he derived only minimal occupational satisfaction. He saw his job as a means to an end, to finance his life, but was already planning an exit strategy by the age of fifty.

He realised his lack of drive, and perhaps even disinterest at times, had not gone unnoticed by his colleagues, but he had long since been comfortable living within that perception.

His main passion, which he shared with his wife Susan, was hill walking. Many weekends, more so in the summer, would see them head to the Grampians or Cairngorms to bag another Munro or Corbett from their list.

Today he was sat in one of two unmarked Police cars deployed in the surveillance of Wilson's Abattoir, with another two officers placed inside the building. Carry-out coffees had long since been finished. Crumbs from a croissant were scattered over trousers and floor. As was common on surveillance operations, time was dragging, and his mind was beginning to wander towards planning a possible trip to climb Càrn a' Ghèoidh. He and his wife had already picked most of the low hanging Munro fruit, in terms of their proximity to Aberdeen, but, for some reason, had never tackled Càrn a' Ghèoidh, despite it being comfortably achievable on a day trip from the city.

The expected Deliveroo had come and gone, without any bogus delivery in the relatively narrow window of opportunity after the legitimate one. The team knew that the chances of a successful operation were rapidly diminishing, but they would have to maintain their vigil for an hour or two yet.

MacDonald was considering which would be the best route into Càrn a' Ghèoidh, and parking options nearby, when his eye was caught by a group of seagulls above the back entrance to Wilson's. There had been a few there most of the morning, but their numbers had swollen perhaps because of some recent additions to the giant bins in the abattoir's rear yard.

He marvelled at how they used their natural ally of the wind to soar and hover, with only occasional flapping of wings to counter a gust of wind, and maintain them in the area of potential feeding interest. One gull in particular seemed especially adept at resisting the buffeting effects of the wind and kept a remarkably constant aerial position. Unnaturally constant in fact .

MacDonald reached for his binoculars but, almost as if it knew it had been spotted, the drone moved sideways rapidly out of vision behind a neighbouring building.

CHAPTER 15

Saturday 21st December

It had been a windy night. A steady thirty mph, force six, punctuated by forty mph gusts. The fallen leaves, at least those not so waterlogged that their own weight prevented them becoming airborne, were being propelled around Aberdeen like whirling dervishes. Trees groaned and cracked as their trunks and branches were stretched to, and sometimes beyond, their structural limitations. An occasional, half shredded plastic bag fluttered on a wire fence.

The normal image of a hanging body is of a head bowed, tragic figure with lifeless dependent limbs. A lonely, still, vertical statement. A testament to either a desperate personal battle, or a decision taken by others.

This body was oscillating between five o'clock and seven o'clock and, in addition to the lateral movement, was also slowly rotating one hundred and eighty degrees clockwise, and then one hundred and eighty degrees anti-clockwise. The chain which had been used for the hanging creaked on its anchor point.

Although it was still dark the first signs of dawn were beginning to bleed into the morning sky, and it wouldn't be long before the city would be relieved of its night time shroud.

The first dog walkers of the day were preparing themselves and their hounds.

And the body would be found.

Monday 23rd December

Aberdeen, and indeed Aberdeenshire, were gripped in a mesh of fear and intrigue. Anxiety mixed with morbid fascination.

The double homicide dominated conversation in homes, cafes, bars and coffee rooms. Especially coffee rooms.

The Forensic Pathology department was no exception. Even within their own area of professional experience, where they had encountered many gruesome examples of what the human race can do to each other, this was still seen as an unusual and interesting case. Brewster had just briefed Dr Roddy Hall, a consultant Pathologist colleague, when a mortuary technician plumped herself down on a spare seat on the sofa and took her first sip of coffee.

"By the way, Dr Hall, the lab results are back on your next PM this morning. The hanging from the weekend."

"Oh. Ok. Anything interesting?"

"Not really. Just the usual. Alcohol, cannabis and benzodiazepines."

Brewster realised he probably had a jaundiced opinion, due to an in-built bias in the cohort of patients that formed much of his workload, but sometimes he felt that about a quarter of the population of Aberdeen must be on this particular trinity, especially at weekends.

By definition he would not normally be involved in expected or explained deaths, but within his realm of unexpected deaths, encompassing those involving violence such as accidents, suicides and murders, there was a high rate of positive toxicological results. The top three "offenders" were alcohol, cannabis and benzodiazepines, the latter two being class B and C controlled drugs respectively, which, despite their regulated status, seemed to be widely available within the city.

"Was your hanging at Union Terrace bridge?" enquired Brewster in an attempt to steer the conversation away from himself.

"No, it's still mostly jumpers there I think, though less so since the council erected some anti jump measures. Tends to put off all but the most committed now I believe."

"No, our lady was found at Grandholm bridge."

Brewster felt his interest pique a little.

"As in the Grandholm bridge over The Don?"

"Yes. That's it."

"Anything odd about it?" he enquired

"Well. She was a known prostitute and there are witnesses saying she was working the dock area earlier on Saturday night. So it seems a little strange, if she felt a compelling need to terminate her life, that she travelled the best part of three miles from the city centre to do the deed. Mind you, who knows what goes through your head with that drug cocktail on board."

Hall continued, "Her fellow workers didn't report anything unusual that evening, though other witnesses have been hard to track down as 'punters' are, understandably, reluctant to come forward. Also, the oldest profession, unlike most others now, is still one that deals almost exclusively in cash, so there are no financial trails to follow."

"Was there a suicide note?"

"No."

"Anything else unusual?"

"Not really, though I guess the choice of ligature was a little unusual. It was a chain rather than a rope."

"Do me a favour, Roddy, please. Could you ask the lab to do a sub group analysis of the benzodiazepine to see which one it was?"

"Sure. No problem", and while he replied he nodded to his technician who now understood she had an extra task added to her post coffee workload.

"Oh, and would you mind if I sit in on the PM?" enquired Brewster.

"Of course. No problem."

Dr Louise McEwan was elegant, effortlessly so. Bankhurst considered she was probably in her mid forties but she could easily pass for late thirties. As usual she was immaculately dressed with beautifully tailored trousers accentuating her figure, while shiny black hair cascaded over what Bankhurst thought might be a Ted Baker blouse. She wore subtle, but skilfully applied, make-up which complemented her natural beauty. After an appropriate introduction she stood to address the room and immediately had its attention. Her audience wanted to hear what she had to say, and it didn't hurt that she was so easy on the eye.

You're welcome boys. Enjoy! thought Bankhurst

"Thanks DI Bankhurst. I appreciate the introduction and also the invitation to come along to the MIT. It's certainly a fascinating case."

"I thought it might be useful, at the risk of teaching granny to suck eggs, to remind us of the difference between spree and serial killings. As you will know, I'm sure, a spree killer will commit multiple murders at more than one location in a limited time frame, without any cooling off period. These are often considered one event, even though they are spread over different locations."

" A serial killer, on the other hand, will commit at least three murders at different locations, over a more prolonged period, with a cooling off period in between."

"On the face of it, and although we only have two known victims to date, we could be dealing with a serial killer here."

"As I understand it the first victim was only discovered fortuitously at the butcher, and may well have gone under the radar if it wasn't for the artificial heart valve. This in turn caused raised awareness, which no doubt contributed to the discovery of the second victim. So it's entirely possible there may be other, as yet unknown, victims. The two that we do know about had a cooling off period in between, so the pattern would fit a serial killer."

She continued, "As far as serial killers are concerned it is generally accepted in Criminology that there are four types."

"Firstly, there is The Visionary. These individuals are usually psychotic and feel compelled to murder because they have auditory or visual hallucinations that order them to kill certain types of people."

"Secondly, we have Mission-Oriented killers. These target a specific group of people who they believe are unworthy to live, and without whom the world would be a better place."

"Then, we have The Hedonistic killer who kills primarily for the thrill of it. They enjoy the act of killing, and may even be sexually aroused during the act."

"Finally, there is the Power-Oriented killer who kills to exert the ultimate control over their victim. They are not psychotic but are obsessed with capturing and controlling their victim, and forcing them to obey their every command."

"My difficulty, as a criminologist, in trying to assess which type of serial killer we are dealing with, and constructing a profile, is the same that is facing you guys...the paucity of useful information to work with. I would tend to rule out The Visionary, as someone so sufficiently disturbed to execute these crimes would, I believe, have a degree of mental illness that would almost certainly have, by now, declared itself to family, friends or the medical profession, and be under some sort of supervision. So, I feel it is more likely our killer belongs to one of the other three groups."

"I **can** say that, as a general rule, the killer is very likely to be male, middle or lower class, white, living on their own, aged between 25 and 50, and probably in employment."

"I know that's probably not a huge help but I am of course very happy to re-appraise the situation as and when new information becomes available."

"Are there any questions?"

"Hello. I'm DS Baxter. Is it significant that it seems only to be the heart of the victims that have been found?"

"I would imagine it probably is, but I'm really not quite sure at this stage what that could be. It may be some form of symbolism, but referring to what exactly...I don't know."

"DC MacLennan, Ma'am. Do you think it is likely he will reoffend?"

"Yes. I do. Whichever subgroup he is in he may well have a different motivation to kill again, but the driver will be powerful and unlikely to be ignored."

This response produced a low grade hum of conversation in the room, but no further questions. Bankhurst thanked McEwan, who returned to her seat accompanied by a ripple of applause.

"Any updates from the floor?" enquired Bankhurst.

"We've gone back and looked at historical ANPR data for the night Munro was abducted. There aren't too many cameras in rural Aberdeenshire, but we picked up our van of interest on the AWPR* earlier in the evening, heading north-eastwards. No sign of a return journey that night, unless he stuck to rural roads."

"OK. Good. Add that to the board."

"What about social media?"

"She was a very light user it seems. No Facebook, Instagram or Twitter accounts. We've also checked for any use of dating sites, but drawn a blank there too."

"We've been looking in more detail at her family. Her sister in Westhill we know about, of course, but she also had an older brother who lived in Inverurie, but he died two years ago of a heart attack. He did, however, work at the Inverurie paper mill when it was open."

"Ok. This is good. Keep working away. We need to find a concrete connection between our victims."

Bankhurst closed the discussion and went over to thank the criminologist in person once again before walking her to the door. She couldn't help but wonder how on earth she got her hair so shiny.

What a time to have such a girly thought! she pondered.

Having admonished herself she, nevertheless, made a mental note to follow the theme up at a more appropriate time and place.

*Aberdeen West Peripheral Route (bypass)

CHAPTER 16

"Testing. Testing. Sound check."

The mortuary assistant ran through the normal checklist required before a postmortem. The sound was particularly important when there were observers in the gallery, including, on this occasion, one of their own. The presence of Brewster along with the visiting CID officers had not gone unnoticed by the staff.

Trolley wheels squeaked slightly as they were moved into position. There was a clatter of metal on metal as a variety of different sized bowls were positioned in readiness to accept the organs the pathologist would deliver. Instruments were spread out by the mortuary assistant, like a scrub nurse would for a surgeon, and the power saw was checked. Radio 2 was muted, and a rustle of aprons and snapping on of gloves announced the team were ready to commence.

"This is Dr Roddy Hall recording. Monday 23rd December. Postmortem on a thirty year old female identified as Mandy Bremner. The deceased is 1.61cm tall and weighs 58 kg . Before I start the formal postmortem, it was noted that there are two tears in her clothing, and there has been no obvious postmortem discharge of faeces or urine into said clothing."

As an afterthought, and for the benefit of the lay audience, he added "which is sometimes seen in hanging...be it suicidal or homicidal, but not usually in strangulation."

"The external appearances are of a reasonably well nourished female consistent with her stated years. She has evidence of nicotine staining on the fingers of her right hand. She has a tattoo of a flower on her right ankle, and a further tattoo on her right scapula of what appears to be a Chinese character."

"There is cyanosis of the lips, hands and feet."

"There is evidence of livor mortis in the lower limbs, but there are also some subtle livor changes in the lower lumbar area. This suggests it is likely the body was moved postmortem from a supine position to a vertical position."

"There are petechial haemorrhages of the sclera, eyelids and face in keeping with either strangulation or hanging."

"An absence of tongue protrusion is noted, as is an absence of unilateral dried saliva trail."

Brewster whispered to the other gallery personnel, "Both of these mitigate against a hanging."

Hall continued, "There appears to be two ligature abrasions in the neck. One follows a horizontal circumscription around the neck, and the associated tissue changes suggest this was antemortem. The other, less obvious, abrasion rises towards the left ear, and the associated tissue changes suggest this was postmortem."

"There are also superficially incised curvilinear abrasions on both sides of the neck, in keeping with injuries from the victim's own fingernails."

"There are broken finger nails on the right index and right middle fingers. The finger nails of the left hand are intact."

"There is evidence of postmortem abrasions on the trunk consistent with the body being moved postmortem, and would be consistent with being lifted over a bridge."

"There are subtle changes in both heels consistent with the body being dragged postmortem."

"These are the main external findings. I will now proceed to neck dissection."

"Blade please... just opening superficial neck tissues...need to dissect further...give me a few minutes...ok, that's interesting..."

"The main findings of the neck dissection were evidence of bleeding within the soft tissues around the larynx, a cricoid fracture and a thyroid horn fracture."

Hall went on to methodically complete the postmortem as per protocol, but the rest of the examination was essentially unremarkable, in keeping with a young adult female. He stepped away from the table and turned to the gallery.

Brewster, and indeed the CID officers present, knew what was coming but they welcomed Hall's succinct and clear précis none-the-less.

"In summary, the postmortem findings strongly suggest antemortem strangulation followed by postmortem hanging. There is evidence that the deceased actively tried to prevent her strangulation."

"This was a homicide, and not a suicide."

"My full report will be ready this afternoon."

Click. The intercom was switched on.

"Thank you, Dr Hall," said Bankhurst, "appreciate that."

"Was there any semen present?"

"No. Presumably she insists on her clients using condoms."

"OK. Thanks." Click.

Bankhurst turned to Iqbal.

"Zafar. Can you get SOCO to go and process the Grandholme bridge site ASAP please?"

"We'll also want them to have a good look at the clothes and ligature."

"Aye. No problem, Boss."

"What about a FLO?" added Iqbal.

"Sure. The family have already been contacted, and statements taken, due to the apparent suicide, but this puts everything in a different light. Makes sense to have FLO involvement."

""I'll speak to *upstairs* and request the MIT take this case on board at the moment. We've no way of knowing if it's connected to our main case, but it is a homicide. It could hardly be closer to The Don without actually being in it, so it would make sense to work it in parallel. As it is, we've got the majority of CID working in the MIT anyway, so I'm sure they can cope."

One of the advantages of an early identification of a murder victim, particularly with the significant weight of an MIT driving the investigation, is the rapid accumulation of data. By 4pm in the afternoon, the white board details of the latest victim, Mandy Bremner, had been significantly augmented.

MANDY BREMNER age 30
25a Nerine Street, Southfield, Aberdeen
Body discovered 0730 am Sunday 22nd December by a dog walker
Estimated time of death 10-12pm on Saturday 21st December
Lives with daughter Taylor Bremner (13) and mother Jean Dalgleish (54)
Smoker 10 day
P/T cleaner and P/T sex industry worker
Previous arrests for possession, solicitation and breech of the peace
Previous IVDU but clean for several years
Still uses oral controlled substances
Borderline hazardous alcohol consumption
Hepatitis C positive
Mobile phone missing but triangulation data showed the phone moving from the docks area to Grandholme at about 10-30pm on Saturday . Phone switched off or destroyed at that point
Facebook and Instagram accounts interrogated. Nothing of note at moment
In debt to total of £1500 spread across two cards
No unusual financial activity
No known enemies
Well known within sex industry

Other information:
CCTV shows 3 dark coloured vans in the docks area on Saturday evening. Two plates identified. No ANPR hits.
? used different vehicle

? changed to different plates (but how would they know to do that?)
No eye witnesses of unusual activity in dock area or Grandholme at relevant times
VICE squad contacted. Nothing to report.

As with McRobert and Munro, Bankhurst wanted to interview the nearest relative herself and, along with Iqbal, made the relatively short trip to the Southfield estate where a squad car remained parked outside. As it was, the FLO was just finishing his visit and was making his way to the front door when the bell rang. He thought he could recognise the silhouettes of his colleagues through the glass of the front door, and wasn't disappointed when he opened the door. A brief conversation followed in the corridor before he double backed to the living room.

"Hello, it's me again, Mrs Dalgleish. These are the two detectives I was speaking to you about: DI Bankhurst and DS Iqbal."

"Hello, Mrs Dalgleish. We're really sorry to have to meet you in these circumstances."

Bankhurst trotted out her standard post bereavement line. She had never been comfortable with *Sorry for your loss,* so had stuck with what had served her reasonably well over the years.

"I know you'll be aware that we are now treating your daughter's death as a homicide, and not suicide."

"I kent she wouldnae have committed suicide. She would never have done that to the bairn."

"Do you know if she had any enemies, or felt threatened in any way?"

"Nae that I'm aware of. Mind you, there's aye a risk when you do what she did for a living."

Bankhurst felt a sense of relief as she hadn't been sure if Bremner's *other job* in the sex industry had been known to anyone but herself, and was anticipating a potentially awkward conversation with her mother.

"You knew about her different types of part time job then?"

"I kent she was on the game if that's fit you mean. She tried to hide it, but I'm nae daft, ken."

"She used to say she was gan oot to clean a doctor's surgery, oot of hours, but I've never seen a cleaner wear some of the stuff she does...used to."

"And she aye had plenty cash on her, which naebody else does these days. Mind you, it kept this family clothed and fed, so I'm nae judging, ken."

"Do you know if she's ever been attacked before?"

"Nae that I ken."

Bankhurst continued using standard interviewing techniques until she was satisfied there was nothing more to be gained from continuing the process. She had the impression that Bremner's mother, although devastated by the loss of her daughter and the implications for their family unit, had gained some comfort from the fact that she had not departed the world by her own hand.

By the time Bankhurst and Iqbal returned to Nelson Street, she noted the first column on the white board dedicated to Bremner, which had only been started after the late morning postmortem, was already almost full. She reviewed the information and felt satisfied about the amount of data accumulated in a short time frame. She knew information would provide power and forward momentum to the investigation. She had hoped that some of the research would have yielded specific information, to include or exclude Bremner, from the existing investigation, but that hadn't happened .

It would be the following morning before it did.

CHAPTER 17

Tuesday 24th December

"I've got the lab on the phone with the forensics from the clothes and chain," announced MacLennan. He passed the phone to Bankhurst who took the call.

A series of *thanks...I see...Yes...I see* followed. It wasn't often the lab phoned them directly, and the MIT room hushed and focussed on the call.

"OK, thanks a lot. Appreciate you phoning. Bye for now." Bankhurst ended the call.

"There wasn't much on the clothing apart from the two tears we knew about which would be in keeping with a struggle. They did, however, find two things of interest on the chain. The first was a few fibres found at the end nearest to the anchor point. These have now been identified as likely to be a form of leather. They postulate that the running noose ligature used to simulate the hanging could be a large canine choker chain from which the leather handle has been removed. It is very possible this could be the murder weapon, which was then used to fake the suicide.

Bankhurst paused and took a breath in, not really knowing whether she had done so to steady herself or for dramatic effect.

"The second finding was a trace of blood on the chain...the DNA from which is an exact match for Danny McRobert. We now have an indisputable connection with one of the other two victims and, therefore, confirmation that we are dealing with a serial killer."

An immediate swell of noise washed around the room, which Bankhurst did nothing to quell. It was a highly significant development, and she recognised the team would need time to process it before returning to order.

When she felt the reaction had abated to a satisfactory level, she continued.

"OK. Can we contact Dr McEwan and ask her if she could come back again this afternoon? I really want her take on this, as it seems such a different MO from the first two victims. What the hell is going on?"

"I also want an appeal for witnesses for the likely site of abduction in the docks area, and the faux hanging at Grandholme. Make sure you offer an anonymous option, in case we can entice some of her punters to come forward. Can we ask Comms to get in touch with the P and J and Northsound radio?"

"Also, let's speak to Vice and ask them to brief their sex industry contacts, advising extra care and vigilance at the moment."

"And, of course, keep researching all three victims. We need to find a link!"

"Any questions?"

"Do we tell the press that the murders are linked?"

"That's a tricky one," acknowledged Bankhurst, "we don't really want to alert the suspect that we've made the connection, but on the other hand we perhaps have a civil duty to inform the population to take extra precautions over the Festive Period... especially as people may be going home late from parties 'under the influence.'"

"I'll speak to DCI Anderson about it."

True to her word, Bankhurst took advice about a press briefing from DCI Anderson who, in turn, shared the weight of the decision with Superintendent MacNiven. The consensus, after some debate, was not to publicly link the Grandholme death with the previous two victims for the time being. Time would tell if it was the right decision.

Bankhurst had returned to the MIT room, and was engrossed in her screen. She became aware of a pleasant, familiar perfume and was just about to look up to locate the source when Dr Louise McEwan spoke.

"Hi, Lily, thanks for asking me back. I hear there's been a development."

"Yes. There has. Thanks for coming, Louise."

Bankhurst noted another pair of beautifully fitted trousers and a quality blouse, and vowed to up her own game a notch.

McEwan listened attentively as Bankhurst briefed her on the details of the third victim, and the forensic link with the other two.

"Wow, that's quite a deviation from the previous MO!"

"What do you make of it?" enquired Bankhurst.

"Well, the first two victims were a product of some quite sophisticated planning and execution, if you consider the abductions, transport of victims, presumed dissection of the body, freezing and storage of at least one organ and the delivery of the hearts into the meat industry.

This very much suggests someone methodical. Someone in control. Although the reasoning remains a mystery, the intent, presumably, was for occult disposal of the organs, as it was only a fortuitous discovery that triggered the investigation in the first place.

This, however, smacks more of disorganised and reactionary behaviour. Although an attempt was made to simulate suicide, the perpetrator ensured the discovery, unlike with the earlier victims.

It is a disconcerting development as it may mean he is becoming unstable for some reason, or it could also be a response to the discovery of his previous work. Either way, he seems to have accelerated his programme, whatever that is, which is clearly not good. The only silver lining is that he could become undone perhaps if he adopts a less calculated and more capricious approach, which in turn is more likely to generate mistakes."

Bankhurst made a mental note to look up the word *capricious,* but the gist of the sentence had been understood.

"The obvious concern, of course, is at what human cost?"

"Ok. Thanks, Louise. Appreciate your input as always."

"Listen. If I don't see you again before, and, no offence but I hope I don't, have a good Christmas."

"Thanks, Lily. What about yourself? Will you manage some time off?"

"I'll need to come in for a bit tomorrow."

"No you won't! An authoritative voice joined the conversation. DCI Anderson had approached, unseen, from behind.

"You'll have a day off with your family...and that's an order," he added in a softer voice.

"Look, my kids are all grown up and spread around the country. It's just me and Rona this year. We'll just be having a quiet day, so I can easily come in. Might in fact be better for us both if I get out from under her feet for a few hours!"

"Anyway, we've no idea how long this thing is going to drag on, and we'll all need time off to recharge our batteries at some stage."

"Well, if you're sure, Sir."

"I am...and make sure you get away sharpish this afternoon too!"

Bankhurst felt she had been given an early Christmas present. The gravity and intensity of the investigation since the discovery in the Cult's butcher had been significant. Broken sleep had become the norm. She was indeed feeling worn out, so Anderson's offer was well received, and further enhanced her opinion of him. She doubted many of her other senior officers would have done the same.

She also appreciated the offer of an early finish. Crackers and garlic dip had still to be picked up, and it was always prudent to buy in an extra bottle of gin when her parents visited.

Wednesday 25th December

It was the best of times it was the worst of times

Bankhurst knew this was the opening line to a Dickens novel but she couldn't, for the life of her, remember which one. No matter, it was the sentiment of the text that perfectly summed up her Christmas Day, she thought.

She had always been a big fan of Christmas Day, and cherished all the Yuletide festivities, something she had inherited from her mother. Her friends would tease her that she was a little too invested at times, but she didn't care. She always had the tree and decorations up from the 1st of December and, normally at least, would enjoy the build up and anticipation of the 'big day'.

Andrew, naturally enough, was "super excited" but she wasn't sure if he was normal for an eight year old ,or perhaps he too was on the way to being another Christmas fanatic.

Over the years her family, like countless others up and down the country, had evolved their own particular programme for the 25th. Starting with the standard Christmas Day template, the individual nuances of timing and content had slowly become established in their own particular regimen.

At times she managed to take some comfort from the familiar routines, and the delights delivered by a three generation celebration, but her concentration was regularly interrupted by the thoughts of the unspeakable evil that was lurking within the community; her community; where she, and her family, lived and worked. She couldn't fully relax, even with the normally soothing effect of the alcohol offered by the traditional champagne for the presents opening, and wine with the meal. She couldn't shake the burden of responsibility and expectation that had come with MIT leadership, and a feeling of guilt about being out of the loop for 24 hours.

She had resisted, with great personal effort, contacting the skeleton MIT who were continuing to work on Christmas Day. By the time the evening came, and her father had completed the family routine by falling asleep on the couch with his mouth open, she was counting the hours before she could rejoin the fray.

Thursday 26th December

Bankhurst had woken early and was ready to leave for work at 7:30am. Her morning glucose test had reflected the excesses of Christmas Day, and she had given herself four extra units of insulin to compensate. The rest of the household was still asleep and, trying to keep it that way, she closed the door gently behind herself, and tread lightly to her car.

Dawn was in full flourish and the bright sky promised a crisp, sunny winter day, a welcome relief from the somewhat stormy weather of the previous few days.The downside of such a morning was a thin layer of frost on her windscreen which required attention, and she was glad of the warmth offered by her new gloves as she scraped the screen.

The city, with its streets and pavements almost deserted, reminded her of driving to work during the Covid pandemic when all but essential services were working from home.

Progress was swift and, before she knew it, she was pulling into a parking space at Nelson Street. The car park seemed reasonably full already, and Bankhurst suspected she wasn't alone in wanting to re-engage with the hunt for the killer. Her suspicion was well founded as, when she entered the MIT room, she was heartened to see most desks filled and there was already a satisfying audible murmur of activity.

She went round the room exchanging Christmas greetings, and asking her colleagues about their Festive celebrations. There was the usual range from "pretty quiet really" to " full on family war" and by the time she came to Iqbal she was on autopilot.

"How was your Christmas?"

"Gonnae no do that, Boss?" Iqbal replied in a slightly terse Glaswegian brogue.

"What?"

"Ask a Muslim about his Christmas Day."

"Oh. Christ. Sorry, Zafar!" blurted Bankhurst, as she

compounded the faux pas with her choice of profanity.
He allowed an offended expression to linger on his face for a few seconds before a broad smile creased his face.
"Ha ha, gotcha, Boss."
Bankhurst felt a slight sense of relief that she had only been pranked, and joined in with the smile, while feigning to give her DS a clip round the ear.
"To be honest, Boss, like a lot of weegie Muslims, I had a nice curry and binge watched a few of your Christmas movies. A wee guilty pleasure. Some of them are dead brilliant, by the way."

Bankhurst returned to her desk, and requested an update from the MIT Christmas Day team.
"Not too much to report, Boss. We're still gathering data but nothing really standing out."
"I've been checking the anonymous witness phone line this morning, Boss, and someone claiming to be one of Mandy Bremner's customers left a message late last night. He sounded a wee bit pished to be honest. He'd maybe had a few drinks which emboldened him to phone."
"Anyway, apart from giving her a service review that Trip Advisor would have been proud of, he did mention he'd seen a blue van cruising around the dock streets mid Saturday evening. He didn't think too much about it as, by the very nature of the area, there are usually a few slow moving cars on the go, as punters search for their service providers, but it was the fact it was a van that caught his eye. Apparently that's a bit unusual."
"Don't suppose he commented on the make or model?"
"No such luck."
"Anything about the number of people in the vehicle?"
"He said he had a vague feeling there was also someone in the passenger seat, but he couldn't be sure."
"Before he hung up, he added that he was going to miss her and, for what it's worth, I thought he sounded genuine, and not a time waster."
"OK. That's good. Doesn't move us forward too much perhaps,

but all information is potentially useful. Keep on it everybody. Thanks."

Bankhurst made herself her first coffee of the day and took it back to her desk. The steam rising from the coffee reassured her it was satisfyingly hot, and she wrapped her hands around the cup.

She peered at her screen and wondered where to begin. By the end of Christmas Day, she had decided to take a fresh look at the case from day one to see if there was anything they were missing. By now, particularly since the MIT had been convened, there was a mountain of data to consider, and she was pondering what would be her best strategy when she became aware of someone by her side.

"Morning, Ma'am. I'm DC Yuill," said a woman who looked not much older than eighteen, thought Bankhurst.

"Morning. Have you got something for me?" countered Bankhurst.

"I'm not sure, Ma'am."

"Go on."

"I've been drilling down into the finances of Fairlieknowe Farm. They've been running at a loss for three years now, with several borderline years before that. I don't know how they are keeping their heads above water, unless they have some private savings we don't know about."

"I went back to look at farm invoices in more detail, and I was struck by how relatively large the expenditure was on dog food. Am I right in thinking Fairlieknowe is an arable and poultry farm?"

"Yes, that's correct," confirmed Bankhurst.

"Not a big demand for working dogs then?"

"Fair point. I certainly don't remember seeing any when I was there."

"I've found on-line orders, and it appears that 90% of the dog food ordered was puppy food."

"So, they had a litter perhaps?" suggested Bankhurst wondering where the DC was going.

"I've been doing some calculations, and there was enough food ordered to feed a small army of puppies."

Bankhurst started nodding her head, "As in a puppy farm you mean?"

"Yes. Exactly. And it might explain some off record income keeping the farm afloat. I imagine the illegal puppy trade would be strictly cash only."

"OK. This is excellent work, DC Yuill."

" Thanks, Ma'am."

" Right," she said with some authority, "let's get Angus Munro in here for questioning this morning!"

She couldn't immediately think how the development might be relevant, but it somehow felt important and worthy of further prompt exploration. Her intuition would turn out to be accurate.

CHAPTER 18

Angus Munro looked pale and worried. Damp patches were appearing on his shirt and he had an agitated look on his face. His eyes darted from one side of the room to the other and he drummed his fingers anxiously on the table.

Bankhurst had resisted the temptation to start the interview soon after his arrival and she observed, through the one way window, the effect of leaving him alone with his thoughts and conscience for thirty minutes. He had declined the offer of legal assistance, so would have no support for his interview.

So much the better Bankhurst thought.

Whether it was the softening up period, or that he didn't possess sufficient strength of character, but he offered no resistance to the subsequent direct questioning.

"Good Morning, Mr Munro. As you may remember, I am DI Bankhurst, and this is DS Iqbal, who you haven't met before."

Munro nodded and shifted position in his chair avoiding direct eye contact.

"We want to ask you about some irregularities we have identified in the farm accounts, and the goods purchased for the farm."

Munro looked slightly confused, but Bankhurst also thought she detected a nuance of relief on his face.

She decided to get straight to the point.

"Have you been operating a puppy farm at Fairlieknowe?"

"Er...aye...we have."

Bankhurst was a little surprised at the lack of any denial, or attempt at evasion. He again looked, if anything, a little relieved. Perhaps he had been under the impression that the abrupt demand for his attendance at the station meant that he was somehow being considered as a suspect in his mother's homicide, and the alternative line of enquiry was much the lesser of two potential evils.

"Tell me about that."

"Well...you have to understand the farm was running at a loss... we were even contemplating putting it on the market... it was my Mum's idea..."

He paused again as if to gather himself.

Bankhurst held up her hand.

"Look, Mr Munro, I'm not looking for justification for what you did, or apportioning blame...although I'm sure you realise that such activity is illegal. My focus is the abduction and murder of your mother, and other related murders. I want to know as much as I can about the puppy farm business."

"Well, we were running it for the last two years or so. When Mum disappeared I got rid of all the stock as my heart wasn't really in it; you really need at least two people to make it work."

"Before that, we could have thirty to forty puppies at a time. It was strictly cash and off the books. Obviously, we couldn't advertise directly. We tended to use local on-line selling agencies, like Rubber Tree, and free newspapers to advertise that we had puppies for sale. We mostly dealt in black labradors as they're very sellable."

"We had numerous e-mail accounts and half a dozen mobile phones, so it wasn't obvious the same source always had puppies for sale all year round. Some people probably suspected we were less than legit, but turned a blind eye when they saw beautiful labrador puppies at half the price they would normally have expected to pay."

" Scruples can sometimes be sacrificed if the price is right," he added.

"Did you ever have anyone who objected to the system?" enquired Bankhurst.

"Not really. We had a few who didn't buy, especially those who asked to see the parents; a request we couldn't honour. But nobody kicked up a fuss, and we never had any RSPCA inspectors calling, or anything like that."

"And, just to be clear, no threats at all?" pressed Iqbal.

"No. Certainly none I was aware of. It was relatively easy money, to be honest, and once we got started we just kept going, as it was the only part of the farm that was turning a profit."

"We'll need a list of all your customers. Do you have that?"

"I doubt it. Mum took care of that type of thing. It was all strictly cash. No invoices or anything. People contacted us, they came, they bought, or they didn't. I've still got the mobile phones, and an old laptop we used for the business if you like. That would give you a lot of mobile phone numbers and e-mail addresses."

"You realise this is potentially important information, Mr Munro, that we should have known days ago," said Bankhurst in a terse manner. "This amounts to obstruction of an investigation".

"Well…no…why would I have thought it could be relevant in any way? Things were hard enough as they were, and I didn't want to fess up to anything illegal."

"I appreciate it's a difficult time for you, Mr Munro, but you realise we may have to return to this in due course."

"Aye...I do."

"However, for now, we're focussing on the homicides."

"You can go. An officer will accompany you home, and pick up the mobiles and laptop."

"Do not withhold any further information from us, Mr Munro!" lectured Bankhurst in the sternest voice she could muster.

"No, Sir..I mean…Miss," he replied in the meek voice of a scolded schoolchild.

Bankhurst and Iqbal returned to the MIT room and brought the team up to date. The information was being added to the white boards when Reflex Babinski commented, "Did McRobert not have a caution for dog abuse on his rap sheet?"

"Yes, he did," confirmed someone from the body of the room with a slight excited tone, and then, as an afterthought, added, "but it wasn't added to the white board as it wasn't thought to be relevant."

Bankhurst felt an annoyance that the detail had been omitted, and was inclined to say so, but stopped herself as she realised it was not unreasonable. If too much detail is added to the boards, it is often difficult to see the wood from the trees and, on the face of it, this particular piece of data, at the time, was but a twig.

She let it pass.

Her annoyance was, in fact, soon replaced with a rush of adrenalin, and a sense of excitement. She thought she could feel her pulse quickening and no doubt her face would be turning the annoying blush pink that she associated with embarrassment or excitement. Looking at her colleagues in the room, she realised the significance of the discovery had been appreciated by most of them as a ripple of animated conversation spread around the space. It was left to Bankhurst to verbalise the conclusion.

"This could be what we've been waiting for. A potential link between our first two victims. Could it be possible that animal abuse, specifically dog abuse, is the connection? It also gives us potential motive."

"Some kind of animal extremist exacting revenge for perceived animal cruelty perhaps?" suggested Baxter.

"Indeed," agreed Bankhurst.

Bankurst had recalled McEwan's mini lecture and wondered if this might point the finger towards a mission-oriented killer. Someone who, for some reason, targets a specific group of people who they deem unworthy. In this case animal abusers.

She paused to gather her thoughts. The team was waiting for guidance. Her guidance. Although the butterflies had returned to the pit of her stomach, she felt empowered, and not weakened, by them. She felt strong and in control. This was a moment to be decisive. To be clear. A series of precise directives followed.

"Reflex, get me everything on McRobert's caution."

"Yes, Boss."
"We need to have a close look at Bremner as well. I want to know any detail, no matter how small, relating to her interactions with animals, especially dogs. Re-interview the family on this theme."
"Ask Dr McEwan to come back over. I really want her input on this."
"Yes, Ma'am."
"Check the missing persons list for the last year and see if anybody has any links, no matter how tenuous, to animal abuse."
"Yes, Boss."
"And get me everything we have on animal activist groups, especially those with any connections to the North East."

Bankhurst inhaled deeply. It felt as if she hadn't breathed since starting her instructions; perhaps she hadn't. She had been entirely focused in converting her thoughts into delegations.
"Good work, everyone."
Having completed her instructions, Bankhurst left the room, which had undoubtedly been re-energised by the development. She walked the length of the drab, poorly lit corridor leading towards the rear of the building, passing notice boards displaying faded posters that nobody ever read.
An appealing aroma was leaking from the kitchen, and Bankhurst wondered if there would be something tasty on the lunch menu. She had a lightness of step as she climbed the stairs to Anderson's office.

CHAPTER 19

The MIT juggernaut had ploughed through a vast amount of data and re-interviewed appropriately by the time the group re-gathered formally in the late afternoon. Dr Louise McEwan had agreed to attend to hear the update, and offer her opinion.

"Ok. So where are we at?" enquired Bankhurst as a way of focussing final attention and starting the session.

She looked towards Babinski and, with an inflection of her head, invited him to start.

"So, McRobert was cautioned three years ago for alleged abuse of his Staffordshire terrier. It was his word against that of the accuser, so he was never charged. I approached the RSPCA who say they have an anonymous informant section on their web site. I asked them to look into previous accusations against McRobert, and they phoned back half an hour ago. They have three previous similar accusations recorded but for one reason or another, mostly lack of concrete evidence, they were never followed up."

"Presumably it wouldn't be out with the skill set of somebody with advanced IT knowledge to hack their site, and mine their data for possible targets?"

Bankhurst directed the question at the IT expert in the team, Neil Jardine.

"No. It wouldn't be much of a challenge, even to a relative novice hacker," he replied.

"In fact," he continued, "if I was to put myself in the shoes of the suspect, and my IT skills allowed it, I would also consider hacking the local advertising sites."

"You mean like Rubber Tree?"

"Yes."
"That was where the Munros advertised."
"I know. If you hacked the system you could conceivably run a programme searching for multiple e-mail addresses and mobile numbers, all tethered to a single post code."
"Because, unless you move your business around, which would be very challenging, that's the one constant."
"Exactly."
"And another way to identify potential targets."
"Indeed."
"Ok. That's great. Thanks, Neil."
Bankhurst continued, "So this links to possible motive, and identification of victims. We also need to assume that we are dealing with someone with advanced IT skills. Remember, as well, the drone that was spotted at Wilsons. He is clearly comfortable with technology."
"Still remains a mystery to me how he knew we were going to be there that day," commented MacDonald.

"What about Mandy Bremner? Have we found any possible link with any form of animal abuse?"
"Not a thing, Ma'am. Quite the opposite. According to her Mum she loved animals, especially dogs. Mad about them apparently."
"Ok. Noted. Thanks."
That's a pity in some ways, mused Bankhurst, but thought better of verbalising it.

"What about mispers with links to animal abuse?".
"Nothing so far, Boss, but still working through them."
"Ok. Keep on it."

"Sharon, what have you got on animal activists?"
"Quite a lot in fact, Boss. Perhaps more than we might have expected. It's no surprise, I guess, that there is a spectrum of activism from fairly benign to extremist views, but the latter has now spawned some animal terrorist cells, including in the UK. In fact, there's been some on-line rumours about an active group

in Scotland."
"They're quite difficult to track down as they are often fairly small cells working independently of one another, and not in direct communication with any command hierarchy. They very much try to keep under the radar... for obvious reasons."
"I've put a list of animal activist groups with potential links to Scotland on a new white board."
She pointed to the details on the relevant board.

ALF Animal Liberation Front
HSA Hunt Saboteurs Association
SHAC Stop Huntingdon Animal Cruelty
ALB Animal Liberation Brigade
ADL Animal Defence League
PETA People for the ethical treatment of animals

"Now, I must stress that these groups are not all linked to extremist activity, but it's possible our suspect may have been affiliated with one or more such groups, and then graduated—if that's the right word—to terrorism."
"By the very nature of the organisations, they're not going to be forthcoming with a list of their members past and present...we certainly can't anticipate any cooperation."
"Most of the communications, such as they are, between the most extreme cells are on the dark web, so we'll need IT help to try to hack into these if possible."
Baxter looked in Neil Jardine's direction as she said it, and he responded with a nod.
"No problem. Will see what we can do."
"Also, there may well be other groups we haven't identified yet, as we're still working on it, so this list may yet get longer. We also need to bear in mind that he, or they, may be a completely independent unit not connected to anyone else."

"What are your thoughts, Dr McEwan?" enquired Bankhurst.
Dr Louise McEwan, smartly dressed as ever, had been standing at the side of the room for the duration of the update, listening

with intent and growing interest. Despite TV programmes to the contrary, most of her job as a criminologist was relatively mundane and repetitive. These types of cases did not come along very often, and she was secretly quite thrilled to be involved. The responsibility of such involvement, however, was not lost on her and, like the other senior members of the MIT, she felt some weight of expectation. The case was evolving into one that might be reviewed at national, and possibly even international, level in the future, and she hoped what she was about to say would stand up to the professional scrutiny that might follow.

She had made a few headline notes to fall back on, if necessary, but she hoped, as she always strived to do, to speak to the topic without reference to them.

"Thanks, DI Bankhurst... and thanks for inviting me to attend."

"You've all certainly been very busy since I was last here, and have made impressive progress... so, first of all, congratulations on that."

"This is undoubtedly an interesting, and potentially very important, link that you've made."

"First of all I'd like to comment on the potential profiles of animal terrorist cell members. These individuals, as you can imagine, have fairly entrenched ideologies. They feel exasperated by what they perceive as inaction and underachievement by traditional activist groups, and believe violence is the only route left open to them.

They often cleave themselves away from existing groups, and seek out kindred spirits on the dark web."

"It's thought that if a terror cell is formed, it becomes the primary source of social reality for its members. The recognition and reinforcement of said members enables a terrorist cell to provide social acceptance and validation of what they do."

"They are likely to be middle class, male and, certainly in this country, caucasian. Many will be in employment and appear to fit into conventional society."

"They usually view acts of terrorism as a way of shining a spotlight on their struggle, but some of the so-called *Extremity Revenge* sites actually encourage activists to be judge, jury and, where necessary, executioner. For them it may be more about revenge than publicity, and this may be what we are dealing with here, as it seems that they were not intent on discovery, at least not in the early stages."

"So, do you think it's likely we are dealing with more than one suspect?" enquired MacDonald.

"You do get an occasional lone wolf but, generally...yes...they work in small cells of two or three."

"That might tie in with the witness statement from the docks where he thought there might have been a second person in the van," commented Bankhurst.

There was a general nodding of heads, and a slight pause, before McEwan felt the time was right to continue.

"Secondly, I've been having some thoughts about the third victim. Previously, we wondered if this was a sign of panic and poor thinking from the perpetrator... or perpetrators. Now, I'm wondering if it might actually have been just the opposite. Quite deliberate, and carefully considered in fact."

"By the time of Mandy Bremner's abduction and homicide, the suspect knew we had already started a murder investigation. What better way to muddy the waters than to select a totally random victim, of no direct interest to the animal terrorist group, and also use a different MO? A classic distraction technique, to cause confusion and misdirect resource."

"It was a fairly clumsy attempt at a faked suicide, and they must have known there was a high chance of discovery. Indeed, that is what they actually wanted. There would have been no point if it had just been written up by the Police and the Procurator Fiscal as an unfortunate suicide and forgotten about. They needed to attract our attention. This is where the choice of locus is interesting... they seemed to almost know that we had some interest in The Don area, and by staging it there made it more likely we would be drawn in."

"And, of course, they couldn't resist using a dog's choker chain as the murder weapon. This could either be a sign of arrogance, confidence that they were beyond detection, or perhaps even that they were moving from pure revenge towards ideological publicity."

"And sadly, as ever, sex workers make relatively easy prey."

"So, poor Mandy Bremner was just in the wrong place at the wrong time?" commented Baxter.

"Indeed."

"And, of course, that would explain why we couldn't find any connection with the other two victims?"

"Exactly."

"Ok, that all makes sense," added Bankhurst.

"Really appreciate your opinion as ever, Dr McEwan."

"You're welcome. Please, feel free to get in touch again at any time."

McEwan tried to create the impression of a low bar for her personal re-involvement as the case continued to hold her fascination, and her investment in it made her reluctant to cede responsibility to other colleagues.

"OK, thanks everybody," continued Bankhurst, "great work today."

CHAPTER 20

Friday 27th December

Another day. Another dilemma for Bankhurst. She was due her annual diabetic retinal screening appointment in the afternoon and, because she was taking a half day of personal time off, had arranged to have her two monthly haircut on the same day. She weighed up the potential bad optic of taking time out for a hair appointment during an MIT investigation against the feel good factor it would give her. She was due highlights at the appointment so, in reality, it was never really a fair debate, and by mid afternoon she was welcoming the distraction of banal holiday chat with her regular, and trusted, stylist.

As it happened, it was perhaps her most considered decision of the day. After what had felt like a significant advance the previous day, Friday had been relatively quiet and without incident.

When she returned to the MIT room, apart from drawing a few glances for her hairdo, there was no sign of any colleagues trying to attract her attention to perhaps signify something of interest. Most remained focused on their screens. Her friend, Sharon Baxter, gave her a thumbs up, and a smile of approval for her haircut which was well received by Bankhurst. She mouthed the word 'thanks' in response.

Despite the slow Friday, Bankhurst felt the MIT had gained significant momentum since the Christmas break and was keen for this to continue over the weekend. Although she was rostered to be off Saturday and Sunday, she had already decided to 'go in' for at least part of each day. Forty eight hours was potentially a long time in an MIT investigation, and she wanted to remain in the loop.

She wasn't a slave to her job, however, and even with the magnitude of the investigation, she very much wanted a hybrid weekend, mixing professional and family commitments. She was aware that Andrew had not had her full attention since the investigation started and, particularly with her own parents returning home, she would have to step up to the plate.

She would often try and watch him play football on a Saturday morning but, as his league was suspended over the Festive Period, she considered other possible options. In the end, she decided the best plan would be to involve him in the decision later on Friday evening.

After a debate over fish and chips from the local 'chipper' Andrew, after some procrastination, decided that a Marvel movie followed by tea at McDonalds was his favoured choice.

Bankhurst spent a few uneventful hours at work on Saturday morning before mother and son followed the chosen agenda with Bankhurst thankful for the family time. She wasn't a huge Marvel franchise fan herself but, somewhat against her expectations, she quite enjoyed the film. She definitely enjoyed the McDonalds that followed, however, and the tasty food reminded her why the brand had stood the test of time. A brief pang of guilt at having two 'fast food' teas in succession was soon forgotten.

Sunday had offered further time for family activities, domestic chores and relaxation. Bankhurst was watching TV with Andrew in the early evening when her phone rang, causing her to jump slightly. Her screen displayed a number she recognised and she was immediately on alert. Andrew noticed his Mum putting her game face on, and rolled his eyes. He knew it wasn't going to be a social call, and experience had taught him the potential consequences. Worse case scenario would see him being deposited at Olive's for an unknown length of time, possibly even overnight. While he was happy to have street cred with his friends for having 'a detective' mother, there were times

when he wished his parent had a 9-5 job. He listened attentively.
"DI Bankhurst."
"Evening, Ma'am. This is DS Donaldson. Sorry to disturb you at home but you said you wanted to know of any significant developments. As you know, we've previously had independent data searches done for Wilson's staff and Deliveroo employees. I decided to combine the searches, and there's one address common to both searches... 524b Union Grove."
"There are two male occupants; one works at Wilsons, and the other does part time Deliveroo work. I just thought this could be significant."
"Thanks DS Donaldson for calling... it's no problem... and you're right, this could be a significant finding."
"Have they not been interviewed before?"
"I checked that, Ma'am. Grant Gilchrist... he's the guy who works at Wilson's... has been interviewed, and cleared. Nothing of note in his history, or interview, and there was CCTV and witnesses placing him at the staff meeting at the time of the Deliveroo delivery."
"We haven't been able to get hold of Piotr Nowak ... the Deliveroo guy... yet."
"Ok. Thanks. Definitely worth a closer look. I think we'll definitely pay them a visit tomorrow. Good work, DS Donaldson... it's Grant, isn't it?"
"Yes, Ma'am."
"Thanks for phoning, Grant. Appreciate it. Anything else happening?"
"Not that I'm aware of, Ma'am."
"Ok. Thanks. Bye for now."
"Good night, Ma'am."
Andrew, along with his mother, breathed a sigh of relief and unmuted the volume on the TV. He immediately resumed his relaxed position on the couch and re-engaged with his programme, though his mother continued to look into space for a while pondering the new information, and what the next day might bring.

Monday 30th December

Union Grove is an urban residential street to the west of Aberdeen city centre, dating from the 19th century. Most of the street is given over to three and four story privately owned, granite tenement buildings. Wrought iron fences contain small front gardens, belonging to the ground floor apartments, while there are larger communal green areas towards the rear, backing on to a lane. Over the years, the outside toilets, and shared toilets on the mezzanine landings, have gradually been replaced by modern facilities in each apartment.

As Bankhurst and Iqbal drove up the street, she noticed a rash of satellite dishes, almost as far as the eye could see, protruding from the front of the tenements. She also noted the tell tale signs of City Fibre installations everywhere, with superfast fibre cables being run from the pavement to a junction box on the wall, and then spliced to serve several different apartments. This was a very well 'connected' street, thought Bankhurst, and she wondered what the residents of yesteryear would have made of today's high tech world.

Trees lined both sides of the street, and every hundred yards or so were giant communal bins, with the obligatory squabble of seagulls taking advantage of any overfilling.

As they approached 524b, a van obligingly pulled out from directly outside the front door, and Bankhurst gratefully parked her car in the space created. The two back up squad cars parked on the other side of the road on the double yellow lines that ran the length of the street on the odd numbered side. One or two curtains, in ground floor apartments, twitched as residents strived to ascertain what was requiring such an obvious police presence on their street at that time of day.

Bankhurst and Iqbal got out of their car, ducking their heads slightly under branches of a rowan tree to get to the pavement. Only a few of the most tenacious red berries remained on the branches, the others having long since succumbed to cold weather, weakened stems and gravity.

At the side of the front door, six bells and nameplates were displayed, though not all were populated with data, including flat b. Bankhurst noted two key safes, and presumed they were for less able residents, or Airbnb apartments.

They pressed the bell and waited for an answer through the intercom. Several seconds passed before a somewhat sleepy voice enquired, "Who is it?"

Iqbal took the lead.

"It's the police. Open up."

"What?"

"Police. You need to open the door— now."

"Give me a couple of minutes to put some clothes on."

"No chance, pal. Open the door now, or we're coming through it!" Iqbal barked.

Bankhurst thought that was a little extreme as they were no more than people of potential interest at this time but, even so, they wished to give them as little time as possible to hide anything. It had the desired effect as there was an audible click and the door opened.

A few paces along a corridor smelling of damp cement took them to the door of the apartment, and they could hear a Yale lock being turned.

Grant Gilchrist was dressed only in his boxer shorts, and was trying to pull on a T-shirt as he let the officers into a poorly lit hall.

"What's this all about? I've already spoken to you lot."

"We need to ask you, and your flatmate, some more questions. This address has become one of interest to us in the murder investigation."

"What? No way!" he protested.

Bankhurst pointed to a door that was open just enough to suggest the room behind it was the living room.

"May we go in?"

"Aye… Ok… on you go. I'll put some clothes on and be with you in a minute."

"While you're at, it get your flatmate Nowak, up. We need to speak to him," ordered Iqbal who still seemed to be in his *I'm going to break your door down* persona. Bankhurst gave him a look that invited him to calm down a little.

"Good luck with that," called Gilchrist as he went into his room to get dressed, "he's in Boston… USA".

The latter was added, Bankhurst assumed, to remove any doubt that he wasn't in Boston, Lincolnshire, but both she and Iqbal had automatically made the connection with the USA in any case.

"When did he go there?" enquired Bankhurst.

"Three months ago… he's doing a PhD in Biochemistry, and he's gan to Boston University for four months. He's nae due back until the end of January."

Bankhurst and Iqbal looked at each other and shared a sense of deflation.

"Which University is he at?"

"Aberdeen."

Iqbal was making notes, and added the university, and department, to be checked in due course..

"So, he's not been back at all?"

"Na. Couldn't afford it, I don't think."

The conversation from the bedroom paused as Gilchrist dressed allowing the two detectives to take their surroundings in. They were in a somewhat cold, open plan lounge-kitchen at the front of the house adequately illuminated by a bay window overlooking the street.

The room was untidy, but not particularly unclean. A generous amount of dishes were, however, piled in the sink awaiting attention, and a basket full of clothes sat on the floor in front of the washing machine. There were the usual white goods in the kitchen, and the fridge door was adorned with a liberal assortment of magnets, including those representing football teams, holiday destinations and some that were not familiar to

Bankhurst. The living space was shared by a large settee, an easy chair and two gaming chairs positioned in front of an impressive array of IT equipment.

Typical male flat thought Bankhurst.

Gilchrist duly appeared fully clothed, and made his way across the room to switch a heater on.

"Thanks for that, pal. It's a bit Baltic in here," offered Iqbal in an attempt to soften his approach slightly.

"Aye, we've nae central heating... bit of a bummer at this time of year."

Gilchrist sat in the easy chair and put on an extra fleece to ward against the cold until the room heated up.

"So, you work at Wilsons?"

"Aye, I'm sure you ken that."

"Do you have a driver's licence?"

"Aye, I do though I havnae got any wheels at the moment."

"Do you ever drive a blue van?"

"No."

"Where were you on the evenings of 20th November and 21st December?"

"I haven't got a clue to be honest. Probably here."

"Can anyone vouch for that?"

"I doubt it."

"Would you be willing for us to analyse data from your phone?"

"Well ... I dinna ken."

"It would potentially eliminate you from our enquiry. We'd not be interested in anything unrelated to our investigation, if that's what you're worried about."

"Aye... I suppose so."

Iqbal took over the questioning.

"Have you any link with animal activist groups?"

"What?"

"People that campaign for the rights of animals."

Gilchrist allowed himself a laugh.

"No!" before adding, quite forcibly, "you've got to be kidding.

Give me a break!"
"What about Nowak? Does he ever speak about animal issues?"
Bankhurst wasn't sure why he asked the question, as Nowak had what seemed like a cast iron alibi.
"Er… no."
"You seemed to hesitate a bit there, Grant," commented Bankhurst."
"No. No. He definitely hasn't."
"Do you mind if we have a wee look round?"
"No. Go on. Knock yourself out."

The two detectives had a closer look at the kitchen-lounge area before checking the two bedrooms and bathroom. Gilchrist's bed was unmade, as might have been expected given his rude awakening, and he had a few clothes lying around the room competing for space with shoes, football boots, books and a traffic cone.
Nowak's room, again as might be expected, was generally tidier; the bed was made, and there were no scattered articles of clothing. A bike was leaning against the wall, and, lying on the floor of one of the cupboards, was a well worn Deliveroo bag. Otherwise, the inspection was unremarkable.
They returned to the living area where Gilchrist was checking something on his mobile phone. Bankhurst wondered whether he was actively editing his phone, or had just automatically picked it up, as seemed to be the current norm to fill in time while waiting for something or someone. She knew she was guilty of the same habit herself.
"Can you please put your phone down, Grant?"
"Aye… ok… I was just checking my Whatsapps."
"I think we've finished here now, but we'll need to check with Border Control that Nowak is where he claims to be."
"Aye… go ahead… but I can show you a picture of him this week at a Boston Celtics game if you like," he said with a slight note of triumph in his voice.
Iqbal ignored the retort.

"We'll need your phone for a couple of days."
"Two days! What am I meant to do in the meantime?" he protested.
"I'm sure it won't kill you to go a bit retro for a while," suggested Iqbal.
"Easy for you to say," he retorted.
"I'm sure you've got other ways of connecting to the outside world, Grant," pointed out Bankhurst, as she nodded towards the adjacent impressive collection of keyboards and screens .
"Huh," he replied.

The two detectives retraced their steps to the car, and ducked once more under the branches of the Rowan tree. Iqbal nodded to the patrol cars indicating their presence was no longer required. He suspected they would be heading for a coffee break. As they pulled away from the kerb, Bankhurst was aware of something niggling at the back of her mind, but couldn't bring it into focus. She let the thought drift away, and returned to concentrate on her driving.

Bankhurst allowed herself a fifteen minute break to enjoy her coffee, and catch up on her e-mail and social media. She also had a quick look on her favourite clothing sites to see if there were any items remaining from the Boxing Day sales that might catch her eye. As she was a common size, and had been slow off the mark, it was no surprise that her search was fruitless.
She rejoined the MIT, and brought them up to date with the visit to Union Grove.
"There's something I'm suspicious about, but I just can't put my finger on it. Sharon, can you see if you can convince one of the neighbours on the other side of the street to accept a CCTV camera for a couple of days. Let's keep an eye on that address for a bit."
"Will do," replied DS Baxter.
"Also, we need to contact Border Control and check the details of Nowak's passport and recent travel."

"Can you do that, Hugh?"
MacLennan nodded.
"And let's chase Digital Forensics up later today about Gilchrist's phone, as we've only got it for a limited period."
"Why is that, Ma'am?"
"Well, he handed it over voluntarily... after a bit of persuasion, and I said we would only have it for forty eight hours."
"I would love to have a warrant for that property, and all their IT, but we just don't have enough evidence yet. Both occupants have, on the face of it at least, good alibis, there are no forensics implicating them and nothing to connect them with any animal activist organisations."
"We're lucky we've actually got his phone,"she added.
"One last thing... I want a detailed look into these two, and their backgrounds, for any sniff of animal activism."
"Will do, Boss."
Satisfied that she had done all she could, she left the MIT room and set off to brief Anderson.

CHAPTER 21

Tuesday 31st December

Bankhurst stood up and cleared her throat, but still didn't have the attention of the MIT room. A couple of less than subtle bangs on the table with her George Ezra coffee cup did the trick.
"Ok, feedback time. Where are we at?"
"Sharon?"
"We've had a camera up and running across the road in Union Grove since yesterday afternoon. Nothing remarkable so far."
"Ok, what about Nowak's university credentials?"
"Check out, Ma'am. Aberdeen University confirms he is a Biochemistry PhD student on secondment to Boston University. I've been trying to get a hold of his mentor at Boston Uni, but no joy so far. Time difference may have something to do with it."
"OK, thanks."
" Any animal activist links with either Gilchrist or Nowak?"
"No, Ma'am, not so far."
Bankhurst scanned the room to see if anyone from Digital Forensics was present, and spotted Neil Jardine near the back of the room.
"Neil. Anything on the phone so far?"
"Nothing so far. Triangulation fails to put his phone anywhere near our areas of interest, and nothing unusual on the phone itself. Just what you might imagine a young male would have on his device."
A few knowing looks and half grins spread around the room.
"OK. Enough of that," said Bankhurst in a gentle chide to her

audience.

"What about Border Control, Hugh?"

"They confirm Nowak flew from London Heathrow to Logan International on 28th September, and hasn't returned since. They did, however, point out something of potential interest... Nowak has dual citizenship."

"And?"

It was only a single word but came out sounding quite impatient. In a split second she had realised what was coming next, and was annoyed at herself for not considering the possibility.

MacLennan looked slightly taken aback.

"Well, his dual nationality gives him two passports..."

Bankhurst regretted her terseness but continued the line of reasoning herself, "so he could potentially fly out to the USA on a British passport and then return again, under the radar, on a Polish one. Commit a crime or crimes and then jet back to Boston on the Polish one again, where he makes sure he sends plenty of photos of himself at Bostonian landmarks. Makes for a great alibi."

Iqbal continued, "Meanwhile Gilchrist, who could still be the inside man, creates a perfect alibi for himself by making sure he is very visible at the staff meeting, while the heart was delivered to the Abattoir by his co-conspirator. Both men successfully alibied!"

"Good work, Hugh. Can you follow this through and get in touch with the Polish consulate to see if they can throw any light on his movements under a Polish passport?"

"Yes, Ma'am."

Bankhurst spotted Zimmerman leaning against the wall in his usual place by the door.

"Alan, how are the media just now?"

"Oh...you know...baying at the door as usual."

"OK, let's give another statement to try and appease them before the New Year break. Keep it fairly generic meantime. 'Following several promising lines of enquiry' etc. We don't want to give

away anything for free to the suspects."
"Will do," replied Zimmerman.
"Ok. Good. Thanks, everyone."

As it was Hogmanay, an assortment of snacks, chocolates and soft drinks had appeared on one of the tables. Bankhurst, always a sucker for a salt and vinegar crisp, snaffled a few on the way past. She doubted it would be her last visit to the festive trough, and in her head she was already calculating the adjustment in her insulin dose that might be required.
What the hell, it's Hogmanay.

Despite her snacks, Bankhurst was hungry by lunchtime when she met up with Baxter in the canteen. Both detectives chose to tackle the chicken curry on offer as the special of the day.
They agreed it was passable, but didn't exactly set the taste buds alight, though the naan breads were excellent and partially saved the culinary day. Conversation was upbeat and oscillated between recounting family festive stories and the case. Both detectives felt the investigation was on an upswing, and hoped a breakthrough might be imminent.
Unfortunately that sense of optimism would be dashed by the end of the afternoon feedback session.

DS MacLennan reported back that Nowak's mentor in Boston confirmed that he had seen him every two to three days of his secondment, and didn't recall any longer absences. In addition, the Polish consulate was able to state that Nowak had not travelled on his Polish passport. There was, therefore, no evidence to suggest he was doing anything other than pursuing his academic studies three thousand miles away from the crime scenes in North East Scotland.
There was a strong sense of being back to square one, and the morning optimism was replaced by a rather more sombre mood as the daytime MIT shift broke up for the Hogmanay celebration. A few decided they were going straight to the pub to replace the Nosecco and 0.0% lagers of the MIT room with the real

stuff, while Bankhurst made her way home to relieve Olive, and consider what she was going to rustle up for tea.
In the end, and somewhat against her better judgement, she acquiesced to Andrew's pleading to get a Chinese carry-out from Cults picked up by Deliveroo. She wasn't a fan of such delivery services, and not just because of the involvement with the current case. She generally thought it was a lazy option but any such moral judgements were trumped by the advantage of having a couple of decent sized glasses of wine, and not to have to worry about driving.
Andrew had also been promised he could stay up until 'the bells', but had crashed out by 10-30pm. He had the slightly sweaty head that always indicated he was in a deep sleep, and he remained undisturbed as his mother carried him through to his bed. Bankhurst herself felt exhausted and had no great desire to stay up until midnight. She got undressed, removed her subtle makeup, and cleaned her teeth with her electric brush. After finishing her recommended two minutes, and generating a smiley face from her brush, she detached her toothbrush head and placed it beside Andrew's. As she did so, something clicked in her head, and a clarity of thought that was previously denied made her realise what had been bothering her about 524b Union Grove.

CHAPTER 22

January 1st

"There's someone else living at that address!"
"Happy New Year to you too,"replied Iqbal who was the duty DS on for the holiday MIT.
"Oh, sorry, Happy New Year!"
She reached out for an embrace, which was reciprocated, and she lingered in his firm grip perhaps slightly longer than was strictly necessary. She thought his aftershave might be Kouros, which she approved of, and she hoped her own perfume had been appreciated.

She had entered the MIT room and headed directly for Iqbal, desperate to offload her theory, somewhat at the expense of social etiquette. Having realised her mistake, she took the time to wish everybody a good new year before returning to topic.
Iqbal was fully alert and waiting for her to continue.
"It was the toothbrushes," she continued.
Iqbal looked confused, but said nothing, inviting her to continue.
"I knew there was something niggling me, but I couldn't put my finger on it. Then it dawned on me that there were two toothbrushes in the cup on the sink in the bathroom. Who doesn't take their toothbrush away with them on a prolonged trip?"
"When I got to think about it, there was also an anti-perspirant in Nowak's bedroom. Another thing he would have taken with him. What male owns two anti-perspirants, I ask you? I suspect there's one or two in this room who don't own one!"

"Oooh...harsh, Boss...but probably true!" conceded Iqbal, with a generous smile and a laugh.
"Then there was that pile of dishes waiting to be washed in the sink. Surely too many for one person to have generated? There has to be another resident."
"Gaun yersel, Boss. I think you're bang on," replied Iqbal.
"The question is, who?"

Bankhurst explained her theory to the MIT, and asked for a report on the CCTV from the other side of the street.
A fresh faced detective raised his hand. "DC Jarvie, Ma'am. The overnight team has been analysing the video data. Nothing much happened since a few revellers came in at 03:00. They reckon there's a total of about thirty people gone in and out of the address in the last thirty-six hours or so. They've pulled images of each individual and saved them to a file."
He pointed to his screen inviting Bankhurst to come and have a look. She and Iqbal stood at the back of the DC as he clicked on the appropriate file. A series of images, some better than others, were presented on the screen, and Jarvie scrolled down to allow all of them to be studied. Near the end, Iqbal shouted, "Stop!"
He leaned in closer to the screen and pointed to an image of a male, perhaps in his late twenties.
"Is that no that wee baw bag who gave you a hard time at the press conference, Boss?"
Bankhurst leaned a bit closer herself. "Yes. I think you're right."
"Journalist for the P and J. What was his name again? Something like David or Davy."
"What the hell is he doing there?"
"Surely he couldn't have got wind that we are interested in this property?"
Jarvie opened another file that logged activities against a time frame. "He entered the address at 4:30pm, using his own key, on the 30th. Yesterday he left at 07:45 and returned again at 4:30pm.
"The wee scroat's been at work!" exclaimed Iqbal, who seemed

to be working his way through his Glaswegian lexicon of derogatory terms. "He's living there!"

"So," continued Bankhurst, "either this is a major coincidence that he happens to live in the same apartment block that interests our investigation, or he could perhaps be a person of interest himself. Could he, in fact, be the 'third resident'?"

Bankhurst felt a tingle of excitement spread through her body. She'd had a feeling, a sixth sense, that the Union Grove property had something to tell. Her hopes of the previous day had been quashed at the afternoon meeting, but had now been rekindled. She didn't want to get ahead of herself, but she couldn't deny the palpable sense of anticipation that was coursing through her body.

"Peter Davies is his name, Ma'am," shouted one of the MIT from a couple of desks away.

"Have just checked the on-line P and J."

She turned her screen round to show the profile and picture of the twenty-eight year old Crime reporter.

"Right," she said, speaking to the image on the screen, "let's find out everything we can about you, Peter Davies."

She raised her eyes from the screen to make sure her message had been heard. A flurry of activity indicated it had.

"I'll contact the duty sheriff myself and ask for an emergency warrant," said Bankhurst.

"We need to pay them another visit...and this time we're not coming away empty handed!"

It took a few hours for the warrant to be granted, and the appropriate paperwork completed, and in that time a significant percentage of the MIT computing power had been focussed on Peter Davies. By the time thoughts were turning towards lunch, a significant amount of data had been accumulated, including details about his upbringing, education, career, hobbies and social media activity.

One of two children to Isobel and John Davies, he was born and bred in the city. He had attended the local High School with academic results in the top 20% of his intake, achieving a prize in English. He appeared to have taken a gap year after school, though there were no details available on what he did or where he had gone. After the presumed gap year, he enrolled at Aberdeen University where he graduated with a 2:1 in English, and followed that with a postgraduate course in journalism, before joining the P and J news desk. He subsequently moved to the Crime desk at the same newspaper, where he still worked. It appeared from DVLA data that he was the current owner of a six year old grey VW polo.

He had never married and his sexuality, and current relationship status, were unknown, though his Facebook profile suggested he was likely to be single. He had no criminal record.

As was often the case, it was social media which proved the most illuminating. Neil Jardine from IT reported that, although Davies had done his best to hide any overt support to animal activist groups, presumably as this might not go down well with his employer, he just couldn't help himself 'liking' various posts on Facebook over the years. These posts related either directly or indirectly to animal welfare and the overall trend analysis suggested someone with a strong, and persistent, interest in the issue.

Jardine also expressed a keen desire to get access to Davies' phone and other IT hardware ASAP, as they were likely to be much more informative.

Armed with her warrant in front of her, and two squad cars behind her, Bankhurst was driven by Iqbal along the now familiar route of Union Grove, from east to west. It was 1:00pm and the streets were deserted. Residents were either still sleeping off hangovers from Hogmanay celebrations, or staying inside as everywhere was closed.

As a result, there were no legitimate parking spaces, so all three vehicles parked on the double yellow lines across from 524b, generating another round of curtain twitching.

Bankhurst noted, as she crossed the road, that the last berries had given up the ghost and left the skeleton rowan tree to endure the winter; nature and lengthening days would entice it back into life in Spring. Parked three spaces along the road was Davies' grey VW Polo.

This time Bankhurst and Iqbal had six uniformed officers with them as they rang the bell, with a burly sergeant leading the way.

"Police. Open up!"

"For fuck's sake. Not again!" was the, perhaps not surprising, response from Gilchrist at the third visit in almost as many days.

"Open up. Now!"

"OK, OK. Fuck me."

The lock clicked and the entourage made their way along the close at a brisk pace. Gilchrist had the door open for them so no momentum was lost as all eight officers entered the flat though, as the hall wasn't big enough, they soon spilled into the living room.

Bankhurst held up the paperwork.

"I have a warrant to search these premises, and remove any items we feel may have been involved in criminal activity."

"This is getting ridiculous!" protested Gilchrist.

"Is there anyone else in the flat just now?" continued Bankhurst.

"No!"

"We have reason to believe a third person may be residing at this address."

Gilchrist's demeanour immediately changed from indignation to somewhat culpable looking.

Bankhurst sensed the change, and pressed home any advantage while he might be on the back foot.

"Is Peter Davies staying at this address?"

"Er...yes...he is...but it's no big deal. We're just subletting to him. Lots of people do it."

"Why didn't you tell us about him?"

"You never asked! You just seem interested in me and Piotr."

"Seriously!" responded Bankhurst in a terse voice.

"Well, I wasn't going to advertise we were subletting. If the landlord finds out, we'll probably get chucked out."

"Tell us about the subletting arrangement," continued Iqbal.

"So, about 6 months ago, Piotr and I were a bit short of cash and he knew, via a friend, that Peter was looking for somewhere to stay. Our sofa turns into a bed, so we agreed Peter could stay for a few months at an agreed rent, and we pocketed the cash. By luck, Piotr landed the Boston secondment and Peter has been able to use his room the last three months. Everybody was happy."

"Has he ever spoken to you about issues relating to animal welfare?"

"Aye, he has. In fact, that's the one thing that can get him a wee bit hot under the collar."

Bankhurst and Iqbal exchanged glances.

"So...that's why you hesitated when we asked you if Nowak had ever spoken about animal welfare. He hadn't ...but Davies had."

Gilchrist looked at his feet.

"Where is he now?" pressed Bankhurst.

"I don't know. He got a text about an hour ago and just grabbed his phone, laptop and rucksack before leaving in a hurry on Piotr's bike. Didn't even say where he was going."

"But you surely can't suspect Peter of anything? He wouldn't say boo to a goose!"

"Have you never heard of the banality of evil, Mr Gilchrist?" enquired Bankhurst before answering her own question, "No, I don't suppose you have."

Gilchrist looked bemused, and decided silence was his best option.

With a nod of the head from Iqbal the officers began a systematic search of the flat. After an hour, various items of clothing, all IT hardware and the Deliveroo kit were bagged, labelled and removed to the waiting vehicles.

Gilchrist looked crestfallen, and very much like he wasn't enjoying the start of the New Year.

"Ok, pal. You need to come with us to the station for questioning," announced Iqbal.

"What!" replied Gilchrist, recovering a little of his indignation.

"Well, either that or we **will** arrest you," responded the DS.

"Why?"
"Because at best you are guilty of obstruction of justice and at worst you are up to your neck in this...not to mention possibly defrauding your landlord."
"Aye...ok, ok...I'll come. But, I'm telling you here and now that I'm not guilty of anything, apart from trying to make a wee bit of cash on the side."

Progress was quick across the city but, as Bankhurst and Iqbal turned into the Nelson Street car park, they were immediately met with an unexpected site. Two fire engines with blue lights flashing were parked outside the main door with half a dozen firemen looking busy either coming in and out of the building, or speaking on shortwave radios.The entire staff of the building had been evacuated, and had actually gathered at the proper assembly point.
Perhaps the fire drills do work thought Bankhurst.
Some of them had managed to grab their coats, but most looked frozen, and there was much stamping of feet and rubbing of upper arms. There were no flames evident, and the only fumes came from two opportunistic smokers who had taken advantage of the enforced evacuation to light up.
Unbelievable! thought Bankhurst.
As it happened, they had timed their return to the station to perfection as, after another burst of short wave radio activity, the senior fireman announced the building was clear, and that the staff could re-enter. No second invitation was required. The chilled officers, and civilian staff, all but jogged back into the anticipated warmth of the building. A large queue soon built up at the coffee machine as people sought a hot drink to take the edge off the cold. The usual comments were made on why there was never a false fire alarm on a nice summer's day.

Gilchrist, after the ignominy of a squad car trip across town and the subsequent fire alarm drama, was looking deeply worried, if not actually afraid. He was directed into an interview room, and

sat down to await his inquisitors.
As Bankhurst and Iqbal walked down the corridor towards the MIT, the senior officer verbalised the question they had both been thinking since their visit to Union Grove.
"Is it just me, or is it almost like Davies knew we were coming?"
"No, it's no just you, Boss."

CHAPTER 23

Bankhurst summoned attention with her now customary tap on the table with her coffee cup, while hoping George Ezra wouldn't be offended to be repeatedly used in this way.

She updated the team about the raid on Union Grove, and that it appeared that their prime suspect, Peter Davies, was now very possibly on the run. She confirmed that Gilchrist was awaiting formal interview, and that the various seizures from the flat had been passed on to the relevant departments for further analysis.

"Davies left on Nowak's bike almost like he knew we were on to him. Being a crime journalist, he would be more than aware of ANPR technology, and taking the bike, although restrictive in speed and range, would make it a lot easier for him to travel without detection."

"Speaking of which," Iqbal interjected, "where are we on the ANPR analysis for Davies' car?"

"We have him recorded at various sites in and around Aberdeen, including a few on the AWPR, and one trip to Edinburgh three weeks ago. Once or twice he has been at or near our sites of interest, but not on the nights in question"

"Were they before or after?

"Er…let me see...before, by the look of it."

"So, possible reconnaissance trips?"

"Looks very like it."

"Ok, it really feels like this is our guy," stated Bankhurst.

"I want his profile circulated immediately to Police Scotland, the airport, bus station and harbour."

"Also, contact his boss at the P and J. We'll need to confiscate his

work computer...and organise a forensic lift of his car."
"Yes, Ma'am."
"Ok," she looked at Iqbal, "let's go and see what we can squeeze out of Gilchrist."
Both detectives sported a determined look as they set off for the interview room.

Two hours later, Bankhurst and Iqbal left the interview with nothing but a palpable sense of disappointment, and an increasing feeling that Gilchrist was not an accomplice. It looked increasingly likely that Davies had inveigled information about Wilson's Abattoir from Gilchrist, and also opportunistically used Nowak's bike, and Deliveroo kit, while he was abroad. The original flatmates were probably not guilty of anything other than naivety, and the desire to earn a bit of cash on the side.
As he had not actually been arrested, and there was no evidence to link him to criminal activity, there were no grounds for Bankhurst to detain Gilchrist overnight. After four hours, she agreed to his release, and a relieved looking man exited Nelson Street into the darkness of the evening.
The temperature had been dropping steadily throughout the afternoon, and the first precipitation of the day began falling as light snow. Gilchrist pulled the collar of his coat up and made his way to the nearest bus stop, with no great expectation that the January 1st timetable would grant him a bus any time soon.
He made a snap decision to go and stay with his sister overnight to reduce any possibility of another police visit the following day. They would have to find him first.

January 2nd

Bankhurst looked at herself in the mirror of the Nelson Street female toilet.

Not too bad she thought.

Although she had cursed the dampness in the morning air, her hair had not suffered too badly, and she remained determined to try and prolong the newly styled look for a few more days. She flicked an errant strand back into place, straightened up to improve her posture and adjusted the waistband of her trousers. While she occasionally objected to societal expectations that females should always look their best, most of the time she was happy to invest the necessary time and finance.

Feeling presentable, she left the toilet with a swish, and walked with purpose to the MIT room.

"Morning, Ma'am," stated an upbeat DS MacLennan, apparently refreshed from his brief time off.

"Morning, Hugh."

Bankhurst glanced at the white boards to see what had been added overnight.

No sightings
No CCTV images
Phone switched off
No bank cards used
No social media activity
Multiple prints found in car. No matches in the system
Traces of human blood found in Deliveroo bag. DNA awaited

"OK, so you've gone off grid, Peter Davies," Bankhurst was speaking to herself as much as anybody as she continued to scan the board, "but where have you gone? And are you working on your own or in a cell?"

Bankhurst decided an early coffee wouldn't do her any harm; when she took it back to her desk, Neil Jardine was waiting for her.

"Hi, Neil. Hope you've got something for me?"

"I do, as a matter of fact. Digital Forensics have been working overnight on this. We've found a lot of data to confirm this is very likely to be our guy. Some encrypted stuff on his computer, but mostly on the dark web. We eventually hacked his VPN account, and have been able to follow several threads of conversation he's had over the years on the dark web. Seems to have multiple alias names, but favours Pandjib and Dadberusko."

"Any significance to the names?"

"We wondered if Pandjib was a play on the P and J where he works, but we've really got no ideas about Dadberusko."

"There has definitely been a trend over the last three years towards more radical and extreme thinking, with many conversations expressing dissatisfaction with current forms of protest and encouraging escalation to violence. Most seem to promote this as a means to an end...to draw public attention to their cause.

But for some it's purely about retribution...and you definitely don't want to be within their cross-hairs, I can tell you."

"Apart from the conversations, he's visited multiple animal activist sites, particularly those at the extreme end of the spectrum. Some of these have legitimate, less extreme, sites on the regular internet, and some are purely on the dark web."

"Any chance of tracking down the people he's been chatting with?"

"I doubt it. They are, as you might imagine, very secretive about their identities. They use multiple IDs, and multiple VPNs, so we don't even know which country they're in."

"What about accomplices? Any indication he might be in a cell?"

"Nothing concrete I'm afraid...we did, however, find some searches on the dark web on how to source illegal drugs including Flunitrazepam."

"Ah…that fits…thanks, Neil, that's very helpful."

"No problem."

Bankhurst felt a surge of satisfaction. Everything was falling into place. This was definitely their man. Now all they had to do was catch him, and she was now armed with a confidence that they would.

What she didn't know was that they weren't the only ones

trying to find him.

CHAPTER 24

Bankhurst had an early lunch on her own and was back at her desk by 1:30pm, having visited DCI Anderson's office on the way back from the canteen to update him on the significant progress made. She left his room with a warm endorsement in her ear and safe in the knowledge that the good news would be rapidly passed up the food chain.

She had no sooner sat down than a middle aged, sometimes cantankerous DS, George Gillespie, waddled over towards her. A combination of obesity and what she took to be a sore hip made him look a bit like a penguin. She certainly wasn't going to say anything about it as he wasn't exactly known for his sense of humour.

His rasping growl of a voice was testament to a lifelong twenty a day habit, and the strong smell from his clothes as he approached suggested he had not tempered it.

"You might want to look at this," he grunted.

No salutations. No small talk. No acknowledgement of rank.

Typical Gillespie.

She let it slide. He was a good detective, and that cut him a little slack.

"What have you got, DS Gillespie?" Bankhurst could never call him *George.*

"I've been having another look at Davies's ANPR sightings and mobile phone positioning over the last two months. He's been making a fortnightly trip to a postcode seven miles west of Aberdeen. I've done a bit of digging and apparently his aunt and uncle have a small cottage on the outskirts of Kirkton of Skene. They spend October to March in Tenerife and sounds like Davies visits every two weeks to check on the property, give it an airing, flush the toilets etc."

"If I had to make a snap decision about finding a bolt hole within cycling distance, that I knew would be empty, it would be high on my list."

"Mine too," agreed Bankhurst.

"Great work, DS Gillespie."

She thought she could see a glimmer of a smile on his face, but it was quickly suppressed.

Why break the habit of a lifetime?

Within an hour Bankhurst had briefed the MIT and assembled a mobile team in four cars to make their way to the small hamlet of Kirkton of Skene. Her third rural destination of the case, each one radiating out from Aberdeen like the spokes of a wheel. This time she was going almost due west, the others having been more north-west. It was certainly improving her knowledge of Aberdeenshire, though she would have preferred if the experience had had a different driver.

She was in the lead car, and concentrated hard, as she made her way along the, sometimes confusing, lane arrangements of The Lang Stracht, as the entourage made its way westwards to the city boundary. The light traffic eased further as they passed a large garden centre on the outskirts of the city, which seemed to suck in the majority of the passing vehicles, their passengers no doubt glad to have somewhere to go after the New Year closures, and possibly with Christmas vouchers to spend.

And so it all begins again thought Bankhurst. *How long until the first Easter produce starts appearing in the shops?*

Almost immediately after the garden centre, the countryside opened up and the convoy made their way towards Westhill, and beyond to Kirkton of Skene. It was a beautiful crisp winter's day. Not a breath of wind. A light dusting of snow blanketed the fields, the brilliant white contrasting with the striking azure sky. Swathes of roadside Rosebay Willowherb, once resplendent in pink summer blossom, lay reduced to a forest of slender brown

stalks. Bankhurst noted a few rural residents still burned a real fire, the vertical trails of smoke spiralling unmolested skywards from various shapes and sizes of chimneys.
One in the distance was particularly impressive; Bankhurst imagined a family keeping warm around a blazing farmhouse fire.

The convoy was travelling with purpose, but only marginally above the speed limit and without blue lights. It came as a slight surprise to hear a siren towards the rear of the cars, but Bankhurst soon realised it was coming from a fire engine, and not one of the police cars, as a red shape appeared in the side mirror and rapidly closed on her car. The A944 is dual carriageway as far as Westhill and the police vehicles stayed in the inside lane as two rigs powered past, leaving a vortex of spray and vibration behind them.
Iqbal and Bankhurst glanced at one another before he picked up the radio.
"Hello. DS Iqbal here. Can you patch me through to Fire control?"
"OK."
"Fire control."
"Hello. This is DS Iqbal. We're on the A944 heading westwards; we've just been passed by a couple of your engines. Can you tell me where they're going please?"
"Aye...we've a call to a possible house fire out past Westhill."
"Where exactly?" pressed Iqbal.
"Kirkton of Skene."
"Shite!"
"Pardon."
"OK. Can you tell your guys this might be an address of interest to us as well and to be aware. We're a couple of minutes behind."
"Will do."
Iqbal turned and looked at Bankhurst again.
"For fuck's sake!" she said before turning on the siren and gunning the engine, as it dawned on her that the smoke she had seen in the distance was not from a generous farm chimney

after all.
The other cars responded automatically while Iqbal got back on the radio to communicate the reason for the change in strategy.

It took only two minutes, travelling at speed, to reach Westhill and they were soon past the commuter town and on the single carriageway road towards Kirkton of Skene. Both officers looked straight ahead as the now billowing smoke, and the blue lights of the fire engines, drew them to their destination.
They were soon parking up on the grass verge near to the blazing house and Bankhurst's historical dislike of coincidences was further reinforced when her satnav announced, 'You have reached your destination'.
Bankhurst and Iqbal got out of their car but were kept from further advance by the immediate wall of heat they encountered and the senior fire officer in command. His extended arm and hand with splayed fingers indicated the universally understood sign for ***Halt***!
They immediately understood why and needed no encouragement to take a few steps back. The intensity of heat generated by the now fully ablaze house was metaphorically and literally breathtaking. Bankhurst had attended fires before, primarily when she was in uniform, but had never experienced the sensation like immediate sunburn on her exposed skin, and the unpleasant experience of inhaling hot, ash-tinged air.
She took another few steps back and was grateful for the face covering handed to her by Iqbal, who still carried a couple of medical type masks dating from the COVID pandemic.
It was clear that the angry, swirling blaze had the upper hand over the fire personnel, and it was no surprise to hear the Officer In Charge summon extra help on his radio. The roaring, spitting fire was punctuated by periodic pops as windows blew out. The inrush of oxygen was matched by the new flames generated by the venting fire; an explosion of orange and red, with a tinge of blue, were soon licking the side of the building.
A loud cracking noise heralded the partial collapse of the garage

roof, exposing what appeared to be a dark coloured van inside.

It took two hours, and four engines, to quell the fire and, in that time, the house and garage were severely damaged. The blackened, granite walls stood resolute, but the rest of the structure had been reduced to a smoking, black, dripping shell. Exhausted firefighters were taking a break, or beginning to disassemble their equipment. Others stood in readiness by their rigs in case the fire reignited.

The structural assessment party had been in the building for ten minutes when a burst of static on the OIC's radio suggested they wished to communicate.

"OIC Martin."

"Firefighter Watt, Sir."

"Yes."

"There are clear signs that an accelerant has been used...and we found a severely fire damaged body in one of the downstairs rooms."

CHAPTER 25

"Understood," replied Martin.

"Structural report?" he continued.

"Safe with caution, though wouldn't recommend trying the stairs."

"Understood."

Bankhurst, who was now standing near enough to the laconic Fire OIC to hear the conversation, turned to Iqbal.

"Let's get Dexter Brewster out here stat."

"On it, Boss," replied Iqbal as he took his phone out and moved away from the gathering of police and fire personnel, seeking a quieter spot to make the call.

Brewster was in a compromising position when his pager went off. As usual, he had felt pangs of guilt when he slipped out the back door of the mortuary thirty minutes previously and drove the relatively short distance to his liaison. He had found a parking spot nearby and noticed she was standing at the bay window waiting for him. The door opened, he was ushered inside with minimal fuss and the door was closed behind him again.

The house was warm and inviting as usual, and he allowed himself to relax a little. He put his hand in his pocket and felt the reassuring presence of cash. Small talk was kept to a minimum as they both knew time was limited. He got undressed with practised speed, and it wasn't long before he was succumbing to her magical touch. When she felt he was ready, she turned him over and expertly placed him ready for the coup de grâce…and then jumped on him with not inconsiderable force. There was a

dull cracking noise from the lower right lumbar region.
"Good," she said, "that's that side done. Now for the other one."

Margaret Burns had been Brewster's osteopath for more years than he cared to remember. As the pre-eminent osteopath in the North East, appointments were at a premium; he took what he could get. He booked up every three months which sometimes meant taking a chance on being able to accommodate it within his professional responsibilities. Sometimes, like today, he had to slip out for his appointment within working hours. Even though he always made up the time, it didn't stop him feeling guilty during the appointment; today was no exception.
Burns had just skilfully re-positioned him on her couch in preparation for the next manoeuvre. He was in a precarious position on the left edge of the couch, with his body rotated such that his right leg was dangling towards the ground, when his pager went off. The shrill bleep startled him and made him jump slightly, the result of which was to pitch him onto all fours on the ground.
Therapist and patient both saw the funny side and dissolved into giggles, before Brewster recovered some composure.
"Sorry, Margaret, but I'll need to make a quick call."
"No problem. Go for it."
Brewster, by now vertical again, dialled the number of the mortuary and at the same time noticed a reflection, from the shiny surface of a unit in Burns's treatment room. A rotund man in his pants and socks holding a mobile phone to his ear.
Not a pretty sight he thought *especially with the pot belly in profile!* He pulled in his abdominal muscles, but with only marginal benefit to the reflected image. A quarter turn to the right removed it from his sight and mind.
The mortuary receptionist explained that DI Bankhurst had specifically requested for him to assess a body that had been found at a potential crime scene at Kirkton of Skene. She passed on the postcode and Brewster instructed her to let Bankhurst know he was on his way.

Cursing his luck at receiving a call during his osteopathy session, he explained the situation to Burns, got dressed quickly, left some cash on a shelf and quickly made his way towards his car promising, as he left, to e-mail her about his next appointment.
He wasted no time in keying the postcode into his satnav, selecting a Billy Joel playlist and pulling out into the late afternoon traffic.
After twenty five minutes, he was adding his car to the already sizeable collection of emergency vehicles scattered around the Kirkton of Skene address.
Force of habit dictated that he put his Duty Pathologist sign on the dashboard, though it was very unlikely he would fall foul of a traffic warden at such a rural location.
He donned his Tyvek suit, grabbed his bag from the boot and headed towards Bankhurst who was waving her iphone torch to attract his attention in the poor light. The air, thick with the smell of burning, was irritating to the eyes and a tear was running down his face by the time he reached her.
"Evening, Dexter. If it wasn't so serious, I feel like I should be making a quip that 'we must stop meeting like this'."
"Aye, indeed. I was thinking the same thing myself...and me right in the middle of my osteopathy session when you phoned!"
"Oh, sorry about that...who do you see?"
"Margaret Burns."
"Is she good?"
"The best...but don't even think about trying for an appointment. It's 'kent faces only' now she's reduced her hours a bit."
"Ok. Noted. Pity."
Small talk completed to both parties' satisfaction, Brewster invited the change of topic.
"So, what have you got for me, Lily?"
"Let me bring you up to speed," she replied.
Bankhurst spent the next 5 minutes briefing Brewster on the investigation, including the evidence that had directed them to the Kirkton of Skene address. She also explained that the fire had

been set with an accelerant not too long before they had left the station, and that they had been overtaken by the fire engines on a blue light run to the same address.

"Not a coincidence then?"

"Probably not."

"The firefighters found a body on the ground floor...badly burned as you might imagine."

"Indeed," said Brewster as he gazed at the charred remains of the house, now illuminated by powerful searchlights.

"One of the firefighters will escort you in."

"Fair enough. Let's go," he said with a nod of his head to acknowledge his escort who was patiently waiting for the conclusion of the briefing.

Fifteen minutes later, Brewster appeared from the wreckage of the house blinking as his eyes adjusted to the powerful spotlights.

Having sought out Bankhurst and Iqbal, he looked keen to offload his observations.

"Badly fire damaged body in typical pugilist attitude. Not possible to determine age, gender or accurate time of death at the moment.Almost certainly dead before the fire though."

"Oh. Why so?"

"Well, he or she has a through and through bullet wound from the left to right temple."

"Christ! Any firearm nearby?"

"No."

"Any casing or bullet?"

"None recovered so far...though it is a complete mess in there it has to be said."

"Ok. Thanks, Dexter. Is it ok to move the body now?"

"Yes, if the SOCOs are happy, then so am I."

"Very good. Will the PM be tomorrow morning?"

"Will definitely be tomorrow, but more likely in the afternoon. We'll need a PMCT beforehand in the morning. Can be especially useful, in my experience, in severe burn victims, as many of the other osmologies we look for at a PM are rendered useless by fire damage."

"OK. Thanks again. I'll phone tomorrow to find out the exact time as I would like to attend."

"Very good...oh, by the way, I'm sure you'll have this in hand already but could you track down their dentist and have any records, especially x-ray images, sent over please? I'm going to ask the Forensic Odontologist for their opinion, and they'll be able to compare the PMCT oral images with those of their dentist."

"Already on it," she replied.

"Thought as much," responded Brewster as his opinion of the young (*everybody looks young these days!)* DI continued on an upward trajectory.

CHAPTER 26

January 3rd

After the morning MIT update, Bankhurst felt like she was just marking time before the postmortem. She was reminded of what it felt like to have an afternoon exam at university. A broken night's sleep followed by an interminably long morning when she couldn't settle to concentrate on anything, the void often being filled by increasing anxiety. Time dragged and she couldn't wait to get on with it, the butterflies settling in her stomach as soon as she started the paper. She was becoming aware of a similar feeling and was relieved when lunchtime came and she could pass some time with Sharon Baxter, prior to making the short trip on foot to the mortuary for the two o'clock postmortem.

"Before I get started, I would like to say how indebted I am to my Radiology colleague, Dr Henry Strathburn, for performing and reporting the PMCT so quickly, and indeed to Dr Aiden Skene for his expert Odontology advice."

"On that note, I can confirm that we have just heard from Dr Skene that he is 99% sure that the deceased is Peter Davies."

Bankhurst and Iqbal, once again sitting together in the gallery, exchanged glances and nods.

"I would also like, if I may, to paraphrase the main findings from Dr Strathburn?"

It was a rhetorical question, but he afforded himself a quick glance at the gallery over the top of his glasses to make sure there were no dissenters.

"The scan confirmed severe fire damage including bilateral

lower limb thermal amputations, heat induced fractures of the right femur and left humerus, severe muscle contractions and significant damage to the internal organs. There was no evidence of ante mortem fracture.The lower abdominal contents were slightly less affected and he could see evidence of a prostate gland, thereby confirming male sex.

He confirmed typical entry and exit wounds on the left and right temples respectively, and there were no retained metallic objects likely to be from a ballistic origin."

"Most of the blood was coagulated secondary to extreme heat, but the lower spinal column and cord were less severely damaged; he was able to recommend I look for a fluid sample there, in the form of cerebrospinal fluid, for carboxyhaemoglobin, toxicology and DNA sampling."

"What does the carboxyhaemoglobin tell us about, Dexter?" enquired Bankhurst over the microphone.

"It can help tell us if someone was still alive at the time of the fire or had predeceased it...although I will also get a pretty good idea myself about that when I inspect the respiratory tract and lungs shortly. To be honest with you, the bullet wounds as they are, and the fact that he was found in the sitting position, it is highly likely he was dead before the fire."

"How so the sitting position, Dr Brewster?" asked Iqbal who didn't feel comfortable yet with addressing the pathologist by his first name.

"Well, virtually no-one will obediently sit still while a fire threatens to engulf them. They usually make some attempt at escape and are often found in the precubitis ... that is face down...position, perhaps crawling towards a possible exit. Being found sitting is highly suggestive of third party involvement, or extreme intoxication, although in this case we also have the bullet wound as a very good reason for his inertia."

"Aye, ok. Thanks, doctor."

"Ok. I shall begin. The external appearance is of a severely fire damaged corpse showing extreme skin burn changes and advanced carbonisation. There are bilateral below knee amputations, likely to be thermal in origin, and triple contracture flexions of the upper limb muscles giving a pugilist attitude. There is partial evisceration of the upper abdominal organs. There is a wound on the left temple in keeping with ballistic entry and a wound on the right temple consistent with ballistic exit."

Brewster then proceeded to the dissection of the corpse and also managed to obtain some spinal fluid for testing. He spoke throughout mainly for the benefit of his voice activated dictation system, but it also doubled as a useful commentary for the visiting detectives.

The main finding, which hadn't already been documented either by the PMCT or external assessment, was a lack of soot in the respiratory airways and a lack of fluid in the lungs, both indicating death took place before the fire.

"Any questions from the gallery?"

A slight hiss of static suggested one was forthcoming.

"Any estimate of time of death?" enquired Bankhurst.

"It's actually notoriously difficult in severe fire damaged bodies. Body temperature and rigor mortis are unhelpful and the eyeballs are completely destroyed so we can't get any ocular fluid to check potassium levels. I'll have a closer look at the stomach contents to see if that might throw any light on things."

"Can you tell if the shot was close range or further away?" asked Iqbal.

"Again, that's difficult because of the severe carbonisation. Difficult to assess for any powder burns."

"Any thoughts on the entry and exit wounds?"

"Side on shot might perhaps indicate a surprise attack, or that the shooter knew the deceased and couldn't look him in the eye when he shot him...but then again that's probably more your department, detective."

"Aye, fair point, Doc," agreed Iqbal.

When the detectives arrived back at the MIT room there was a message for Bankhurst to attend a meeting at 4pm with "senior staff".

She wasn't altogether surprised, given the latest developments, by the missive. The further murder, this time also with firearm involvement, not to mention the fact that once again the suspect seemed to be one step ahead of the MIT, would not sit well with higher command.

She was, however, a little surprised, when she entered the door of DCI Anderson's office at the appointed time to find, somewhat cramped in the relatively small space, DCI Anderson, Superintendent MacNiven, Chief Superintendent McCulloch and IT specialist Neil Jardine.

Her face betrayed the fact that she was slightly taken aback and Anderson, as perceptive as ever, moved quickly to quell any anxiety.

"Don't worry, Lily, this isn't a lynching squad!"

"Thanks, Sir. I wasn't expecting quite this big a gathering."

"I'm sure you must have been expecting **some** form of meeting DI Bankhurst," sneered MacNiven.

"Of course, Sir. If I hadn't received the message I would definitely have been seeking senior staff guidance."

Keep calm Lily, keep calm she told herself internally.

"I'm sure you can see why we're concerned, DI Bankhurst," added McCulloch.

"Indeed, Sir."

Despite indicating her understanding he proceeded to tell her anyway.

"This is now the fourth murder...that we're aware of...in this current spree. There's obviously been an escalation too involving firearms and arson and, on the face of it at least, possible intra-cell homicide."

"If that wasn't bad enough, and this is where it becomes deeply worrying, there is now every reason to believe that the suspects have inside knowledge informing their decisions and actions."

"Indeed, Sir," agreed Bankhurst once again.

"Now it doesn't take a genius," continued McCulloch, "to deduce that either we have someone on our team involved, passing contemporaneous information directly to the suspects, or they are hacking our system. That's why I asked Neil Jardine to attend the meeting."

He nodded at Jardine indicating it was his moment to contribute which he duly did after clearing his throat slightly.

"Thanks, Chief Superintendent McCulloch. We know already that at least one of the suspects has relatively advanced IT knowledge in that they are comfortable navigating the dark web and may well have hacked the RSPCA and similar websites trawling for potential victims.

It's not a huge leap to consider the possibility they could have penetrated our system defences. As I'm sure I don't have to remind you, as users of the system, that HOLMES is frequently prone to running slow, if not actually crashing. Budgets, as ever, are tight and we sometimes have to make difficult decisions on what percentage of the resource is spent on high end hardware and software, or what might be ring fenced for quality firewalls. The two are sometimes mutually exclusive. Organised Crime, and other groups, are not subject to the same budgetary restrictions that we are, and can be in the vanguard of IT developments. It is not inconceivable that their abilities could outstrip our defences at any given point in time."

"Is it possible to check for any breeches?" enquired Anderson.

"We can try, but they may not always be detectable. What we can do is make sure our systems are as robust as they can be. We'll check for any available patches or updates and make sure they're installed ASAP."

"I shouldn't say this perhaps but if we did find any evidence of a breech or breeches, it would certainly strengthen our hand in future budgetary negotiations."

"Mm, well…that's a discussion for another day, Neil," countered McCulloch, before continuing, "the other scenario, which is perhaps even less palatable, is that one of our own is directly involved."

"I've put together a small team of, what I take to be, trusted officers to check each member of the MIT looking at their backgrounds, associates, social media behaviour etc."

"We can't ignore this any longer. DCI Tony Simpson will head the team and report directly to me. They're obviously going to have to try and do this 'hush hush' and there is no time to lose. I have tasked the team to begin this evening and they will be working 24/7."

"Understood, Sir," responded Bankhurst as she felt McCulloch's comments needed bookending.

"And another thing," added Shifty MacNiven, with what appeared to be slight glee in his voice, "we want twice daily reports from tomorrow onwards."

"Sir," accepted Bankhurst with little choice in the matter, but who also recognised scapegoat preparation when she saw it.

CHAPTER 27

January 4th

The morning had not started well. Olive, completely out of character, had been fifteen minutes late, the burden of which was inherited by Bankhurst as she set off in the morning traffic. As a result, Bankhurst missed her normal, less busy, traffic slot which only magnified the deficit such that she arrived at the MIT room ten minutes late for the morning briefing in a slightly flustered state.

Her tardiness sat uncomfortably on her shoulders, but she owned it and stood tall as she apologised to the room. Her discomfort was further heightened when she realised the overnight team had stayed on for the handover.

[5]

Without wishing to detain them any longer she quickly invited a summary of the overnight effort.

DS Hamish MacDonald had been senior officer on night duty and he wasted no time in starting a laconic response.

"The Fire service and SOCO have now been able to check the entire building, garage and vehicle. There are no further corpses, though two cans were found, which they assumed had been used to carry the accelerant.

No firearm or bullets were found.

The garage was less severely damaged, and the blue Ford van was confirmed as our vehicle of interest.

A large, partially damaged, chest freezer was found which contained no obvious human body parts, but there were two legs of lamb, some frozen chips and a bag of Marks and Spencer petit

pois."
This provoked a ripple of sniggering, but MacDonald wasn't in the mood to encourage it so he pressed on, but not before Bankhurst had noted the discerning choice of peas. Andrew would have approved.
"Of more interest was a small fireproof safe that was found under the stairs. The safe, and the content, had actually been partially damaged by the severity of the fire, but were still salvageable.
The only item in the safe was a phone."
An enthusiastic murmur spread around the room; mobile phones being pure gold for investigative teams and, even though neither the owner of the phone, nor the extent of any damage, has been determined, the potential significance of the find was fully appreciated. The possibilities were intriguing, especially as the Acquisition Department in Digital Forensics were highly skilled in extracting information from even quite severely damaged phones.

"Thanks, Hamish. That's great. I take it Digital Forensics are working on the phone?"
"Yes, Ma'am."
"What about CCTV and ANPR?"
"No CCTV near house, I'm afraid, and no 'pings' on ANPR either but, then again, we don't have any specific numbers to search for."
"Ok," responded Bankhurst as she pointed to the night team, "off you go and get some kip. Thanks."
The six strong overnight team were quick to take their leave and Bankhurst re-focussed the room.

"OK, so it looks very much like Davies has been taken out by another member, or members, of his cell. They obviously realised he had been exposed and decided to shut him up before we could get to him.
It hardly needs saying but we are clearly dealing with a ruthless

and highly dangerous adversary who is intent on covering any tracks that lead to them."

"Apart from taking out Davies, and removing his phone and laptop, the arson looks like a crude attempt at destroying forensic evidence. In their haste, however, they missed the fire safe under the stairs and the garage is less damaged than the house. We await forensics with interest."

"We need to look at every aspect of Davies's life in detail, particularly his associates. We need to interview, or re-interview, anyone connected with Davies including flatmates, friends, colleagues and family."

Grant Gilchrist is going to love that! thought Iqbal.

"I want the ANPR data to Westhill from two hours before and after the fire analysed in detail and every vehicle checked. If they've had so much as a parking ticket, I want to know about it."

"Yes, Ma'am."

"Where are the rest of the bodies?" she asked rhetorically.

"We need to find them. Thermal imaging is probably out given the time frame and winter temperatures. Let's get the cadaver trained dogs to check out the woodland areas near Kirkton of Skene."

"Can we also chase the DNA result on the CSF sample taken at the postmortem and compare it with samples from the Union Grove address. Although the odontologist was pretty sure we need to get 100% confirmation the corpse is Davies."

"Lastly, we should warn the Firearms Unit that we may need some AFOs at short notice."

Bankhurst spent ten minutes delegating various tasks before asking "Any questions?"

"When are we going to address the elephant in the room... Ma'am?" growled DS George Gillespie, leaving just enough of a pause before the 'Ma'am' to avoid any accusation of insubordination, but which nevertheless bordered on disrespectfulness.

Bankhurst did not immediately respond to the bait and took a moment to compose herself.

"OK, I assume you are referring to the fact that the suspects have an uncanny act of always being just ahead of us?"

"Aye," he replied in a rasping, almost aggressive grunt, while continuing to hold her gaze without blinking.

"There's clearly a concern that they have access to our data. Generally there's only two likely ways this could be happening and... trust me...they are **both** being looked into," retorted Bankhurst in an assertive tone.

So much for softly softly thought Bankhurst. *Never mind, they're probably thinking it anyway, and perhaps best to have it out in the open.*

Bankhurst held Gillespie's gaze for a few seconds and then looked left and right defying further comment, but there seemed to be a sudden need to inspect footwear and nothing further was forthcoming.

Satisfied that she had maintained her authority, and had an appropriate strategy moving forward, Bankhurst stood up to finish the meeting but paused when the door opened and Neil Jardine entered, raising a hand to attract her attention.

"Hi, Neil, have you got something?" she asked, trying not to sound too excited.

"Yes. We've unlocked the phone. Looks like a burner phone for emergency use. There's not much on it ...but there is one name in the contacts list... somebody called Baz."

The level of interest in the room went up a notch immediately at the apparent error from Davies.

"There's one SMS exchange with the contact who, as you might expect, has an untraceable number.".

"When was that?" enquired Bankhurst.

"Thursday 19th December."

"So, after the second Inverurie victim and before the third hanging victim?"

"Correct," confirmed Iqbal.

"Can you display it on the screen, Neil?"

"Yes...should be able to...give me a minute."

With a flurry of hands, cables and mouse clicks, Jardine soon had the SMS displayed on the smart white board.

PD: I think we need to cool it for a while.
B: No. Keep going. We have to use this window of opportunity.You know what your job is and I know mine. We just need to be strong.
PD: I don't know B. I'm getting cold feet at the moment.
B: FFS! NEVER personalise a message, even with an initial! Delete this message and destroy the phone. I'll get you a new burner. Pull yourself together and focus!"

"So, Davies never destroyed the phone. Could be carelessness perhaps... or maybe he was keeping a little insurance against his colleagues," suggested Iqbal.
"Indeed," agreed Bankhurst.
"And the 'window of opportunity' referred to could be Nowak's USA secondment?"
"Sounds possible."

"Ma'am?"
"Yes, Reflex."
"I've done a quick bit of research on the name Baz."
"Go on," invited Bankhurst.
"It can be a Muslim name, meaning Falcon, but it's also quite a common name in Poland, apparently meaning king."
"OK, thanks Reflex. Can you also do a search for any Bazes in the system and also check the electoral register for anyone living in the North East with that name. It could also be an abbreviated name for Bazil or Basil, so include them in the search too."
"Will do."
"OK, thanks everyone. Good work," said Bankhurst as she resumed closure of the meeting. As the MIT returned to concentrate on their individual tasks, Jardine leaned closer to Bankhurst and whispered.
"Can I have a wee word in private, Lily?"
He nodded to the corridor indicating a suitable venue for the conversation.

"Sure, Neil," responded Bankhurst and she followed him out through the door eager to find out what could be so sensitive as to require a private audience.

Although there was no-one else in the corridor, he resumed the conversation sotto voce.

"It's early days yet but we've got some provisional results back on our internal investigations. There's only one person on whom we've turned up anything .

"Ok... and who is that?"

"DS Sharon Baxter."

CHAPTER 28

Bankhurst felt a deep, nauseating feeling spread within her. How many times had she discussed the case with her friend Sharon Baxter both formally, within MIT meetings, and informally over lunch? Without any inclination to do so she, nevertheless, felt obliged to ask the natural follow up question.

"OK. What have you got?"

"Well, nothing too serious, but we have found a trend in 'liking' various animal welfare sites on social media over the last few years."

"Specifically?"

"Anti foie gras, anti-fox hunting and the like."

"Hardly at the radical end of the spectrum," she commented with some relief. "I probably have similar feelings myself if it comes to that."

"That's as maybe, Lily, but you haven't posted about them on-line."

Bankhurst realised that she would not have been exempt from any internal investigation, but Jardine's statement brought into sharp focus that her own life, including on-line activity, was under scrutiny. An uncomfortable prospect for anyone.

"And remember the iceberg principle," he continued, "sometimes minimal, benign conventional web activity can be associated with much greater, more radical dark web behaviour."

"OK, so where do we go from here?"

"We keep digging and have an open mind...and that applies to everybody, not just Sharon. I just thought you ought to know."

"OK, Neil. Thanks for the heads-up. Appreciate it."

Bankhurst re-entered the MIT room but was aware, in the space of two short minutes, that something had irrevocably changed. The onus of the new information weighed heavily on her, and she realised that her relationship with her best friend in the meantime could not, and would not, be the same.

She felt the need to do something. Rather than dwell on, and possibly overthink, Jardine's bulletin, she needed to focus on something; she decided to personally interview Davies's parents. Rather than seek out her 'trusted lieutenant', Iqbal, she decided to take DC Hugh MacLennan with her, recognising a potentially valuable teaching opportunity for the young detective.

Although mostly focussed on service provision, Bankhurst was also conscious of the need to be a teacher for the next generation, and she had not forgotten her own experiences of senior colleagues who had taken the time to pass on their knowledge to her. Classroom lectures were one thing, but pearls of wisdom from experienced field officers were quite another.

Davies' parents lived in the Rosehill area of Aberdeen in a typical granite two and a half bedroomed semi-detached house. Davies was the youngest of two children and, as both his parents were now in their seventieth year, Bankhurst calculated that he must have been quite a 'late' child.

She opened the gate and walked the short distance, on a slightly mossy lock-block path, to a front door flanked by two tall planters containing festive red cyclamen. She paused slightly to gather herself before ringing the bell. She could only imagine how difficult it would be to lose a child, but to have the double tragedy of finding out your own flesh and blood was also a killer would be unimaginable.

The distant sound of the bell inside the house was followed, after a few seconds, by the various subtle noises declaring someone was slowly making their way to the door.

A lock turned, the door opened and John Davies, looking five to ten years older than his given age, inspected his callers. Bankhurst introduced herself and MacLennan and, with a weary nod, Davies beckoned them inside, initially to the hall and then subsequently to the lounge where, in the bay window, stood an unlit Christmas tree, a testament to sorrow.

A red-eyed elderly looking lady, who Bankhurst took to be Isobel Davies, sat motionless in an easy chair to the left of the fireplace. Looking exhausted, Bankhurst imagined she had had precious little sleep the night before and, even if she had finally managed to close her eyes, she would have awoken only for the darkness of the night to be replaced by the reality of an even greater daytime darkness.

John Davies slumped into the mirror image chair on the other side of the fireplace opposite his wife while Bankhurst and MacLennan were offered, and took, a seat on the sofa.

Bankhurst took in her surroundings. A patterned carpet clashed, in her mind at least, with floral curtains which extended just below the window ledge on either side of the bay window.

The 1970s style furniture was tired looking and probably overdue replacement but, at the same time, was a good match for John and Isobel Davies. Photographs, proudly displayed on the walls, charted family milestones, including school classes, graduation ceremonies and marriages. Bankhurst's eyes were drawn to two, side by side, graduation photographs of Peter Davies and his sister Joanne. Proud, smiling faces giving no indication of the diverse paths they would subsequently follow.

As it turned out, the interview, and therefore the visit, was largely unrewarding, other than confirming Davies's apparently unremarkable middle class Aberdonian upbringing. Perhaps not surprisingly his parents were difficult to engage. Isobel Davies, in particular, was untalkative almost to the point of muteness, while John, although trying his best to respond to his visitors, was obviously finding it challenging, and would intermittently break down into sobs.

As a parent herself, Bankhurst was acutely aware of their pain.

With an increasing feeling that the interview was twenty four hours too early, she repeated her earlier condolences and started preparation to leave. As she passed the family photographs again, her eye was drawn to what appeared to be a final year photograph of Aberdeen High School. She scanned the faces and located a fresh faced Peter Davies in a crumpled uniform, white shirt and loosened tie. Bankhurst thought the boy next to him looked vaguely familiar, but couldn't quite place him.

"Do you know who that is, Mr Davies?"

"He dried his eyes and squinted at the photograph. Oh, that's Brian, I think - friend of Peter's. I can't remember his surname. Went off to medical school, I seem to remember."

"Ok. Thanks. I just thought I might have recognised him...but obviously not," replied Bankhurst, and she put the matter out of her mind.

The two detectives retraced their steps to the car and on the way back to the station Bankhurst tried to extract some teaching points from the bones of the visit though, in truth, she had little flesh to work with.

After a late coffee, Bankhurst circulated around the MIT room bringing herself up to date with the various strands of the investigation. She was relieved that Sharon Baxter was off site interviewing Davies's colleagues as she hadn't been looking forward to the first meeting with her friend since Jardine's exposé.

The liaison was, in fact, postponed further due to an unforeseen development as DCI Anderson appeared in the MIT room just before lunchtime and insisted Bankhurst take the afternoon off. He recognised that she had worked for three weeks with only one day off and insisted she needed to look after herself to stay fresh. He promised to personally oversee the MIT for the afternoon and made a joke about needing to keep his hand in anyway. Before she knew it, she was climbing into her car and formulating a plan for her unexpected free time. After whipping round the nearest supermarket to home, and depositing the shopping, she quickly changed into sports gear and made the short journey to her local gym. Forty minutes later, she had worked up a decent sweat on a treadmill and reached the end of her Ed Sheeran playlist. A suspicion of a dip in her blood sugar was confirmed by her Freestyle Libre meter, giving an easy excuse to treat herself to a latte and Empire biscuit in the gym cafe before heading home for a prolonged, hot shower.

She enjoyed having the luxury of more time than she would normally have in the morning to dry and straighten her hair which also afforded her an opportunity to check her social media and do a bit of surfing before Andrew appeared home with Olive. After a quick chat, and an early discharge for Olive, mother and son discussed their days and it wasn't long before the earliest aroma of chilli con carne was wafting through the house. Video games were played while tea cooked and, as usual, Andrew's superior skillset won the day.

Without realising it, Anderson's intervention had come at an opportune time for Bankhurst who felt relaxed and rejuvenated by her unexpected leisure time followed by a good night's sleep. She had no idea, as she set off for work, that she would need every ounce of energy and resolve for the day that lay ahead.

CHAPTER 29

January 5th

It started as a fairly prosaic morning. The MIT meeting revealed that, as expected, DNA testing confirmed the corpse from the fire as Davies.

Further confirmatory evidence of his involvement had come from soil samples taken from a pair of boots found in his Union Grove room. These had been analysed by a Raman spectrometer, and the pattern of minerals, elements and organic matter were a close match to the suspected locus for McRobert's Donside abduction.

ANPR data inspection from the same night had been unyielding, as were searches of nearby forests by cadaver sniffing dogs.

Similarly, fairly extensive interviewing of Davies's contacts had failed to produce any associates of interest.

The only piece of good news was that Neil Jardine and his team had, as yet, been unable to produce any further possibly incriminating evidence against Sharon Baxter, or any other member of the MIT for that matter.

Feeling a bit more positive than she had been the day before, Bankhurst decided it was time for the first coffee of the day.

DS Iqbal was holding court with a couple of colleagues at one of the desks in the MIT room. He had a knack for finding some humour in even the darkest of times and was enjoying making his fellow detectives laugh.

He noted Bankhurst returning to the room and toned down his rhetoric. The smell of her coffee drifted across the room and it put him in mind to get his own.

"What's the brew like today, Boss?"

She was just about to answer when she was interrupted by a DC from the next desk who said she had John Davies waiting on the line to speak to her.

"Just about drinkable," she replied as she made her way to pick up the handset.

Iqbal returned to finish where he left off and was vaguely aware of Bankhurst's half of the phone conversation in the background.

"Hello. DI Bankhurst here...Hello, Mr Davies...That's no problem...How can I help you?...Uhu...Uhu... I see...I see...OK, thanks for phoning, Mr Davies. That's very helpful. Appreciate it...Bye for now...Bye."

She hung up the phone and gazed into the distance for a few seconds before snapping back into focus and walking across the room to Iqbal.

"Zafir, can you hold the fort for a couple of hours? There's something I just need to check out."

"Nae problem, Boss. Anything I can help with?"

"Not just yet. Might be something or nothing. I'll let you know."

As it turned out, it was closer to lunchtime when Bankhurst appeared back in the MIT room looking slightly flushed in the face. There were two post-it messages stuck to her screen. One was to phone Genetics about DNA results from the freezer in the garage and one was to go and see Alan in Comms ASAP. She looked at both messages, appearing to weigh up her options, before starting out in the direction of the Comms office.

She gave a brief knock on the door, but had already half opened it before she heard the, "Come in," from Zimmerman.

"Hi, Alan, you wanted to see me?"

"Yes, Lily. Thanks for coming. Have a seat," he requested as he pointed, unnecessarily, to the only available chair.

Bankhurst did as bidden and waited for Zimmerman to speak, though when he did she was surprised to hear a question rather than a statement.

"How long have you known?"

"Known what?"

"Come on, Lily. Let's not play games. How long have you known?"

"Just the last couple of hours really, Alan…or should I say Baz?"

"Touché," announced Zimmerman whose expression changed to something altogether more sinister looking.

"Touché," he repeated in a lower, more resigned voice.

Bankhurst immediately realised the danger she was in. Zimmerman had confirmed her strong suspicions, and all but admitted to being part of the serial killing cell, and obviously knew the net was rapidly closing in on himself. In effect, he had nothing to lose. He was already likely to be implicated in three, or possibly four, murders; adding an extra victim might not be an onerous burden in his eyes.

Bankhurst noticed that Zimmerman's guest chair had been moved slightly from its usual position such that his not insignificant frame now stood between her and the door, blocking any attempt at escape.

A reflex release of hormone prepared her 'flight or fight' response but, as she was in no position to do either, she sat and suffered the physiological consequences of large amounts of adrenalin suddenly coursing through her circulation. Her heart pounded heavily against the inside of her chest wall, her respiratory rate accelerated, her face flushed and she felt a heightened sense of awareness.

Zimmerman detected the changes inadvertently displayed by Bankhurst and leaned over from his chair just far enough to lock the door, with an audible click, while all the while maintaining his gaze on his colleague.

"Don't even think about it," he said in a deadly serious voice, before continuing, "and don't think about shouting either."

"I just want to have a chat, Lily," explained Zimmerman, though both parties knew that the Rubicon he had crossed made that scenario highly unlikely.

After a pause, he continued, “Tell me, how did you know it was me?”

Bankhurst thought she had nothing to lose by engaging in conversation, so complied with the request.

“A school photograph…and the memory of John Davies.”

“Ah…go on, I want to hear the whole story.”

“Well, as you probably know already, I was at the Davies’ house yesterday and noticed a familiar face, apart from Peter Davies, in the Aberdeen High School final year photo. I couldn’t place the name and John Davies could only remember his first name was Brian, and that he went to medical school.”

“However, he phoned earlier to say he had remembered Brian’s surname. It won’t come as any surprise to you that it was Zimmerman.”

“And then it all started to make sense to you I suppose?”

“Indeed,” agreed Bankhurst.

“I was a bit in denial at first, but the more I thought about it the case against you was compelling.”

“In fact, right from when notification of the Inverurie heart discovery came through when we were in this very office together. You went a bit pale at the time which I presumed was due to the fact there had been a second murder but, in retrospect, you must have been shaken to the core that the heart had been discovered at all.”

“You had no way of knowing that, due to staff illness at the butcher, it had been re-frozen and stored for three weeks. As far as you were concerned, it had already gone through the system undetected.”

“Very true, Lily, that was a bit of a shock to the system.”

Bankhurst continued, “Also for some time we had a strong suspicion that the suspects were getting contemporaneous information that could only have come from Nelson Street personnel or the HOLMES system. Who better to access such information than a Comms Officer? Ready accessibility to Police reports on your computer and frequent talks, on and off the record, with investigating officers. Including myself.”

"Also, nobody would give you a second glance if you, as you often did, ghosted in at the last minute to attend an MIT update meeting. Leaning against the back wall, just appearing to do what a good Comms officer might do, keeping up to date ahead of any request for a bulletin. When, in fact, you were gleaning as much information as possible for your own agenda."

"Yes, that was pretty helpful, I have to say," responded Zimmerman.

Bankhurst felt she had a certain momentum and returned to her account of the investigation, as much to buy her some more time as to satisfy Zimmerman's curiosity.

"I did wonder briefly if you might have a brother, Brian, but it didn't take long to establish you are an only child."

"There was also something niggling at the back of my mind and I nipped into your room, when you were at coffee this morning, and checked your graduation certificate on the wall. Sure enough...Brian Alan Zimmerman. Presumably where your nickname Baz came from?"

"Indeed," confirmed Zimmerman, "rather unimaginative of my school mates, it has to be said, but better than some given to others."

"You dropped out of medical school after 2 years, but presumably not before you acquired some dissection skills. I remember Dr Brewster commented that the incisions around the heart looked almost surgical in nature."

"Quite a compliment really, I thought," he responded and then nodded to encourage Bankhurst to continue.

"I checked the station CCTV this morning and noted you left in your motorbike leathers not long after we identified the Kirkton of Skene address as a likely bolthole for Davies. You, of course, knew it was probable he would incriminate you, so you made a snap decision to take him out and destroy as much evidence as you could in the process. You presumably took the back roads to avoid ANPR cameras, and being on a bike you could make rapid progress in and out of the countryside. We have you on CCTV returning to the station about eighty minutes later giving you just enough time for the return trip, shoot Peter Davies and set the fires in the house and garage."

"A triangulation of your phone confirmed where you had been, and sniffer dogs were very interested in the carrier on the back of your bike this morning."

"I suspect if we went downstairs right now to the garage it would be highly likely we would find the gun in that carrier."

"All a bit circumstantial so far, Lily."

"Oh, but I have more."

"I suppose you got gunshot residue from my leathers?"

Bankhurst was taken aback.

"...Yes," she replied hesitantly, before continuing, "how could you possibly know that?"

"See that row of books on my shelf up there," as he nodded above Bankhurst's head inviting her to twist round and view the volumes in question.

"Yes," replied Bankhurst.

"One of them hides a motion sensitive camera, which feeds directly to my smartphone. So while I was having coffee this morning I got an alert and then watched you and a couple of the SOCO lads going over my room, including what I presumed was GSR swabbing of my leathers."

"Although I didn't understand how exactly, I knew you were on to me then. Hence my request for our little tête-á-tête to salve my curiosity, before bringing things to a closure."

Bankhurst didn't care for his choice of words, but tried not to show it.

"I have to say I'm impressed, Lily, but there is one error in your assessment."

Bankhurst waited for him to continue, but instead of saying something further, he reached down by his side and produced a rag covered package which he then placed on his desk with a dull thud. The sweet aroma of gun oil and the undeniable shape of a pistol under the cloth left no room for doubt about her misjudgement, and the implied threat that came with it.

Bankhurst swallowed hard and nodded her understanding.

She racked her brain for relevant topics that might prolong the conversation and delay what 'closure' he had in mind.

"Where on earth did this all come from, Alan?"

"It all started when I was about seven. Our neighbours used to abuse their dog, and I would sneak next door in the evenings to comfort him. I vowed then to do something about it when I grew up."

"Later at school I found out that Peter had similar views..."

"...and you hooked up with him again during your English degree, and took up from where you left off at school?"

"Yes, that's pretty much it. We're quite different in many ways but always saw eye to eye on animal welfare issues at school, and our attitudes hardened at university. Of course, after we graduated, we had to very much go under the radar in our respective jobs."

"But it's a big jump from being an animal activist to a terrorist, Alan."

A flash of anger showed in Zimmerman's eyes and his voice hardened "It's lucky there's a few of us who are willing, Lily, as traditional methods are fuck all good."

Keep him calm thought Bankhurst. *Keep him calm.*

She decided to change tack.

"Is there anyone else in your cell?"

"No. Just the two of us. Peter was always the weak link and often needed to be managed."

Including the ultimate 'management' thought Bankhurst.

"And was the whole thing more about revenge or publicising your cause?"

"Both," he replied. "We often talked about Karma. Payback for the wrongs of the animal abusers. These people deserved to pay the ultimate price for their sins. And they did."

"And the hearts placed in Wilsons...what was that all about?"

"Oh yes, that was my idea," he said with what appeared to be a

note of pride. “I’ve a couple of friends who like to give their dogs raw meat. They get cheap cuts from the local butcher including offal. A particular favourite is heart and, as there isn’t a huge human market for this organ, it’s very likely that one placed in the system will be eaten raw by a dog.”
“So,” he summarised, “strangled by a dog chain and their heart-their very soul-eaten by a dog too.The ultimate Karma.”
Zimmerman almost sounded enthusiastic.
“We knew what we were doing would be discovered eventually... although we had no intention of actually being caught ourselves. The idea, apart from the Karma, was to make it as sensationalistic as possible when it was uncovered. I deal with journalists all the time and they, especially those from the red tops, would love nothing more than a story like this. It would run for weeks and really focus attention on animal cruelty.”

Bankhurst’s mind wondered briefly as to how on earth she could have worked with Zimmerman for years without any hint of his underlying malevolence. She forced herself to refocus and keep him talking.
“Where are the remains of the rest of the bodies?”
Zimmerman hesitated, seemingly unsure whether to answer.
Bankhurst pressed on.
“Their families deserve to know.”
“They’re buried in a corner of Greymore woods, between Echt and Torphins, about six or seven miles from Kirkton of Skene.”
“So the van was a mobile abduction and kill room, and Kirkton of Skene was where the van was kept and hearts stored in the garage freezer.”
Zimmerman nodded a slow confirmation.
Bankhurst made a mental note about the location of the remains.
“What about the gun? Where does a Comms officer source a handgun?”
“Oh, that was relatively easy. Don’t forget I know every inch of this station. It didn’t take me long to hack the code of the

armoury where I knew there were still some guns left from the last armistice awaiting destruction. I just needed a decent distraction to get in and out."

He paused to give Bankhurst a chance to join the dots.

"The fire alarm!"

Zimmerman nodded his confirmation.

Bankhurst realised she was running out of conversation with Zimmerman and he had already extracted the information that he wanted from her.

She felt sweat forming on her brow and her pulse, which had settled for a while as she engaged Zimmerman in conversation, started to quicken again. Like rain drops on a window, two beads of sweat coalesced forming a small rivulet which trickled down her forehead before eventually finding the inner corner of her left eye. The saltiness of the sweat smarted her eye and made her blink.

The silence lengthened as the two colleagues continued to look at one another, the only faint noise a tick from an old fashioned wall clock. Bankhurst noticed that Zimmerman was also sweating and his respiratory rate had quickened. It was as if each was waiting for the other to make a move, but in reality Zimmerman held all the cards and only he could deal.

After what was probably only one minute, but felt like ten, he stood up and reached for the gun under the cloth. He started to sweat profusely and the hand holding the gun was shaking slightly.

"Stand up, Lily," Zimmerman ordered, to which Bankhurst complied, but not without a surge of anxiety.

"Turn around," he continued.

Bankhurst was now desperate. Thoughts of Zimmerman's cowardly shot to Davies' right temple flooded into her brain.

"For fuck's sake, Alan. You don't need to do this. Think of the years we've worked together. Think of Andrew!"

"Relax, Lily. I'm not going to shoot you. I need you for the meantime."

As he was finishing the sentence, he pulled her wrists together and she felt the cold steel and firm edge of handcuffs against her skin followed by an audible and palpable click as they were locked together.

Zimmerman then put a gag in her mouth and tied it firmly at the back of her neck.

He sat her back down while he calmly put on his bike leathers before removing the sim cards from both of their mobile phones.

He then concealed the handgun in an accessible area inside his leather jacket making sure Bankhurst saw the process and understood the implication of easy accessibility.

He picked up his helmet, an old looking coat from a wall hook and a small rucksack which he hefted over his shoulder.

"Ok. Good to go" he announced.

"As you know, Lily, not many people come down to this part of the station, and it's only a short distance from here along to the door to the carpark."

"We're going to make our way there now and go for a wee trip on my Kawasaki. Needless to say, I don't want any heroics from you. I'm so far into this now I've really got nothing to lose, so won't hesitate to take drastic action if I need to."

She wished she could speak to reassure him that she was still recovering from the trauma of believing she was just about to be shot; heroics were not on her mind. She indicated her clear understanding with an exaggerated nod of her head.

After unlocking the door, and checking the corridor, he beckoned Bankhurst to make her way along towards the external door.

"I'm right behind you," he whispered in a cold, menacing voice.

They took only a few seconds to reach the door to the carpark where Zimmerman repeated his reconnoitre, before ushering Bankhurst over to his bike.

He quickly took a spare helmet from the carrier on the back of his Kawasaki, and put it onto Bankhurst before unlocking her handcuffs. The gun from his jacket was retrieved to ensure compliance.

"Put this coat on. You'll need it for the bike ride, and where we're going after that."

"I'm leaving the cuffs off when we're on the bike. You'll need both arms to hold on to me. I wouldn't recommend letting go...it won't end well."

Bankhurst did as she was told. They were soon making swift progress through the city traffic, the bike, particularly with a determined and motivated rider, affording advantages not bestowed on four wheel vehicles.

She appreciated the modest protection offered by Zimmerman's coat, but even with it on she felt a chill penetrating her bones, especially when they left the city boundary. Freed from the shackles of urban driving, he gunned the bike up to high speed. The trees on both sides of the South Deeside Road sped past at an alarming rate.

In her younger days, and perhaps in midsummer, she might have found it exhilarating but on a bleak winter's afternoon with sleet stinging her eyes, and a desperate man in control of the motorbike, the only sensation she had was of terror.

The muscles in all four of her limbs ached as she strained to maintain her grip on both bike and biker, and it was no comfort to feel the outline of the pistol barrel under Zimmerman's leather jacket as she did so.

After following The Dee, on its south bank, for several miles, Zimmerman took a left exit and followed a windy road as it made a slow ascent.

Deeside parkland ceded to a more sparsely wooded landscape of rolling fields demarcated by fences and dry stane dykes in various states of repair. Lights from scattered farmhouses and steadings pierced the afternoon gloom, and the precipitation, at the higher altitude, was now falling as snow. A white blanket was beginning to re-form over the countryside just a few days after the last one had reluctantly disappeared.

Ten minutes later, after cresting another hilltop and beginning a descent on the other side, Bankhurst saw the twinkling lights of a coastal town in the distance .

Given the time lapsed since leaving Aberdeen, the approximate direction travelled and the size of the conurbation before her, she deduced it was likely to be Stonehaven that they were rapidly approaching. She assumed the indirect route taken by Zimmerman to the traditional seaside town was to avoid any ANPR cameras. As they passed the urban speed limit sign, she wondered what possible reason had drawn her captor there.

The answer wasn't long in coming.

CHAPTER 30

Zimmerman had reduced his speed to within the legal limit due to the worsening conditions, and a desire to avoid attracting any avoidable attention. He made steady progress along the High Street, and crossed The Carron Water, before turning left and following narrow roads down towards the harbour lights. After weaving in and out of a few old creels and buoys, he parked his Kawasaki next to a weathered looking yacht, which rose and fell noticeably despite being within the sanctuary of the inner harbour, and tethered to the dock by its hawsers.

Davaar was, in fact, a ten metre long wooden ketch, co-owned by Zimmerman and two other seafaring enthusiasts, which sailed out of Stonehaven over the clement months of the year. Even over the winter months, when the ketch rarely left the harbour, there was always some tinkering or maintenance to be done. Many weekends and days off were spent by the trio pottering around their beloved vessel.

After dismounting the relative stability of the bike, Bankhurst became aware of the buffeting sea wind which rocked her back on her heels slightly. The choppy waters within the harbour were nothing against the backdrop of an angry looking North Sea which she could still just see, despite the fading daylight, in the distance beyond the outer harbour wall. Dark, brooding waves with white crests extended as far as the eye could see into the malevolent seascape.

A shiver of panic ran down her spine as she considered the possibilities.

Had Zimmerman taken them to the yacht to pick something

up, perhaps to use it as a bolthole, or was he, and this was undoubtedly the worst case scenario in her mind, planning an escape by sea?

Zimmerman gripped her hand tightly as a means of preventing escape and also helping her to board *Davaar*. He waited until the yacht rose to its maximum height on the swell, and then assisted Bankhurst from the dockside over the gunwale and onto the small stern deck, just aft of the wheelhouse. Once aboard, he directed her to hold on to a handrail while he quickly unlocked the wheelhouse door, before bundling her inside.

"Sit over there on the floor," he ordered, sounding less like a colleague now and more like the captor he was.

Bankhurst followed the instruction and Zimmerman bent down and reattached the handcuffs, though this time her wrists were also tethered to a solid pipe on the wall of the wheelhouse.

"I'm going back to the shops for some more supplies. We'll need enough to keep us going until Norway."

Bankhurst tried to speak but the combination of gag and helmet prevented any sound being generated that was audible against the, now howling, gale.

Her anxiety levels, already fairly high, managed to find a whole new level. The thought of going to sea in rapidly worsening conditions, in an ageing yacht and with a killer, was terrifying.

She was also acutely aware that she had no insulin with her, and had already missed her lunchtime dose. Although she hadn't eaten anything since mid morning, she knew the combination of a missed insulin dose, combined with stress and dehydration, would very likely be pushing her blood sugar levels higher, a situation that would only worsen with every missed dose.

She quickly calculated in her head that, even in fair conditions, it would probably take two days to cross the North Sea to Scandinavia and, by that time, she may well be in either ketoacidosis or, indeed, a hyperglycaemic coma.

She cursed the impetuous decision that had taken her to Zimmerman's office before she had shared her discovery of his likely complicity. She thought she had been safe, as she had only just found out herself who 'Baz' was, and had no inclination that Zimmerman would be aware of this knowledge. She also took reassurance that his office was in the heart of Nelson Street Police Station, but was unaware that he, in the very same office, had a hidden motion sensitive camera; the same camera which had filmed and broadcast her covert mission, along with a SOCO team, earlier in the day.

Her colleagues were ignorant of her breakthrough, her whereabouts and perhaps whether she was even missing. She was in a desperate situation of her own making. When she analysed the potential outcomes, none of them looked appealing.

Bankhurst forced herself to focus and go back to basics.

There was just enough daylight left to illuminate the inside of the wheelhouse, and she took stock of her surroundings. She was in an approximately 2x2 metre wooden panelled space. Being tethered near the door, looking for'ard, she could see a traditional looking, eight handled, helm above and behind which was an unusual looking instrument which she took to be the binnacle. Between the binnacle, and the compass therein, and the port side of the wheelhouse were what looked like a radar screen, a radio set and various dials which she assumed were related to engine function. On the starboard side of the helm was a small door which appeared to lead to the cabin of the yacht.

She could stretch her neck just far enough to see out the bottom of the window, but had no way of attracting attention and, in any case, the harbour appeared more or less deserted. The only signs of life were lights from a small fishing boat docked at the far end.

I need a weapon! she thought.

She found herself trying to recall a film she had seen with Nicole Kidman and Sam Neil as inspiration for potential nautical weapons.

Boat hooks, flare guns, galley knives and even a harpoon gun came to mind, though the latter was quickly dismissed as an absurd likelihood on a pleasure boat in North East Scotland.
She decided she would keep her mind open to anything that might offer an advantage, but realised the first thing she would need to do would be to convince Zimmerman to release her from her handcuffs.
Although she dreaded the thought of going to sea, at least, she considered, it would strengthen her hand in any negotiation with her captor. She recalled that Zimmerman had said he still 'needed her'.
Apart from being a potential hostage, she considered that he would actually need an extra pair of hands on a yacht for an escape across the North Sea to Norway. With a potential sail of thirty-six to forty-eight hours ahead, he would need some breaks for rest and basic bodily functions. She hoped that this was part of his 'need' and that he would release her from her constraints at sea, safe in the knowledge that he was armed, had significant physical advantage over her and there was no option for her to flee.

Thirty minutes later, the sound of heavy boots landing on the stern deck heralded Zimmerman's return to *Davaar*. He was soon inside the wheelhouse and closed the door behind himself, but not before freezing air and a few snowflakes swirled into the small space making Bankhurst shiver.
Without speaking, he went below deck and reappeared a few minutes later minus his helmet and shopping, but still with full leathers on. He turned the ignition key and the yacht's engine obligingly spluttered into life at the first time of asking.
"Ok, lass, let's see what you're made of."
After a split second of confusion in Bankhurst's mind, she realised he was talking to the boat.
Zimmermann disappeared out the wheelhouse doors again and she heard his footfall fore and aft before he returned inside bringing more cold air with him. She assumed he had been

slipping the ropes and, with a sense of dread, she realised the maritime dice was now cast.

He pulled, what Bankhurst assumed was, the throttle towards him and she heard the engine revving up. Another control was being worked with his left hand and she wondered if it was the rudder. She strained her neck to see what was happening outside but despite Zimmerman's efforts, more revs and some swearing under his breath, *Davaar* seemed reluctant to leave the dockside. Although the rope attachments had been released, it was like there was some magnetic force preventing *Davaar* from cleaving itself from the pier. Bankhurst assumed the combination of swell and the strong onshore wind was trapping the ketch against the dock. She had never been more grateful to the Scottish weather.

Her gratitude was short-lived, however, as with another increase in revs, such as the engine was almost whining, and with the entire yacht shuddering, the bow slowly started releasing from the dock.

"That's my girl!" exclaimed Zimmerman.

CHAPTER 31

Jimmy Hay, the 52 year old skipper of *Ruby*, an 8 metre A913 Trefjar creel boat, was glad to have rounded the first breakwater at Stonehaven harbour into the slightly less turbulent waters beyond. Although the forecast had been poor, he had put to sea at dawn as *Ruby* had been tied up, and therefore not earning, over the Festive period. His own livelihood, and that of his sons Craig and Darren, depended on the creel boat, and they needed to start bringing in both shellfish and income. Besides, his regular customers, particularly the local high end restaurants, were clamouring for crab, langoustine and lobster.

By early afternoon, The North Sea had given up a reasonable haul of crustaceans and, mindful of the deteriorating weather, Hay had set out for home.

His sons were busy, suitably protected by oilskins, sou'westers and the ubiquitous blue rubber gloves seen in any Scottish fishing port, sorting the catch at the stern of the boat. A large, noisy squabble of seagulls swirled and swooped in the wake of the ship keen to take advantage of anything offered up by the fishermen.

As he neared the inner harbour, Hay was taken aback to see the old ketch *Davaar* making its way to the harbour exit. He was familiar with the boat having seen it many times in and around Stonehaven harbour. While he wouldn't say he *knew* the owners, he was at least on nodding terms with the three of them.

A crackling noise on the wheelhouse radio of *Davaar* heralded an incoming broadcast.

"Aye, aye. This is Jimmy Hay of *Ruby*. We've just come in. There's a four metre swell just outside the far harbour wall, and it's forecast to get up to six metres in the next couple of hours. I wouldnae advise putting to sea at the moment. Over."

Zimmermann ignored the message and looked straight ahead.

"This is *Ruby* calling. Are you receiving? Over."

Again he refused to engage.

"This is *Ruby* calling. Are you receiving? Over."

He was nothing if not tenacious, thought Bankhurst, but his persistence was not rewarded by a response from Zimmerman, and he gave up after that.

Zimmermann negotiated the relatively narrow exit from the inner harbour into the middle harbour and turned starboard into the navigation channel leading to the breakwater of the outer harbour. The North Sea lay beyond. Despite him keeping *Davaar* within the three knot port speed limit, Bankhurst felt an immediate increase in the movement of the ketch after they had left the shelter of the inner harbour, and were more exposed to the swell coming in from the North Sea.

Another burst of static on the radio followed.

"This is Stonehaven harbour master."

Zimmerman uttered some expletives, leant over and switched the radio off, at which point Bankhurst felt that another tie with the mainland, and potential safety, had been severed. A shiver went down her spine.

Suddenly, and somewhat unexpectedly, Zimmerman half turned around, while still maintaining control of the helm, and tossed a pair of small keys to Bankhurst.

"Undo your cuffs," he ordered, "and you can take your helmet and gag off too. We've got a couple of days at sea ahead of us and I'll need you to be able to communicate, and also help physically. Besides, there's nowhere for you to go now we're at sea."

Bankhurst jumped at the opportunity of relative freedom and, despite freezing fingers, managed to extricate herself from all her restraints within a couple of minutes. She wasted no time in engaging with her captor but, by now, she was not in a diplomatic mood.

"For fuck's sake, Alan. This is madness!"

"Oh ye of little faith," he replied, before continuing, "don't you listen to her lass," as he patted the superstructure of the ketch.

"Alan. You heard the *Ruby* skipper. It's crazy to go to sea in this weather!"

"No!" he shouted before continuing in a moderated voice, "what's crazy, Lily, is me staying to face a life sentence...I prefer to take my chances at sea, and in Scandinavia. Norway has a huge coastline, and is ideally suited to sailing in unnoticed."

"Alan. I'm diabetic and have no insulin with me."

"Sure you are, Lily, sure you are," he retorted sarcastically.

Bankhurst realised Zimmerman had no prior knowledge of her condition, and she had absolutely no way of proving she was actually a diabetic, far less an insulin dependent one. Her heart sank a little further down the incline it had been on for some time.

"You can go below now," he instructed. "It's about to get a bit lively up here once we get beyond the breakwater. Might be better if you lie down for a bit until you get your sea legs. I'm going to need you up here from time to time, so get a bit of rest now."

"By the way," he added, "I've removed all the knives from the galley, and any other potential weapons, so don't even think about doing anything stupid."

Bankhurst followed her instruction but, contrary to the detail, immediately set about assessing the below deck space for anything that might give her an advantage, no matter how small.

Having defaulted to her training, and risk assessed her perilous situation, she decided she would need to attempt some form of attack-sooner rather than later.

Although she had no glucose monitor with her, she could sense her blood sugar level rising. Her triad of typical primary diabetic symptoms, which traditionally indicated a deviation from good control, were tiredness, thirst and blurred vision. All were present.

Unfortunately, the non specific nature of the first two made them unhelpful, and could simply be due to physical fatigue and dehydration, but the subtle blurred vision she had noticed in the last half hour was a biological signature she recognised and respected. Left unchecked she could be dangerously ill in twenty four to thirty six hours, never mind capable of any form of offence.

Apart from concerns about her diabetes, Bankhurst thought that the further they sailed from the North East coast the less likely she would be to navigate safe passage back, if she did manage to overcome her captor and turn the ketch around. She fully realised any such journey would be fraught with danger but, nevertheless, it seemed her best option.

Dark wood panelling mirrored the wheelhouse design but the cabin was a significantly bigger area with space designated for cooking, dining and resting. A small door marked WC flanked a larger padlocked door leading for'ard. The fact that it was secured immediately caught Bankhurst's attention as worthy of further assessment. She made a mental note to come back to it.

Unfortunately, Zimmerman had done a good job of de-weaponising the cabin. She checked what appeared to be a cutlery drawer and found all knives and forks had been removed leaving behind only a few blunt looking spoons. Hidden underneath the spoons she found an old, wooden handled Lancashire swivel potato peeler, with a small point at the end for removing spud eyes.

"Better than nothing," she said to herself as she pocketed the peeler.

As she set about a thorough search of the cabin, she felt a significant increase in the movement of the ketch which began to pitch and roll on much steeper angles. Drawers and cupboards were compelled to start repeat cycles of opening and closing in response to the see-saw movement of the ketch; anything not secured rapidly ended up on the floor.

She assumed, correctly, that they were now beyond the outer

harbour wall, and at the mercy of the potentially cruel North Sea. She accelerated her search, as best she could, in the increasingly challenging conditions but, after fifteen minutes, had nothing useful to show for her efforts.

In desperation, she turned her attention to the locked door. The padlock, although small, looked beyond her capability to force, but she took some encouragement from the brackets through which the padlock was fastened. The one on the right side looked slightly loose, a suspicion confirmed when she managed to force the end of the potato peeler just underneath the rim. With a few levering actions, she created a space big enough to accommodate the barrel of the peeler, which she then proceeded to yank with all her might.

On the third attempt, a splintering noise was accompanied by a small screw being delivered into the jaws of a crack that had been created in the wood. Bankhurst winced at the noise, but it was instantly drowned out by the howling gale and cacophony of sounds now being created by the ageing ketch as she battled against the sea outside. A further pull and the bracket was released enough to allow her to slip the padlock over and open the door.

She reflexly looked behind her, but Zimmerman remained in the wheelhouse. It appeared her breech of the door had gone unnoticed.

In fact, she needn't have worried about Zimmerman as he was fully concentrated on controlling *Davaar* through mountains of turbulent water sporting white froth whipped up into peaks which then dissipated into fizzing trails. His previous experience of sailing *Davaar* was between Spring and Autumn and, even then, only if there was a reasonably favourable forecast. While he had occasionally been caught in unexpected moderate conditions, during those months, the current sea was a whole new experience for him, and demanded his full attention. The bravado exuded while leaving the inner harbour had been replaced by a hard realism, and he focussed himself on the short term task of negotiating safe passage past the looming offshore wind farm.

Meanwhile Bankhurst, satisfied that she was safe to proceed, wasted no time in clambering down the three short steps which took her into another space beneath the bow deck. She noted a power switch but resisted the temptation of extra exploratory light lest there be any escape through the superstructure alerting Zimmerman in the wheelhouse.

She was met by a strong smell of diesel and the sea. This did nothing to help her feeling of nausea which had started since the yacht had begun rolling with greater energy.

The old ketch creaked and groaned in response to the deepening swell but somehow the noisy pliancy of the yacht reassured her a little as she felt the craft was naturally rolling with, and not necessarily fighting against, the might of the sea.

Reduced light and slightly impaired vision compelled Bankhurst to use her sense of touch, as much as her sense of sight, as she explored the storage space. She could make out an assortment of ropes, chains, buoys and what looked like an old anchor before she spotted something potentially of more interest.

The backpack taken on board by Zimmerman.

It was small and light so Bankhurst took it to the door of the upstairs cabin for better illumination. Inside she found a sizeable wad of Sterling, Norwegian Krone and Euros along with two passports, closer inspection of which revealed identical photo IDs of Zimmerman, but two different identities.

A stolen ID, another purchase from the dark web no doubt.

In a separate compartment were some medications and a mobile phone which raised her hopes transiently until she realised it had no sim card inserted.

She carefully replaced the bag where she had found it and continued her search. A wooden chest contained staples such as toilet paper, soap, washing up liquid, a six pack of baked beans and a first aid kit, but nothing approaching a weapon. She was just about to give up her search when she saw a small wooden box in a dark corner of the space.

She pulled the box towards her, sprung the catch and opened the lid to reveal a Very flare gun and two rounds.

"Now **that** is what I am talking about!" she said in a whisper as she loaded a round and placed the gun inside Zimmerman's roomy jacket. A spare round was put in a pocket.

Having achieved her goal she retreated into the cabin but not before taking a smear of tar on her finger from one of the buoys. She closed the doors, carefully reassembled the padlock and bracket, and applied the tar to help disguise the splintered wood. She briefly considered proceeding immediately to a full-on wheelhouse attack, but by the time she had opened the doors and climbed up, any element of surprise would have gone. Better, she considered, to wait until she was instructed to go to the wheelhouse by Zimmerman, and take her chances then.

She sat back in the sofa-come-bunk to await her opportunity.

CHAPTER 32

Two hours later, Zimmerman had gained some confidence in handling *Davaar* in seas far heavier than he was used to, and had negotiated a way past the offshore wind farm. Now all that remained between the ketch and the Norwegian coast was the occasional ship or oil rig, both of which would be highlighted on *Davaar's* radar.

Below deck, Bankhurst had been waiting patiently for Zimmerman's summons to the wheelhouse, getting up and walking around the cabin from time to time to ward against stiffness. She had identified an almost cyclical pattern to the rhythm of the sea where, after six or seven moderate waves, there was a significantly larger one. The bow of the ship would rise higher than normal before crashing down into the sea with a bang at which point the stern of the ship would come out of the water. The noise from the propellor would reduce in volume but quicken in revs as it met little resistance from the air before digging back into the water again, accompanied by a loud deceleration of the screw, and a shudder being sent through the length of the vessel.

It was just after one such episode that the wheelhouse doors opened suddenly and Zimmerman instructed her to join him.

After checking that she knew exactly where everything was inside Zimmerman's coat she gripped the handrail tightly and climbed into the wheelhouse.

"I'm needing a toilet break," he shouted above the noise of the wind and sea.

"You'll need to control her for five minutes while I go below."

"She's on a good heading just now, and I need you to make sure she stays that way by keeping a tight hold of the wheel. Don't worry if the bow goes under water and the wash obscures your view for a few seconds. It'll clear quickly enough."

"Don't fuck it up or we'll both be drowned," he added.

"Have you got all that?"

"Yes," Bankhurst replied as she tried to think of something that would make him turn away from her and give her a chance.

"What's the best way to hold the wheel?" she shouted .

Zimmerman reflexly turned around to address the wheel.

"One hand at 10 o'clock and the other 2 o'clock".

He was in the process of demonstrating the desired position when Bankhurst took the Very pistol from inside the jacket and aimed it at his head. She had already decided the best way of disabling him would be a shot to the head and, without hesitation, she pulled the trigger..

Unfortunately, at that precise moment, the ketch lurched and the flare, instead of hitting Zimmerman's head, contrived to hit his upper back instead. Although still a powerful blow, he was relatively protected by his life jacket and motorbike leathers, and, crucially, had not been seriously disabled.

While Zimmerman was thrown forward the relatively short distance onto the wheel, the recoil of the gun and flare, being so close to the target, had propelled Bankhurst backwards the length of the wheelhouse. She cracked her head, with a sickening thud, on the yacht's superstructure.

Both parties were stunned for a few seconds while the flare took advantage of the pause to ricochet around the wheelhouse like a demented firework, before crashing through a window and following a short curve downwards into the sea, where it was immediately doused.

No sooner had the flare exited the wheelhouse than Zimmerman turned round slowly, and unsteadily, with a look of murderous intent on his face. He started reaching inside his jacket for the gun. Bankhurst had a searing pain at the back of her head and felt gushes of warm blood cascading down to her neck. Crippling waves of nausea and dizziness spread up from within her and, despite the perilous situation she was in, she felt a compelling drowsiness.

Through her altered state of consciousness, she realised she was out of options, and fate was calling her. Zimmerman was going to kill her. She thought of Andrew's smiling face, his laugh, his damp head when he was fast asleep.

The fleeting images of her son stirred deep maternal instincts. She forced herself to rally for one final effort. She instinctively retrieved the potato peeler from the outside pocket of the jacket, and gripped it as hard as she could in her right hand. Zimmerman had retrieved the gun from within his jacket and was beginning to raise the barrel. Bankhurst used what remaining power she had in her wobbly legs to move towards Zimmerman, and with a swinging arc of her right arm propelled the peeler towards his face with all her remaining might.

The offensive movement caught Zimmerman slightly off guard and he was unable to prevent the assault.

Unfortunately, Bankhurst missed her target.

Or so she thought.

The expected bony resistance did not materialise as, by utter chance, the point and barrel of the peeler had passed straight through Zimmerman's left eye and orbit, deep into the frontal lobe of his brain. In a split second, Bankhurst realised she had hit some kind of worthwhile target as Zimmerman let out a piercing scream, dropped the gun and collapsed to the floor.

He continued to scream in agony for a few seconds, while he writhed on the floor, but the sound rapidly diminished to a whimper, accompanied by a steady reduction in movement until he lay completely still and quiet. Bankhurst wasn't sure if he was dead or not but either way she had achieved her goal of disabling him, albeit not by her intended method.

She didn't have time to dwell on her captor as she had problems of her own. After her final attack on Zimmerman, she had collapsed backwards and lay half propped up against the wall of the wheelhouse. The pulsatile arterial bleeding had stopped, but she still had a sensation of warm blood trickling down from the left side of her scalp to her neck.

What she couldn't feel, however, was the steady trickle of blood from a left skull fracture which was also going on inside her head, between the skull and the dura layer covering her brain. Unlike the external bleeding, it had no escape route and was slowly building up a clot between her brain and skull.

As the clot expanded, the unforgiving bony skull compelled the swelling to press inwardly towards the brain, and the subsequent compression of the left cerebral hemisphere was slowly but surely compromising its function.

Bankhurst realised something was wrong when she tried, after a few minutes' rest, to reload the flare gun. After a struggle, and using both hands, she managed to insert the second flare but when she tried to raise the pistol and fire it through the broken window into the sky her right hand would not follow the instruction she thought she was sending from her brain.

Unable to process exactly what was happening, she switched to her left hand, and seconds later had to absorb the recoil from the gun for the second time in a few minutes. On this occasion, however, she was able to observe a satisfactory result as the flare climbed high and bright into the night sky in a perfect parabola.

Bankhurst collapsed back on the wheelhouse floor and looked at Zimmerman whose remaining, lifeless eye, with a large fixed pupil, confirmed he was dead. She knew she had to try to get up and regain control of the helm, but her body would not cooperate. She couldn't grip anything with her right hand and she was now also struggling to move her right leg.

The uncontrolled yacht yawed violently about its central axis, as it was hit broadsides by a large wave, sending it into a dangerous spin.

Bankhurst's pounding headache worsened and the movement of the yacht rapidly added severe nausea and vertigo to her symptom burden. She rolled over onto her side and vomited copiously. Exhausted, she lay her head down on the wheelhouse floor and it was almost a relief to allow the blackness and silence of unconsciousness slowly wash over her.

The waves outside the helpless craft hissed, spat and growled as the unforgiving North Sea prepared to accept another two souls onto the *lost at sea* register.

CHAPTER 33

13 DOWN was proving difficult.

Hairstyle for workers? (7 letters).

Donald Calvert was duty manager in the control room of Ben Gullion, an oil and gas rig in the Forties section of the North Sea. He had joined the rig on his latest rotation two days previously, but had still not managed to complete the crossword in the newspaper he had taken with him. As he started a tea break, he picked the paper up for what he promised himself would be his last attempt at completion before consigning it to the bin.

Inspiration continued to elude him and he wondered if a biscuit might help. Not that he needed an excuse to visit the biscuit box, as his waist would testify.

As he was stretching over to the tin, he thought he saw, out of the corner of his eye, a brief flash in the darkness of the North Sea. It was gone almost as quickly as it had appeared, and he wondered if his eyes had played a trick on him. He peered into the inky darkness outside the control room but saw nothing else.

He returned his focus to the crossword until, a few minutes later, a very definite and unmistakable illumination shot skyward before beginning a slow luminescent descent.

"Fuck me," he said as he reached for the rig-to-shore phone.

Within a minute, he had been patched through to the Coastguard Operation Centre.

"Hello. This is Donald Calvert, rig manager of Ben Gullion, Fortes field."

"Hello. Stephen McClure. Coastguard Control Aberdeen. Go ahead."
"I've just seen a distress flare about a couple of miles from our rig. It's a wild night outside. Somebody's obviously in trouble."
"Understood," replied McClure, "any radio activity?"
"No. Nothing."
"Any other lights visible?"
"Again. Negative." replied Calvert.
"I've got the coordinates of your rig on our map. In which direction was the flare?"
"Southwest."
"Understood. As it happens we've a Fast Patrol Boat already at sea searching for a ketch out of Stonehaven."
Neither men knew that the two incidents were related but when the message was relayed through to the captain of the Fast Patrol Boat, a detective sergeant standing alongside him on the bridge, with a strong Glaswegian accent, immediately commented, "I bet Lily Bankhurst had something to do with that, by the way."

Earlier in the afternoon, DS Zafar Iqbal's curiosity about his DI's behaviour that morning had turned into concern when she couldn't be located at lunchtime, and failed to turn up for the afternoon briefing. She was nowhere to be found in the station and her phone was off.
Iqbal recalled that it seemed to be a phone call from Davies' father that had triggered Bankhurst to go off site for a few hours, before returning to the station late morning, looking flushed.
He phoned John Davies who repeated what information he had already passed to Bankhurst earlier in the day. Alarm bells duly rang inside Iqbal's brain.
He quickly alerted those present in the MIT room before sprinting down to Zimmerman's office, but there was no sign of the duty Comms officer nor his motorbike leathers.
By the time he returned to the MIT room both DCI Anderson and Superintendent MacNiven had been summoned, as he had requested. He explained the situation to his senior

officers. Anderson was immediately concerned for Bankhurst's wellbeing while MacNiven reserved his angst for what the development would do to the reputation of A Division - in particular himself.

"Ok, we need all hands on deck for this," announced Anderson in a decisive and commanding tone, not realising at the time the appropriateness of his maritime idiom.

"I want an immediate APB, including photographs of Zimmerman, to the whole of Police Scotland, and all airports, bus stations and ports."

"Check ANPR for all city exits for Zimmerman's plate."

"Check Nelson Street CCTV for any footage of them leaving the station."

"Look for any activity on his cards."

"Yes, Boss" came the unanimous and determined response from the MIT.

It took less than an hour before some good fortune provided a breakthrough when the Stonehaven harbour master was surprised to find a familiar face looking out at him when he opened the APB e-mail.

Zimmerman and the co-owners of *Davaar* were well known in the harbour, and adjacent hostelries, and the harbour master had spoken to him in person on several occasions, both professionally and socially.

He phoned the emergency contact number and reported that *Davaar*, possibly skippered by Zimmerman, had put to sea earlier in the afternoon and had not responded to radio broadcasts from himself and a local creel boat skipper. Both were concerned about the adverse weather conditions.

The *Resolute*, a coastguard FPB based in Aberdeen, had been scrambled shortly afterwards but not before Iqbal, after some terse negotiations between senior Police and Coastguard staff, had secured a berth on board.

The *Resolute*, travelling as fast as her engines and the weather conditions allowed, took forty minutes to reach the area of the likely flare launch. For the last twenty minutes of her journey, a small, stationary blip had appeared on the radar screen on the bridge as they closed rapidly on their likely target.

As *Resolute* approached *Davaar,* there appeared to be no signs of life on board and the ketch was out of control.

Iqbal feared the worst.

The four metre swell made any attempt at boarding hazardous, especially as no cooperation was anticipated from the stricken yacht.

Nevertheless, after some encouragement from Iqbal, the FBA captain slowly positioned *Resolute* on the windward side of *Davaar* and, keeping the ketch within the lee of his own ship, created the optimal environment for a boarding.

Two of the coastguard crew, one of whom had basic medical training, accepted the challenge and managed to board *Davaar* before quickly disappearing out of sight into the wheelhouse.

Crackle. Crackle. The radio came to life.

"We've got two people in the wheelhouse, Captain Watt. One dead male and one female who is unconscious with what appears to be a significant head injury."

Iqbal's heart sank and it showed in his face.

"At least she's still alive," commented Watt.

"Aye, right enough," responded Iqbal, though it was hard to be positive even for the normally upbeat detective.

"Is the rest of the ship clear?" enquired Watt.

"Yes, Sir."

"OK. It will probably be too risky to try transferring the injured party to the ship. Let's secure a rope and we'll start towing *Davaar,* which at least will give us a little control."

"Oh, there's one more thing," added the medic, "I've just had a wee look at DI Bankhurst when I was putting her in the recovery position. Her left pupil is significantly bigger than her right."

This didn't sound like good news on the bridge of *Resolute,* a suspicion confirmed after a ship to shore call to Accident and Emergency at Aberdeen Royal Infirmary. The duty registrar immediately suggested that internal bleeding causing clot formation, and pressure on the brain, was highly likely, and that urgent surgery was required to prevent serious brain damage, or death.

Captain Watt relayed the information to Coastguard Control. Twenty minutes later, the scrambled helicopter was hovering over *Davaar.*

Extraction techniques, honed by multiple rehearsals and numerous actual rescues, soon had Bankhurst being airlifted to the chopper on a cradle and, even before the door was fully closed, the pilot had started the journey back to Aberdeen at high speed.

The low cloud and poor visibility meant much of the flight was done on instruments only, and the pilot was slightly relieved to finally see the large H on the helipad at Aberdeen Royal Infirmary.

A reception party whisked the deeply unconscious detective into the Accident and Emergency Resuscitation Room, where a rapid clinical assessment was followed by an equally rapid head CT scan in the adjacent radiology suite. An extradural clot the size of an apricot was pressing on the left hand side of Bankhurst's brain.

With no time to lose, and no anaesthetic required, the Neurosurgery registrar, after a quick shave of the skull and a token splash of iodine on the skin, drilled a hole straight through Bankhurst's left temple. Almost immediately, there was a gush of a semi-liquid clot as it gratefully accepted the drainage portal created, and dribbled down the green drape that had been hastily pinned around her head and neck.

The surgical registrar nodded his satisfaction.

"OK. Let's get her up to ITU. She'll be monitored closely during the night and, if there's no deterioration, we'll repeat the CT in the morning to make sure there hasn't been any further bleeding. Hopefully she won't need a craniotomy."

Although not out of the woods by a long chalk, he knew he had given his patient a reasonable chance of surviving. He was much less sure, however, what long term neurological sequelae she might have.

Time would tell.

CHAPTER 34

January 7th

Images came and went.
Snippets of conversations.
More images. Andrew. Other family members. Friends.
Even her ex, *for God's sake* she thought. *Well he can fuck off!*
A familiar scent. A perfume. No.....an aftershave.
Bankhurst felt her eyelids flickering for a few seconds, before she opened them fully and managed to bring Iqbal into focus.

"There she is! Gaun yersel, Boss. About time you showed up!"
Bankhurst, whose head felt like she had a massive hangover, was glad to be alive and in, what appeared to be, a hospital bed.
Flashbacks of the wheelhouse struggle began to surface.
"Where am I?" she enquired.
"Aberdeen Royal."
"What date is it?" .
"7th, Boss. You've been out of it for two days. Your family have all been here, but I sent them away for a wee break this afternoon."
Bankhurst nodded, unable to muster enough strength for another sentence.
Iqbal buzzed for the nurse who in turn, after seeing that her patient had come round, summoned the doctor.
"Hello, Lily!" the youthful looking doctor said in an overly excited greeting.
"Nice to have you with us. How are you feeling?"
"Pretty shit, if I'm honest."
"Good...speech, and sense of humour, intact!"
"Let's have a wee look at you."

Iqbal took the hint that he needed to make himself scarce.
"Ok, Boss. I'll head back to the station. Somebody has to keep them right since our leader thought fit to abandon us," he quipped.
Bankhurst responded by slowly raising her right arm, hand and upturned middle finger in a gesture to Iqbal, the medical significance of which was not lost on either the doctor, or nurse, who smiled and nodded in unison.

Epilogue

Eighteen miles west of Aberdeen, two cadaver dogs and their handlers had been working an area of remote woodland for two hours. The sergeant in charge was just about to call the dogs in for a break when he noticed one had sat bolt upright and would not move. He jogged over to the dog, who looked at him expectantly.

“Good girl, Bramble, good girl,” he said with the enthusiasm of a handler who trusted the abilities of his dog.

The black labrador licked her lips in anticipation of a treat.

ACKNOWLEDGEMENT

I would like to acknowledge Mrs Claire Milne for her help with editing, and Professor Henry Watson for proofreading. In particular, I would like to say a big thank you to my wife, Julia, for her continual encouragment, assistance with the cover design and being a sounding board for plot development.

ABOUT THE AUTHOR

Ewan Wallace

Ewan Wallace is a retired GP who lives in Aberdeen.

Printed in Dunstable, United Kingdom

78514488R00151

Zen and the Art of Formula Racing

Anita Driver

ISBN: 9798877097971

DEDICATION

This book is dedicated to the hardworking men and women of the paddock. These heroes travel the world for weeks on end, neglecting their partners, children and mental health, all so we can watch oil, crypto and energy drink ads drive in circles. Thank you for your service.

DISCLAIMER

This book was written without the involvement of Formula 1, any Formula 1 teams, or any of the drivers, team principals, or engineers mentioned and quoted in the book. All tradenames used are property of their respective owners.

CONTENTS

INTRODUCTION

Zen and the Art of Formula Racing bridges the gap between the high-octane world of Formula 1 and the tranquil realms of meditation. Through poetry, we explore the unique calmness and focus Formula 1 drivers must harness as they navigate circuits at 300 kilometres per hour. Like Zen practitioners, these athletes find clarity and peace amidst the rush, remaining composed under intense pressure and danger.

The poems found in this book contain real quotes from Formula 1 drivers and team principals. Their reflections and musings offer a glimpse into the philosophy of equanimity that is as essential on the track as it is in life. Let the verses and voices within inspire a harmony between the swift pace of existence and the grounding force of inner stillness.

"You need maximum concentration. You need to focus 100%, so everything influencing your life must be in the right place, and there can be nothing disturbing your mind."

Mika Hakkinen
Formula 1 World Champion
Zen Master

INNER PEACE

ft. Nico Hülkenberg, Kevin Magnussen

With eyes closed, but far from blind,
Seek to quiet the restless mind.

Cutting through a chaotic state,
Turn the tumult into the sedate.

Hear the pattern, a heartbeat's pace,
In the rhythm, a sacred space.

The soul becomes calm, the fears abate,
The most unsporting driver,[1] suck my balls mate.[2]

---

[1] Nico Hülkenberg, 2017 Hungarian Grand Prix
[2] Kevin Magnussen, 2017 Hungarian Grand Prix

SPRINGTIME

ft. George Russell

Awaken the soul, to morning's light,
With spring's first breath, end winter's night.

Life stirs beneath thawing ground,
Leaves turned over, hopes abound.

Green tendrils push through heavy stone,
In oneself, seeds of change sown.

Through the soil, aspirations pass,
I don't know if you can see, I've got a car right up my ass.[3]

---

[3] George Russell, 2023 Italian Grand Prix

SUNRISE
ft. Kimi Räikkönen

Through the trees, a crimson ray,
The first sign of a dawning day.

Washing over land and sea,
Weaving a golden tapestry.

Light and warmth wake the earth,
Another chance for your rebirth.

The daily ritual lets life renew,
Leave me alone, I know what to do.[4]

---

[4] Kimi Räikkönen, 2012 Abu Dhabi Grand Prix

BREATHE

ft. Yuki Tsunoda

Inhale deeply the dawn of the day,
Exhale slowly the troubles away.

Chest rising like a morning tide,
On breath's wings we smoothly glide.

Each inhale, a new beginning,
Each exhale, a sweet unspinning.

With every breath, thoughts are shook,
Fucking Perez, he fucking doesn't even look.[5]

---

[5] Yuki Tsunoda, 2021 Emilia Romagna Grand Prix

MOUNTAINS
ft. Max Verstappen

Mountains stand timeless and vast,
Against the heavens, perfectly cast.

Silent sentries, never dim,
Witness to history's every whim.

Their peaks against the starlit glow,
Stand watch over the lands below.

In their silence, thoughts fill to the brim,
Is this fucking guy blind, what the fuck is wrong with him?[6]

---

[6] Max Verstappen, 2020 Portuguese Grand Prix

MORNING DEW

ft. Valtteri Bottas

As dawn breaks, a soft light weaves,
Through silent trees, 'neath sleepy eaves.

Dewdrops cling to leaves like glass,
Mirrors of moments that quietly pass.

With each breath, fresh and new,
The mind reflects this morning dew.

The world awakens, gentle and proper,
Why the fuck did no one listen when I said this is a two-stopper?[7]

---

[7] Valtteri Bottas, 2021 French Grand Prix

RIVERS OF THOUGHT

ft. Sebastian Vettel

Through the mind, thoughts do flow,
Carving canyons, deep and slow.

Ideas swirl in eddies and bends,
Where the soul starts and reality ends.

In this stream wisdom is caught,
Ideas learned that cannot be taught.

Meandering wide, embracing the new,
What a stupid action, I'm going home, fuck you.[8]

---

[8] Sebastian Vettel, 2010 Turkish Grand Prix

RAINDROP

ft. Toto Wolff

A lone raindrop begins its descent,
A silvery globe from heaven sent.

It graces leaves and kisses flowers,
Dancing through the stormy hours.

It joins its kin in a rhythmic cascade,
Drumming the rooftop, a serenade played.

The raindrop lands, no glitz or spotlight,
No Michael no, that was so not right.[9]

---

[9] Toto Wolff, 2021 Abu Dhabi Grand Prix

WHISPERING WIND

ft. Charles Leclerc

The wind speaks in hushes and sighs,
A gentle murmur beneath the skies.

It carries tales from far and wide,
In every gust, a story implied.

In its breath, a mindful bind,
A caress that soothes the troubled mind.

It whispers wisdom, pure and lucid,
Magnussen is and always will be stupid.[10]

---

[10] Charles Leclerc, 2018 Japanese Grand Prix

CAMPFIRE

ft. George Russell

Beneath the canopy of swaying pines,
Flames flicker, illuminating minds.

The warmth and light are fire's gift,
Walls melt away, a disappearing rift.

Open to the world like a flower in bloom,
Kinship and stars replace feelings of doom.

The ashes smoulder, eyes ready to shut,
What the fuck was he doing, is he a fucking prick or what?[11]

---

[11] George Russell, 2021 Emilia Romagna Grand Prix

CHERRY BLOSSOM

ft. Kimi Räikkönen

A burst of colour against the sky,
An indication that spring is nigh.

The pedals drop, in the wind they dance,
Like pink snow, the sight enchants.

Savour the moment in time and space,
Before it absconds without a trace.

Find wonder and bliss in nature's whim,
That fucking idiot, I want to hit him when I see him.[12]

---

[12] Kimi Räikkönen, 2013 Monaco Grand Prix

SILENCE

ft. Lando Norris

The clatter fades, the echoes cease,
In their absence arrives a release.

Take a breath, put thoughts on hold,
A moment of peace begins to unfold.

The calm envelops, a gentle shroud,
A tranquil mind, no longer loud.

Consumed by silence, nothing intruding,
What the fuck is this dickhead doing?[13]

---

[13] Lando Norris, 2020 Portuguese Grand Prix

GROUND

ft. Charles Leclerc

Beneath our soles, the earth holds tight,
To support the trees with all their might.

The fertile ground upon which we stroll,
Has provided abundance, since days of old.

Radiating warmth, protecting seeds,
From soil's bounty, all life feeds.

When rainwater pools, the dirt can get mucky,
Why the fuck am I so unlucky?[14]

---

[14] Charles Leclerc, 2023 Sao Paulo Grand Prix

BONSAI

ft. Guenther Steiner

In the art of Bonsai, find life's mirror,
With careful snips, the vision grows clearer.

Each branch a choice, each leaf a chance,
Life refined by the bonsai's dance.

Twisting limbs to shape and mould,
Stories of resilience silently told.

Roots gripping tight, in the earth's core,
He doesn't do that to me, he does not fok smash my door.[15]

---

[15] Guenther Steiner, 2019 British Grand Prix

LOTUS POND

ft. Christian Horner

Hidden deep in a garden green,
Lies a peaceful, reflective scene.

Tranquil, still, clear and calm,
A picture of nature, a healing balm.

On the surface, lotus blooms rise,
Reaching up toward azure skies.

Petals unfold with beauty and grace,
That nearly killed our driver, I want him out of this fucking race.[16]

---

[16] Christian Horner, 2021 British Grand Prix

BAMBOO GROVE

ft. Lewis Hamilton

In a grove where bamboo abounds,
The rustle of leaves are the only sounds.

Stalks reach high, swaying in the breeze,
The rhythmic movements put one at ease.

Pandas feed, mice find shade,
The bamboo provides all creatures aid.

So much can come from just one tree,
I can't believe you guys fucking screwed me.[17]

---

[17] Lewis Hamilton, 2022 Dutch Grand Prix

THE STORIES BEHIND THE POEMS

INNER PEACE

ft. Nico Hülkenberg and Kevin Magnussen
2017 Hungarian Grand Prix

During the Hungarian Grand Prix, Renault driver Nico Hülkenberg and Haas driver Kevin Magnussen battled, culminating in Magnussen forcing Hülkenberg off the track and into the grass. Hülkenberg later confronted Magnussen in the media pen, criticizing his aggressive driving style. Magnussen was mid-interview with a reporter when Hülkenberg interjected, leading the Haas driver to retort with a now-infamous line.

Nico Hülkenberg: "Once again, the most unsporting driver on the grid."

Kevin Magnussen: "Suck my balls, mate!"

Hülkenberg and Magnussen would later put the incident behind them, developing a friendly rapport and productive working relationship as teammates at Haas F1 Team in 2023.

SPRINGTIME

ft. George Russell
2023 Italian Grand Prix

George Russell was having a sensational weekend in Monza. The British driver qualified fourth, just ahead of Red Bull driver Sergio Perez. On lap 9 of the race, Russell was instructed by his engineer to manage his tyres. This idea didn't sit well with the Mercedes driver, who could see Perez rapidly approaching in his mirrors.

Engineer: "And George, suggest more management at six, turn six."

George Russell: "I don't know if you can see, I've got a car right up my ass!"

Ultimately, Russell was unable to keep the Red Bull behind him, finishing P5; three positions behind Perez.

SUNRISE

ft. Kimi Räikkönen

2012 Abu Dhabi Grand Prix

Finnish driver Kimi Räikkönen has always been known as a man of few words. However, during the 2012 season, Räikkönen might have wished for his engineer to display a similar quality.

During the Belgian Grand Prix, Räikkönen snapped at his engineer to quiet down on the radio.

Engineer: "We are currently under threat from Michael behind. We need to get past Hülkenberg."

Kimi Räikkönen: "I know what I'm doing, so just be quiet!"

Several races later in Abu Dhabi, Räikkönen would again admonish his engineer for talking too much.

Engineer: "OK Kimi, next car behind you is Alonso. I'll keep you updated on the gap. I'll keep you updated on the pace."

Kimi Räikkönen: "Just leave me alone, I know what to do!"

Later in the race, Räikkönen again found himself annoyed with his engineer's radio chatter.

Engineer: "OK Kimi, we need to keep working all four tyres, please. Keep working all four tyres."

Kimi Räikkönen: "Yes, yes, yes, yes, I'm doing all the time! You don't have to remind every 10 seconds!"

Räikkönen proved that he did indeed know what he was doing by winning the grand prix.

His radio messages from that day became legendary. Ten years later, Räikkönen would return to Abu Dhabi for his final Formula 1 race. To say goodbye to the Iceman, Räikkönen's team added a decal to his Alfa Romeo which read "Dear Kimi, we will leave you alone now."

BREATHE

ft. Yuki Tsunoda
2021 Emilia Romagna Grand Prix

In the second race of his rookie season, Yuki Tsunoda was representing Scuderia Alpha Tauri in the team's home race at Imola. Unfortunately, he had a rough start to the weekend.

During free practice 3, Tsunoda found himself on a hot lap, only to be blocked by the Red Bull of Sergio Perez. Despite it only being practice, Tsunoda was incensed and proceeded to air his displeasure on the team radio.

Yuki Tsunoda: "Fucking Perez! He fucking doesn't even look! He's a fucking cunt!"

Tsunoda's woes continued in qualifying. He crashed out of Q1 without setting a timed lap and would have to start the grand prix from the back of the grid. While Tsunoda was able to gain eight positions over the course of the race, he still finished outside the points in P12.

MOUNTAINS

ft. Max Verstappen
2020 Portuguese Grand Prix

During free practice 2 in Portugal, Red Bull driver Max Verstappen attempted to get past the Racing Point of Lance Stroll. The two would make contact, sending Stroll off into the gravel.

In Verstappen's estimation, Stroll, who had just finished a hot lap, should have moved out of his way. Instead, Stroll stayed on the racing line and opened his DRS; an indication that he was not slowing down to yield to the Red Bull behind him.

After the incident, Verstappen took to the radio to complain, using derogatory and offensive language to lambaste Stroll.

Max Verstappen: "Is this fucking guy blind? What the fuck is wrong with him? Jesus Christ! What a r****d! I have damage. What a m****l! I swear."

Engineer: "Okay, box. Red flags and recharge on, please."

Max Verstappen: "He fucks his lap, I'm trying to prepare my lap, and he just fucks my lap by just opening DRS and staying on the normal line! No respect. But yeah, doesn't matter."

Verstappen would later say it's "not my problem" if people are offended by his words on the radio.

MORNING DEW

ft. Valtteri Bottas
2021 French Grand Prix

During the 2021 race at Circuit Paul Ricard, Mercedes driver Valtteri Bottas was experiencing high tyre degradation. On the team radio, Bottas informed his team that he thought a two-stop strategy would be best.

Despite Bottas warning the team several more times about the poor condition of his tyres, the team opted to keep him on a one-stop strategy. This ended up being a mistake.

Bottas was left on severely degraded tyres, making him extremely vulnerable to the cars behind. After being passed by Red Bull's Max Verstappen, and just before being passed by the other Red Bull of Sergio Perez, Bottas questioned the team's decision on the radio.

Valtteri Bottas: "Why the fuck did no one listen to me when I say it's going to be a two-stopper? Fucking hell!"

Engineer: "We've got Perez who's on a one (stop strategy). Perez at 1.9."

Valtteri Bottas: "My tyres are fucking finished!"

After the race, Bottas's engineer would tersely express regret for the blunder by saying "Apologies about that."

RIVERS OF THOUGHT

ft. Sebastian Vettel
2010 Turkish Grand Prix

Entering round 7 of the 2010 season, Red Bull Racing teammates Sebastian Vettel and Mark Webber were both in close contention for the World Driver's Championship.

During the race at Istanbul Park, Vettel made a move to pass the race-leading Webber, pulling alongside his teammate as they charged down the straight. As the two drivers entered the braking zone for the next corner, Vettel appeared to drift right, colliding with his teammate. Vettel was sent off into the gravel and was not happy about it.

Sebastian Vettel: "Fuck! What the fuck are we doing here? What a stupid action! I'm going home! Fuck you!"

The incident ended Vettel's race and caused Webber to lose two positions, costing him the victory.

RAINDROP

ft. Toto Wolff

2021 Abu Dhabi Grand Prix

The 2021 Abu Dhabi Grand Prix was one of the most anticipated races in the history of Formula 1. For the first time in 47 years, there was a tie for first place in the World Driver's Championship entering the final race of the season. Bitter rivals Lewis Hamilton and Max Verstappen were set for an epic winner-take-all battle for the championship.

The race started with intrigue and anticipation but ended with controversy. A late safety car allowed Verstappen to close the 12-second lead held by Hamilton in the final laps of the race. However, there were numerous lapped cars between Hamilton and Verstappen as they followed the safety car.

Race director Michael Masi then made a decision that would later cost him his job. He could have instructed all lapped cars to unlap themselves, but the time that would have taken would have likely caused the race to end under the safety car. Instead, Masi made the unusual call to instruct only the cars between Hamilton and Verstappen to unlap themselves. This brought Verstappen directly behind Hamilton with time for one final lap of racing.

With one lap to determine the race winner and world champion, Verstappen used his tyre advantage to pass Hamilton. Mercedees team principal Toto Wolff immediately got on the radio with race director Masi to express his displeasure.

Toto Wolff: "Michael this isn't right! Michael, no, no Michael, that was so not right!"

Michael Masi: "Go ahead, Toto."

Toto Wolff: "You need to reinstate the lap before! That's not right!"

Michael Masi: "Toto?"

Toto Wolff: "Yes?"

Michael Masi: "It's called a motor race, okay?"

Toto Wolff: "Sorry?"

Michael Masi: "We went car racing."

Verstappen would win the race and the World Driver's Championship, leaving Hamilton and his fans feeling cheated.

WHISPERING WIND

ft. Charles Leclerc
2018 Japanese Grand Prix

In lap four of the race at Suzuka, Sauber driver Charles Leclerc attacked the Haas of Kevin Magnussen down the main straight.

As Leclerc pulled out from Magnussen's slipstream to attempt an overtake, the Haas driver defended hard. He moved right to block Leclerc's Sauber, causing Leclerc to rear end him. Leclerc would take to the team radio to insult the Danish driver.

Charles Leclerc: "Magnussen is and always will be stupid! It's a fact."

Magnussen would suffer a puncture and body damage, which led to his retirement a few laps later. Leclerc would pit to replace a broken front wing and rejoin the race. However, 35 laps later, the Sauber driver would retire due to a mechanical issue.

CAMPFIRE

ft. George Russell
2021 Emilia Romagna Grand Prix

On a damp day at Imola, Williams Racing driver George Russell had the Mercedes of Valtteri Bottas in his sights. As the two cars raced down the high-speed approach to the Tamburello Chicane, Russell made his move and pulled alongside Bottas.

Bottas edged wide to the right, giving Russell just enough space to stay on track. Russell panicked and veered to the right, dipping his right tyres into the wet grass. This caused Russell to lose traction and spin into Bottas, ending both of their races in a dangerous, high-velocity crash.

Russell complained to his team on the radio.

George Russell: "What the fuck was he doing? Honestly! Is he a fucking prick or what?"

Bottas was equally upset.

Valtteri Bottas: "What a cunt!"

Russell climbed out of his car and walked over to Bottas's Mercedes. As Russell approached, Bottas flipped him the bird. Russell responded by smacking Bottas on his helmet before walking away.

CHERRY BLOSSOM

ft. Kimi Räikkönen
2013 Monaco Grand Prix

On the narrow streets of Monte Carlo, overtaking is no easy task. In 2013, McLaren's Sergio Perez learned this the hard way. The Mexican driver would make several ill-fated overtaking attempts, all taking place at the chicane.

In two very similar incidents, Perez attempted to pass Ferrari's Fernando Alonso and later the Lotus of Kimi Räikkönen. Both overtaking attempts ended with Perez forcing his rivals to leave the track and cut the chicane to avoid a collision.

In a radio message to his team, Räikkönen accurately foreshadowed the events that would later unfold in the race.

Kimi Räikkönen: "That idiot will crash into me if I wouldn't have gone straight!"

On lap 69, Perez again made an overtaking attempt on Räikkönen at the chicane. This time Räikkönen went straight and did not cut the chicane. It resulted in the two cars making contact, just as Räikkönen had predicted.

Kimi Räikkönen: "That fucking idiot! I want to hit him when I see him!"

The incident would result in a puncture for Räikkönen, but the Finnish driver was able to complete the race, finishing P10.

Perez didn't fare as well. Several laps after his contact with Räikkönen, damage to his car forced him to retire.

SILENCE

ft. Lando Norris
2020 Portuguese Grand Prix

Coming down the main straight at Portimão, Racing Point driver Lance Stroll attempted an overtake on McLaren's Lando Norris. As the two racers approached turn 1, Stroll made a move to the outside, edging just ahead of Norris. Stroll then turned into the corner before he was clear of Norris, resulting in contact between the two cars.

Stroll ended up spinning into the gravel. Norris managed to stay on track, but not without picking up some race-altering damage.

Lando Norris: "What the fuck is this dickhead doing? I got damage, I need to box. I got wing damage. Cunt!"

Stroll was assessed a time penalty for causing the collision. His race would end in retirement when he later collided with Max Verstappen. Norris ended up finishing outside the points in P13, in part due to damage caused by the incident with Stroll.

GROUND

ft. Charles Leclerc
2023 Sao Paulo Grand Prix

Charles Leclerc's tenure at Ferrari has been full of heartbreak, and his race in Brazil during the 2023 season was no exception.

An issue with his car during the formation lap caused Leclerc to lose the rear end and slam into the wall. His race was over before it had even begun.

Charles Leclerc: "No! No, I lost the hydraulics. Why the fuck am I so unlucky? Why the fuck am I so unlucky? No hydraulic inside the car. For fuck's sake, still! The engine shut off. Why am I so unlucky? Oh my god! Oh my fucking god!"

Engineer: "Sorry about that."

Adding to the disappointment was the fact that Leclerc had qualified second for the race, which should have given him a great chance at victory. It was later determined that the reason for his crash was an electrical issue that caused the engine to shut off.

BONSAI

ft. Guenther Steiner
2019 British Grand Prix

The 2019 race at Silverstone was a day to forget for the Haas F1 Team and their team principal Guenther Steiner. The team had started the season slowly, and desperately needed to score points.

However, the two Haas drivers, Kevin Magnussen and Romain Grosjean, ended their races early after colliding on lap 1. Both Haas cars suffered punctures, but were able to limp to the garage for new tyres. While Magnussen and Grosjean's cars returned to the race, both were eventually retired due to the damage suffered in their collision.

After the race, the two Haas drivers were summoned to their boss's office. Normally these discussions are private, but the microphones of Netflix's *Drive to Survive* docuseries were on hand to capture everything.

Steiner laid into his drivers for being reckless and selfish and threatened to replace them if they didn't knock it off. When the meeting ended, the drivers exited Steiner's office with Magnussen slamming the door behind them.

Guenther Steiner: "What was that?"

Ayao Komatsu (Haas F1 Director of Engineering): "Kevin just fucking smashed the door, that's not acceptable."

Guenther Steiner: "Foking hell! He's not foking doing that to me, you know? He does NOT fok smash my door! Tell him that!"

LOTUS POND

ft. Christian Horner
2021 British Grand Prix

The 2021 Formula 1 season featured an epic battle between Max Verstappen and Lewis Hamilton for the World Driver's Championship. Entering the race at Silverstone, Hamilton was keen for a race win. Not only was it his home race, but he found himself in a hole after Verstappen had won the previous three races.

On Sunday, Verstappen and Hamilton lined up side-by-side on the front row of the grid, but their duel was cut short by a lap one incident. Entering one of the fastest corners on the Formula 1 calendar, Copse Corner, Hamilton attempted to overtake Verstappen. Hamilton dove up the inside, pulling significantly alongside the Red Bull. When Verstappen turned in, his rear right tyre made contact with Hamilton's front left.

While the contact was light, it was enough to unsettle the Red Bull and send Verstappen flying off the track. His car would slide through the gravel before slamming into the barrier in a massive 51G impact.

On the pit wall, Netflix's *Drive to Survive* cameras picked up Red Bull team principal Christian Horner expressing his frustration with Hamilton's driving.

Christian Horner: "That nearly fucking killed our driver! I want him fucking out of this race!"

Hamilton was given a 10-second penalty for causing the incident but went on to win the race. Verstappen was taken to a local hospital for evaluation. He was released that night with minor injuries.

BAMBOO GROVE

ft. Lewis Hamilton
2022 Dutch Grand Prix

In the final laps of the 2022 Dutch Grand Prix, Lewis Hamilton found himself with a chance to win a race; a feat he had yet to achieve that season. With a dozen laps left in the race, a safety car was deployed.

To Hamilton's dismay, he was instructed to stay out on track while many of his rivals and his Mercedes teammate George Russell hit the pits for soft tyres.

Lewis Hamilton: "Why did you stop George?"

Engineer: "Don't know Lewis, I'll let you know."

Lewis Hamilton: "That was a mistake, mate! We had track position. We had a buffer between us mate and now we don't have that."

Engineer: "Copy that, Lewis."

When the race resumed, Hamilton was quickly passed by three cars, including his teammate. Hamilton got back on the radio to voice his frustration.

Lewis Hamilton: "I can't believe you guys fucking screwed me man! I can't tell you how pissed I am right now!"

Not only did this strategy blunder cost Hamilton a shot at winning the race, but it also cost him a spot on the podium.

After the race Hamilton apologized to the team for his profane outburst.

Anita Driver is for kids.

Find these F1 children's books at AnitaDriver.com and on Amazon.

Charles Leclerc and the Terrible, Horrible, No Good, Very Bad Monaco Grand Prix

A Book of Sadness and Disappointment for Children

Stop, Drop and Stroll

The Lance Stroll Inspired Guide to Fire Safety for Kids

Anita Driver is for lovers.

Find these F1 romance books at AnitaDriver.com and on Amazon.

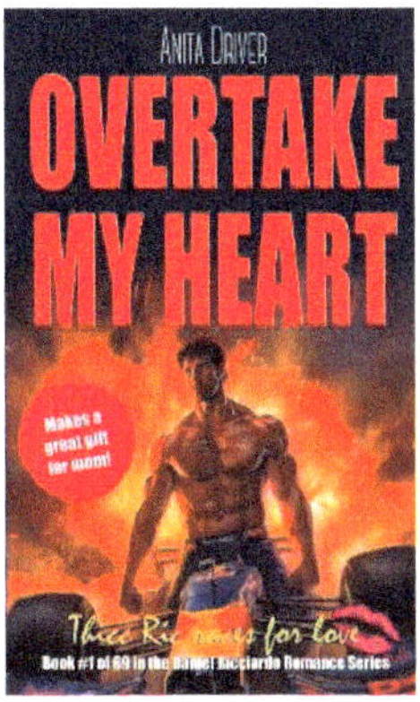

Overtake My Heart

Thicc Ric Races For Love

The Polesitter Always Rings Twice

Thicc Ric Ploughs the Countryside

ABOUT THE AUTHOR

Anita Driver is a Formula 1 enthusiast who has attended every Vietnamese Grand Prix since 2021. She learned to love cars after finding out she was conceived in the bed of a Subaru Baja in the parking lot of a Piggly Wiggly supermarket. She currently resides in a commune in Waikato, New Zealand with her 42 cats who are all named Purrnando Alonso. She once shared a cab with Steven Seagal who gave her a very festive bulletproof kimono that she wears when she's feeling fancy or in danger.

You can find all of Anita's books at AnitaDriver.com and on Amazon.

Anita Driver graciously accepts fan mail at authoranitadriver@gmail.com

STAY IN THE LOOP

Twitter/X: @realanitadriver
TikTok: @anita.driver
Sign up for the email list at AnitaDriver.com

Printed in Great Britain
by Amazon

38395531R00046